BLOOD RITES

THE WARLOCK LEGACY BOOK 8

RYAN ATTARD

Blood Rites

Ryan Attard

Copyright © 2020 by Ryan Attard. All rights reserved. This is a work of fiction. Any resemblance to actual persons living or dead, businesses, events or locales is purely coincidental. Reproduction in whole or part of this publication without express written consent is strictly prohibited.
Email ryanattardauthor@gmail.com

1

Things were getting tense and I was not helping.

The barkeep looked me straight in the eyes. "We don't serve your kind here."

I slammed my money down on the counter anyway, and squared off against him.

"Guess you'll just have to make an exception today."

Next to me, the rest of my team rolled their eyes.

"Smooth," said Benny. I caught him nodding at Robert—a wager had been set.

I ignored them and eyed the bartender again. "I won't ask a second time."

"And I already told you, we don't have it." At his statement, several of the patrons stood up. Their movements were sinuous. Of course they would be sinuous—most of them were cat-people. Not the type who had felines as house-mates. These were were-cats, maybe some kind of subclass; were-lions or -tigers.

"Shit," I muttered.

Daggers and blades were drawn. One guy even had a

mace. I saw Madeline call upon her eldritch magic, her hands glowing in a sickly green light.

"Dude," Robert whined. His rapier quivered in his hands. "Why did you have to go and piss them off?"

"Hey, they started it," I countered.

Patricia, our team leader, held up her staff. "And now we're ending it, thank you, Erik. Everyone get in position."

I raised my sword in a two-handed grip and swung.

The dice rolled.

"That's a miss," said Steve, our DM. "You trip on a bar stool, hitting your head on the side." He rolled his own die. "Two points of damage."

I stared at the twenty-sided red die, utterly stupefied. Next to me, Madeline tried very hard to suppress her laugh, while Robert passed the rest of his gummy bears to Benny, who evidently won the wager.

I set my pencil down.

"Sometimes I really, *really* hate this game."

"Not as much as the dice seem to hate you." The fact that Steve had said that so calmly and deadpan made it hurt all the more.

"Okay, so since Erik is knocked down," Patricia said, "we need another front liner."

"I'll do it," said Benny. Of course, he would say that. The dude's in love with Pat, except she won't give him the time of day and, well... How do I put this kindly?

He's a bit of a dumbass.

I sighed again.

Why, you might ponder, was an actual real-life wizard playing a make-believe Barbarian Half-Orc in the latest edition of a role-playing game?

The answer to that is a long-winded story that ends with me, a wizard with previously limited access to magic having lost all his magic, only to have an archangel (yes, those are real) help me restore it.

All of this after I got myself killed, resurrected as part of a demonic summoning, got a second demon stuck in my head, went on a murder spree, and literally had to pull the damned thing out of my noodle.

Thus, I give you roleplaying with dice that hate me.

It was all part of my healing process. Rediscovering my magic had helped me unlock other parts of myself that I had kept hidden away under trauma. My life since age eleven had been little other than monsters and destruction. I faced horrors on a daily basis—hell, it was my job to.

But I had finally decided that it should not come at the cost of my soul.

In an effort to connect with people around me and open up, I joined a Wicca group, which albeit not lasting for very long, led me to this bunch.

Patricia was a bottle blonde with pixel-perfect skin who spent most of her free time from college going on shopping sprees and modeling online. In the context of the game, she turned out to be a competent leader. Benny, apart from being head over heels for Pat, was the cool guy of the group —at least in his opinion, which was reflected in his play style of a handsome rogue. Next to him was Robert, our Dwarven Bard. Finally, Madeline was Robert's second cousin, transferred over for college reasons and despite being the quiet type, she played a psychotic Tiefling Warlock on our enemies. Steve, Benny's roommate, was our DM and possibly the most sarcastic human being I'd ever met.

And I live with a demonic talking cat.

All of them had small traces of power—the real kind— within them. Magic, like pretty much anything else, is trainable. Some people start with a very small amount of magic but with enough training can get to a point where they can do something with that energy. Not that they were going to be slaying monsters any time soon.

And besides, I didn't hang around them because of magic. I did it because they were my friends.

Yes, plural.

Look at me, emotionally maturing and all.

The game ended with our victory—notwithstanding one unconscious Half-Orc—and Steve decided to stop there for the session. We ordered another pizza, passed around some beer, and basically talked about dumb stuff for another half an hour before Patricia decided it was time to head back to her dorm. Madeline decided to walk with her, and I followed them out about fifteen minutes later.

Abi was waiting for me in my car.

"How's dragon-land?" she asked.

I got in. "Do I smell fries? Abi, this is a Mustang. Why are there fries in my Mustang?"

She reached behind me and set a bag of fast food down on my lap. "I got hungry," she said, pulling onto the street. "And I saved you a cheeseburger."

I opened the wrapper and started wolfing it down. "Marry me," I mumbled in between bites.

"Maybe when you learn how to use a napkin," she replied. "Jesus, didn't you guys just have pizza?"

"Yeah," I said. "So?"

She shook her head, but surrendered the goods. After a few minutes she caught my expression. "What?"

"Nothing," I said. "I'm just thinking."

She turned a corner onto my street. I saw my office building slash apartment just up ahead. "Thinking is good. Or so I've heard." A pause. "What are you thinking about?"

I looked at her. "I'm happy. I have no idea how it happened, but I think I'm actually happy. Things are going okay, nothing's tried to take over the world for more than a year-"

"You haven't been thrown off anywhere high for quite a while, I noticed," she added. "You always seem to do that."

"I think I was a bird in a past life," I said.

We parked on the street and got out. I still had my fries.

"Well," she said, fishing out the keys. "I would make some snarky remark, being the badass that I am..."

"Of course."

"But I'm going to choose to allow this hippie crap on account that you actually deserve some peace."

I nodded.

I did. By God, I really did deserve some peace and quiet.

And that's when Abi's mom burst out from the bushes.

2

"Vampires!"

"What?"

Ishtar grabbed onto her daughter, eyes wide with fear. "Vampires! Coming after me!" Then to me: "Please!"

Her whammy hit me like a freight train. Ishtar had passed Abi her succubus genes, but unlike my apprentice—whose history with Lilith, the Sin of Lust, had permanently altered her DNA and turned her into a hybrid—Mommy Succubus was the full package.

When last I had met Ishtar, her sex appeal had been subtle. You never knew it hit you until you were begging on your knees for her attention. This time however, it was forceful.

She was desperate.

Luckily, I've been practicing.

The mental shield I erected pushed my senses to their limit, and that was how I heard the soft *whoosh* of the crossbow.

Blood Rites

I spun, sword in hand, and heard the bolt bounce off the flat of the blade.

Three of them dropped from the night sky like black raindrops.

Vampires are nothing like they have been depicted in recent movies—everyone keeps trying to put a spin on them. Some turn them into feral monsters with bat wings and elongated claws, while others make their skin sparkle and send longing stares to barely-legal teens across biology class.

Reality is less sexy.

These creatures were once human, who either by ritual or some other neck-bitey method, turned into monsters that drank blood, becoming undead. They are tough to kill, they are on the weaker side of supernatural strength—which meant they could only bench-press a Prius instead of a Ford F150—and are fast enough to outrun most predators and dice up the majority of their prey.

That'd be us, humans.

I faced vampires before. No biggie. But as I squared off against these three, I began noticing certain things about them.

The closest one was in full armor. Breastplate, vambraces, pauldrons, greaves, the whole nine yards, and he carried a longsword. Another carried a lance, not a spear, one of those medieval weapons with a long needle-like point meant for piercing armor. He stood slightly behind the swordsman.

Their friend, Mr. Crossbow, was busy reloading at the rear of the group, where any long-range fighter should be.

It was a perfect formation: sword to engage me, lance to poke and parry and wound, crossbow to end me, or leave me open for the sword.

My gun appeared in my right hand, and I was blasting off rounds before I had fully leveled it. The swordsman lunged in, desperately blocking with his armored forearm. I saw blood spray from his arm.

Our swords clashed, his giving way under his wounded arm. I slipped to the side and tried slashing at his flank. The lancer slipped his weapon between us. I knocked it aside, blocking the tip with the underside of my gun. The crossbow bolt sunk into my shoulder, just as the bowman was struck by an invisible force.

Abi lowered her hand and reached for her pocket. The golden rod elongated into an etched staff that seemed to glow under the night sky.

I disengaged and slid to a halt just in front of her.

"Get her out of here," I said. "I'll take care of them."

Abi nodded. There was once a time when she would have argued. Not this time. This time she held her weapon —a manifestation of Sun Wukong—in front of her in the shape of a baton and grabbed her mother.

The door to my office sprung open. A black cat was waiting. I nodded at him. He nodded back.

I turned to my opponents. The swordsman was flexing his freshly-healed arm. I pulled the bolt out of my shoulder. Flesh immediately started mending. I pumped a fresh clip into my pistol, then held both sword and gun in either hand, right and left respectively.

"Round two."

"Halt," said the swordsman. I saw his fangs jutting out behind his lips as he spoke. "We are only after the demoness. Stand aside, wiz-"

I shot him in the face.

The crossbowman let loose a third bolt but I was ready for him. A streak of azure energy shot towards him from my sword strike. The bolt disintegrated and the streak caught his side as he scurried off.

The lancer thrust his weapon. I knew he was keeping me at bay, giving the swordsman enough time to recover. I dodged and shot him. His lance tip sliced across my hand and I dropped the gun. He managed to kick it away. I blocked his weapon and locked it under my arm. At the same time I heaved and turned us around. The bolt shot through his back. The vampire screamed.

Here's the thing about being faster and stronger—it doesn't necessarily mean you're tougher. Pain tolerance has nothing to do with superpowers. It's a mental thing.

I was used to pain. The vampire clearly was not. He dropped his weapon. I thrust Djinn, my short-sword, into his gut.

My magic coursed through it. The double-edged blade glowed azure and lengthened, shooting out to more than ten times its size. The blade pierced the crossbowman in the chest and I grinned.

"Boom," I told the lancer.

I pulled out the blade from his stomach but the energy blade was a separate magical construct. As such it stayed there, impaling both vampires like a skewer to a shish kebab.

I took one giant leap backward and willed the spell to explode. Two seconds later it was raining vamp chunks.

The swordsman snarled. I turned. Our swords met. I noticed for the first time the markings on his forearm. The wound had healed but left a strange dark violet marking snaking out from the bullet hole.

The swordsman swung around. He knew what he was doing. The longsword had greater reach and mass, and he knew how to apply them. I kept defending and trying to get past his guard. He kicked me away and was suddenly at my side. His blade sliced at my knee. The cut was shallow and quick, but it was enough to slow me down by a fraction.

That was all it took.

His next blow found a margin of error in my guard and the sword sliced along my chest. Not taking any chances, he swung his sword around, and Djinn was sent flying.

"The infamous Erik Ashendale," he said, holding the tip at the nape of my neck. "I have studied you, wizard. Your tools allow your magic. I have disarmed you, and thus you are powerless."

I looked up at him. My chest cut was already healing but it didn't concern the vampire. I guessed he could always give me a fresh one.

"Guess you're not caught up, huh?" I asked.

The vampire looked down.

Two holes appeared on either side of his pelvis. I was holding out both index fingers in a gun shape.

He gasped and bent over as pain registered. The sword clattered on the ground. "How...?" he began.

"You shouldn't believe everything you hear, buddy," I told him, standing up. "I got my mojo back. In fact, I just hit you with the same spell my apprentice threw at the crossbow asshole. Truth be told, she's more adept at the mental, psychokinesis thing. It requires a certain amount of subtlety." I grinned. "But, that ain't really my thing. I'm more... Well, here's a demonstration."

I held out my hand.

Brilliant orange-red flames shot at him, consuming the vampire and reducing him to ash.

3

I shut the door and looked at the cat. "Wards?"

"All secure," he said.

Yeah, the cat talks.

Also, not a cat.

Amaymon is a demon, and also one of the primordial Elementals of the universe, in his case Earth. The whole Elemental thing is quite interesting actually. Every dimension—Earth, Hell, Heaven, Avalon, Asgard, Elysium—has its own version of the four Elementals. They just don't always manifest in one coherent being.

Or talk.

Or shit in my potted plants.

He bounded off to a corner and curled up on himself, watching me with yellow eyes that seemed to bore through one's soul. Which they could, for all I knew.

I shook my head and turned to the present problem.

"Hey, Ishtar. Nice of you to drop by. How are things going, good? Oh, and please feel free to elaborate here, but why are there *mercenary vampires* chasing after you?"

Ishtar looked at her daughter and grinned. "Is he always such a diva?"

"Oh, you have no idea," Abi replied.

"You, can it," I told her. "You-" I pointed at Ishtar, "start talking."

"Mom," Abi said. "What did you do?"

Ishtar leaned back. I readied myself.

See, a full succubus' powers are nothing to scoff at. You might think a sex demon would be all fun and games—well, they are—but when you end up a shriveled husk, barely holding on to your vitality, trust me, the giggles die down real quick.

I could feel her power, her seduction, pulling at my instincts. Ishtar was beautiful. And don't take my word at face value. In another life, she had been a pornstar who was forced to retire (since succubii are technically immortal and women in porn already have a very limited shelf-life) and become a mogul of adult media.

Oh, and she was working with Alan Greede.

Yes, *that* Alan Greede, the Sin of Greed, the guy who had killed me (or at least had a massive hand in it), the guy who had brought demons and dragons (yep, and I rode one) to our plane of existence.

My nemesis.

Back then I had learnt not to underestimate Ishtar's powers, and most of all, her resourcefulness. I still have nightmares from when she drugged an entire room of people, my sister and the Grigori included (I was there too, but more as a tag-along), and forced us all into an orgy that had turned murderous within seconds.

All because she needed a distraction.

I readied myself.

It never came. Instead Ishtar slumped backwards, sweat on her brow, her breasts heaving, and her skin paper-white.

"Mom?" Abi's voice was drenched in worry.

"It's okay, sweetie," Ishtar said. "I'm just tired."

Our eyes met. For a second I thought she was going to tell me something, and then I recognized the fear of wanting to keep one's secrets. Which pretty much cemented my hunch.

Something was preventing Ishtar, Succubus Supreme, from accessing her powers.

And she wanted to keep it to herself.

Fine, I thought. *For now. I'll judge after I hear her out.*

I glanced at Amaymon. He wasn't ever this quiet. His eyes were focused on Ishtar. Something was spooking him, but he still didn't know what or he would have said something.

Like I said, he's never that quiet.

I headed to the kitchen and made enough coffee for the three humans in the room, and then took out some biscuits and offered them to the succubus.

"I don't know who they are," she began.

I groaned. Abi made a similar noise but added another that sounded like "mom". Amaymon hissed.

That, ladies and gentlemen, is what it sounds like when an entire room calls you out on your bullshit.

"I don't!" Ishtar insisted. "But I *might* have an idea…"

"They were organized," I told her. "These weren't some punks looking out for petty revenge. They had a mission and they knew how to operate well as a unit. Their weapons reflected that. The formations were standard but well-practiced. I'm guessing a militia, or an army."

She cocked her head at me. "I keep underestimating

you, Erik Ashendale." She grinned at her daughter. "I bet he's amazing in the sack."

Abi blushed bright red. I nearly choked on my coffee.

"What?" Ishtar said. "Oh, don't tell me you two still haven't... Abi, daughter dear, I thought we talked about this."

"Mom," Abi said, pleading. "Stop."

Ishtar chuckled, then turned serious. "Life is too short, sweetie."

"*Mom!*"

"Okay, fine." She looked at me. "Your guess is right on the money, Erik. That was a scout team from the army of His Vampiric Majesty, King Rashid."

I blinked at her. Then turned to Amaymon.

"Vamps have a monarchy?"

"Several," he answered. "Right when America was being settled, some creatures from the Old World came over to conquer new land. You had all sorts finding nooks and crannies, and then of course, you had the natives."

"The Indians?"

"No, the native *creatures*. Never mind the Caribbean ones, just the Native American ones were enough to cull most forces." He chuckled. "Did I ever tell you the story of how Cortez got mauled by a Jaguar avatar? The Church had him reanimated and that's how he managed to conquer South America."

"Cortez was a zombie?" Abi asked.

"Among other things," Amaymon replied. "Honestly, that was the least of his concerns. Back then the Church handed out reanimation spells like Sunday crackers. It was the only way to keep the expansion going."

"Back to the point, Amaymon," I said.

His tail flickered. "Right. So basically, the vamps were

mostly concentrated around Africa. Northern Africa to be precise."

I frowned. "I thought they were Eastern European. You know, with the accent."

"No, that's just funny," Amaymon said. "And *those* vamps are an off-shoot of the original ones. See, Africa is the cradle of life, so most things—the ones with fangs and claws, as well as monkeys with opposable thumbs—originated from there. The vamps figured that the desert would be a nice barrier between them and their natural predators down south. The cold desert winds helped. Then, as trade routes opened up, they migrated north into Europe. That's where the capes and cowls and medieval castles come in."

"And who is this King Rashid?" I asked him.

"He's the big daddy," Amaymon replied.

"Alpha?"

"Alpha of alphas. One of a handful that still survive. Certainly the only one with any visible power," he replied. "Pretty much any vamp you see answers to someone, who answers to a bigger someone, who for sure answers to Rashid. Essentially, all vampires are under his command."

I whistled. That is a lot of vampires and a lot of firepower to have.

"And tell me, Ishtar," I asked her, "how did you manage to piss off the king of vampires?"

"I stole something," she admitted. "Five years ago." She sighed. "He seems to remember."

"Yeah, who would have thought the millennia-old vampire remembers what you stole from him less than a decade ago?" I asked.

She raised an eyebrow at me. "Sarcasm is the lowest form of humor, Erik."

"Then it suits me perfectly, since I don't feel particularly tickled at the moment."

"There is a solution to that, you know. I have taught Abigale plenty of sexual-"

"Can we please stay on the goddamn topic?" I snapped. Abi got even redder. Now her hair and face were indiscernible.

Ishtar huffed. "If you must know, I stole a scepter from his treasury. It was the price I had to pay for Greede's help."

"Greede made you steal it?"

She raised her eyebrows. "He didn't *make* me. He could never *make* me do anything. But I needed his help and that was the price for it."

"What's so special about this scepter?" asked her daughter.

Ishtar shrugged. "I have no idea. All I did was host an orgy to distract the King and his guards-"

"Yeah, that's your go-to move, isn't it?" I shot.

"Why fix something that's not broken?" Her grin reminded me of every trickster I ever met. This woman was not a victim, I had to remind myself. She was just a predator who had happened to find a fish big enough to threaten her.

"Anyhow," she went on. "I have no idea what the scepter does, nor do I have any interest. Greede never mentioned it again. Then following the debacle two years ago, I went on the run. I had to cross Egypt, which also happens to be Rashid's main territory. I thought I could sneak past. Clearly, I was wrong. Considering their orders to bring my head on a platter for him, I had no choice but to kill a few of my pursuers and run off to the only place that could give me sanctuary."

She fluttered her eyes at me.

I was not impressed.

"You spent all this time hidden," I said. "Why did you have to go through Egypt at all? Why not just find a hole somewhere, or keep moving?"

"That was the plan, Erik," she said. "Until something beyond my powers infected me."

"Huh?"

She sighed. "Greede did something to me. I don't know what, but I haven't felt the same." She looked at Abi. "Not since we joined forces against the abominations he created. I was looking for answers."

"Did you find them?" Abi asked.

Ishtar shook her head.

I was about to say something when Amaymon's head shot up.

"Company."

"Friendly?" I asked.

"It's your sister." He hissed again. "And my brother."

No. That was decidedly not friendly company.

4

There are times when you have to think on your feet. Most people just freeze up, but I have had my fair share of narrow scrapes and narrower survivals so my on-feet thinking capacity was rather high.

I nodded at Amaymon who leapt from his seat. His body morphed into that of a stocky teenager wearing all black. I held out two fingers—it almost looked like a peace-sign. It wasn't.

Over the years I had seen the need for safe houses, and so I kept a few stashed around the city and surrounding areas for just such occasions. Trust me, when you've been backstabbed by friends and family all your life, you learn to keep a few aces up your sleeve.

The safe house I indicated to Amaymon was not the most fortified one. Sure, the cheap—abandoned—apartment was mostly run down, but it wasn't as bad as it looked, especially since I had got Abi to cast several illusion spells around it to ward off curious eyes.

Within two steps, Amaymon was on Ishtar. He grabbed her arm and hauled her off. She didn't even have time to squeal. He dragged her out the back door and I felt his power spike for a brief second as he presumably sank into the earth and disappeared. Both him and Ishtar were going to reappear a few seconds later at the safe house.

My sister knocked again. I could feel her irritation. It's not a twin thing (fraternal, thank the universe), I just knew her well enough.

"I'm coming," I yelled. "Keep your damn panties- Oh, hey Gil."

Okay, so I'm not the best actor in the world.

Sue me.

My sister raised her eyebrows. I wasn't sure if she bought it; my sister often raised her eyebrows at me.

Five feet and change, wearing an honest-to-God olive-green cloak, with her blonde hair in a thick braid behind her and a frown on her elfin, delicate face, the only thing we had in common was our green eyes.

Gil was everything I was not. She was the smartest person I knew, a strategic mind that would put Sun Tzu to shame (not that I would ever tell him that—he'd stop giving me free dumplings). She had managed to take my father's massive estate and business to a whole new level, she had united the last of the warlocks and locked them all under her employ, and now she sat at the top of the Grigori.

I...

I couldn't decide what to watch on Netflix most nights so I usually slept to Youtube videos of cooking shows.

Looming behind her was her familiar, Mephisto. Tall, pale and eternally creepy, Mephisto had been in my family's employ since... Well, he's a demon, Amaymon's brother in fact, so who knew how long he'd been with my family.

Much like Gil and I, Amaymon and Mephisto had nothing in common. Hell, even their animal forms were different: Amaymon chose a cat, Mephisto a dog. Mephisto was a perfect butler, serving his role as manager, financier, advisor and bodyguard all in one perfect rotation; I have to bribe Amaymon with treats and belly rubs, the last one he prefers from the hot redheaded apprentice as opposed to me.

I can't blame him.

The third figure was a surprise.

"Greg?" I asked.

He smiled warmly. Greg the Kresnik was wearing his usual white cloak, under which I knew he kept various pieces of armor and a collapsible spear, along with a bazillion knives and stakes and holy water, and pretty much everything one would need to slay the forces of the undead.

That last part worried me.

What were the chances that the foremost warrior against the forces of darkness showed up at my doorstep minutes after said forces of darkness were chasing after someone I had just hidden away?

"Brother," Gil said. "I suppose you've heard by now." She pushed her way past me and gave Abi a friendly nod. They always got on well together. "There are vampires in town."

Well, there went my hopes for a coincidence.

I shut the door behind them. "Hey Gil, Greg, Mephisto. Won't you come in? Can I offer you some tea?"

Gil sat down and glared at me. "This is serious business."

"Maybe coffee? Oh, and biscuits. Abi, do we still have biscuits?"

"I dunno, ask Amaymon," she replied.

"Yes, where is my dear brother?" Mephisto asked. His voice was like a beautiful snowflake—running down your spine just as you settled warm and cosy in bed. "I swear I could sense his presence just a second ago."

Amaymon chose that moment to saunter back in. "Ah, fuck, you still here?"

He dragged mud all over the floor.

"Dude," I said.

"Pansy. A lil' mud never hurt nobody." He clicked his tongue. With a light kick to the door, the mud sluiced out and the door made a loud bang and Gil's veins started popping out of her forehead.

"If you please..." she began.

"Tea, coffee?" I interjected. "Hey, Amaymon, where are those biscuits?"

"I ate them."

"Coffee sounds lovely," Greg added, his Slavic accent slightly pronounced. Gil shot him a look. He shrugged. "Is cold today."

"Did you replace them?" I asked my demonic familiar.

"No."

"Why not?"

"Because I don't have any money." He brushed past me as he went to the kitchen to grab a beer. I felt two light taps on the back of my hand.

Ishtar was safe. No one had followed them.

I kept my poker face. Or rather, my annoyed-at-Amaymon face, which, let's be honest, is not really that hard to maintain. He opened the beer, drained half the can and belched loudly.

Gil sighed. Her tiny hands balled into fists. I noticed bite marks. Gil had taken to gnawing on her fingernails again—never a good sign.

"Right," I said. "The floor's all yours, dear sister."

Abi gave her an apologetic look. Gil decided to be the

bigger woman and not tell me to go screw myself off a cliff. I made them all tea and coffee.

See? Who says family can't get along?

"We need your help," she began.

"I figured as much," I replied. "This have anything to do with the vamps you mentioned?"

She nodded. "How many have you encountered?"

"Three. Ran into them while I was on a job," I said. The key to lying is that you don't lie outright. You *nudge* the truth a little.

I turned to Greg. "Good to see you, buddy. Unfortunately, it's always under dire circumstances."

He nodded. "That it is. Most unfortunate. But good to see you too. You seem healthier."

Greg was one of the good guys. He looked like the guy from *God of War* and *The Witcher* had a baby together, and he was a force to be reckoned with once he started cutting loose, but as far as I knew, he had never tried to betray me, or backstab me, and the only two arguments we had ever had were about following orders and dating my sister.

That last one was more me threatening to cut off his dick.

And judging by his and Gil's body language he hadn't taken it personally. They seemed happy, and I was happy for them.

"When you say we..." I started.

"The Grigori," Gil answered.

"What's your status these days?" I asked. The Grigori were a touchy subject for me.

I used to date their former leader. Then I'd held her when Greede and his myrmidons had killed her in front of me, along with the majority of the powerhouses the Grigori had.

Part of my recovery was grieving. Mourning Akasha's loss was not something I had opened myself up to easily, but once I had, my magic flourished. Anael's influence (an archangel and Virtue of Love) had unlocked my powers but it was I—and a year's worth of therapy—that had managed to stabilize my life again.

Gil looked at me for two flat seconds, appraising me. The last time we had all been in the same room I had just lost my magic and fallen into a depression. I had given up.

Now she needed to see the fight back in me.

"I stepped up to the second seat," she said. That had been Akasha's place. Gil was a worthy replacement. "Effectively, I run the whole operation now."

"Isn't there a first seat?" I asked.

"Yes," Greg replied. "But we do not know where it is."

I cocked my head. Somehow I didn't think he was talking about the chair.

"It?"

Greg nodded. "It." He said nothing more.

Gil looked around. "This is actually also part of our reason for coming here tonight. Pardon me."

She raised her hand. White light billowed from it. I felt my ears pop from the change in atmospheric pressure. The smell of ozone filled the air for a second.

Then it all died down.

"Your defenses will suffice," she said.

"Pretty lights," Amaymon slurred from his corner. He slurped his beer. "Next time you use magic without a warning, you'll lose the hand."

Mephisto stood up, slowly. Amaymon did the same.

"Both of you, chill," I said.

They ignored me. So I stood up.

Not many humans can claim the following, but I have

enough magical power to rival that of a demon. Now, granted, these two are still out of my weight class, but I could give them a run for their money and ruin their evening.

And they knew it.

My magic made the cups shake and rattle, and the house began to shake.

Both demons gave each other one final stare and sat back down.

I sat down too but I didn't settle. My heart was racing.

"Impressive, brother," Gil said. "I see you're acclimatizing to having your powers back very nicely."

"Thank you, Gil," I said.

"And I do apologize," she said. "Amaymon was well within his rights to threaten me. He is your guardian after all."

I waved my hand. "Let's all just have a pleasant talk." I directed the last syllable towards the demons.

Mephisto looked at me, cold and blank. Amaymon flipped me off as he went to get another beer.

"What just happened?" Greg asked.

"Ashendale family meeting," I told him. "Actually this one looks to be quite boring. No one is going to the emergency room yet. Maybe we're losing our touch, eh sis?"

"Shut up, Erik, and listen."

"Warm and cuddly, that's us."

She rolled her eyes. "The Grigori has a mission that requires your aid. And should this mission be a success, we may then invite you to join our ranks." She narrowed her eyes. "As our third seat."

I choked on my coffee.

"Third? What about him?" I said, pointing at Greg.

He waved his hands. "No, no. I was always number four. I stay that way. No hassle. I not like promotion."

"Why me?" I directed towards Gil.

She shrugged casually. It was unsettling.

"Because you are the strongest. And the most experienced. And happen to be in a perfect position as a liaison for those places the Grigori can't access." She sighed. "Jared was a douche of the highest degree. He abused his power. Quite frankly, I think Akasha gave him the seat just so she could keep him close and pile all the paperwork on him."

"There's paperwork, too?"

"Oh, yes," Greg said with a sly grin. "Like I say, I do not like promotion."

Gil shot him a withering look. "Trivia aside, we actually need you." She smiled for the first time that evening. "I am actually in the process of filling our ranks with the best from every specialization category. We lack a wizard."

"Wizards are below specialists," I told her. "It goes adept, wizard, specialist. If you want the top, I'm not it."

"On the contrary, brother," she said. "You managed to raise the bar for what wizards should be able to do. And with your powers restored, I doubt anyone can match you in terms of versatility."

She was right, of course. But I wasn't going to admit that.

It was for her sake, her ego was too big as it was. I'm thoughtful like that.

"The rest I have already filled out," she went on. "Reports on the first seat are vague so I have no idea what they can do. I am, of course, a warlock. You would be the wizard. Greg is a Kresnik. Aside from that, we have a Biomancer, a Druid, an Abjurer, a Golem-maker, a Pyromancer, and I am keeping open the tenth seat for liaisons and probationary members. Much like I was."

A seat she had inherited from our psycho dad. I chose to move past that bit and focus on the information she had given me.

"The Abjurer would be the moustache dude," I said. "From my trial."

"Mustafa," she said, nodding. "He remembers you."

"Fondly?"

"No."

"It was to be expected."

"You set Amaymon on him."

"He's welcome," the demon called.

"The Golem-maker is Evans," I said. "Wait, did you say Pyromancer? You mean, Luke?"

Greg grinned at her. Gil handed him a twenty-dollar bill.

"Yes, Erik. Luke. The guy who's been working for me for two years."

"Who was working for Greede before."

"We all make mistakes."

"He set me on fire. On multiple occasions."

"But you're fine now."

"But I had nice coats."

"They looked ridiculous."

"Says the chick in a cape."

"I thought you and Luke were past that," Abi said. "Remember, the thing with the aircraft carrier?"

I huffed. She was right of course. Luke and I were now allies. I daresay he had even earned my trust. Just a little bit of it. "I loved those coats," I murmured.

Then in my normal voice,

"So what's the job? I'm not saying I want the position, and I sure as shit will not be working for *you*, but if there are vamps roaming the city then I take it personally. So, where are they and how do I kill them?"

"You do not," Gil said sternly. "You will certainly not propose any violence against these esteemed vampire guests, lest you put us all in open war with them. No. Killing. Vampires! I forbid it!"

I looked at Greg. "Did she just tell me *not* to kill the vampires?"

He nodded. I could tell by his expression he wasn't happy. Mainly because he was frowning heavily, and when a big Russian man frowns, you know about it.

I turned to Gil. "And why, pray tell, am I forbidden from killing said vampires?"

She grimaced. Gil wasn't thrilled about it either.

"Because we are being graced by a visit from His Vampiric Majesty himself," she said. "King Rashid is coming to discuss the possibility of a peace treaty between our kinds. And he's requested you personally."

5

I beat the sunrise the following morning as I made it towards the apartment where Ishtar was being kept. If the mother was anything like her daughter, then she would not be awake for another few hours at the very least.

Part of me wanted her to be well-rested.

An even bigger, more cynical part of me thought that when the woman was half-groggy and sleep-deprived, she wouldn't be able to lie as well.

The cynical part won. At least I was bringing coffee, bagels, and chocolate-chip cupcakes. Breakfast of fugitives.

She was snoring softly on the couch, the TV still on. I switched it off and sat down opposite her.

Back in the olden days, I would have had to set up the room for this sort of magic. But one of the benefits of teaching Abi the basics was that it had reinforced them in me. Sure, my family curse had prevented me from actually *using* any of that knowledge before, but now that I could, I found it rather easy.

I sat there and simply looked.

Ishtar's aura was weak and dim. She was healthy, mind

you, just less healthy than one would expect from a supernatural being. I knew she was a predator by definition. Not the claws-and-teeth kind—if I could compare her to a big cat (and I think she would appreciate that) she was less of a tiger and more of a leopard. She was not the strongest around, certainly not the toughest, and she preserved her kills, taking a little over time as opposed to gorging herself on one giant meal.

The dark-grey and pink sheen were to be expected. Big energy centers in her lower torso and forehead—yellow, orange, and red for the lower, purple and pink for the upper —indicated that she was alive and functional. Thin blue strands emerged from her throat chakra, turning pink.

And then there was the massive clump of grey-white and indigo attached to where the back of her neck would be.

That was not normal. In fact, it looked like a massively overgrown pimple, ready to burst at the slightest touch. It writhed, sinking itself slowly into Ishtar's aura, draining a tiny bit at a time.

On the couch, Ishtar moaned and muttered something. She turned slightly in her sleep before opening her eyes.

"Erik!"

The sound of her panicked voice sent red and dark orange flooding all around her. The blob sipped more and more, becoming more irate, and then it lashed out.

The attack was psychic.

It came at me in waves, first breaking through my spell, returning my sight to normal, then punching through my defenses. My mind reeled as I fell to the ground. Images flashed, crisp and clear as the day I had experienced them.

I was in my father's study. A demon stood before me, a cross between a spider and a tick. A cacodaemon, the Sin of Wrath. The demon that had taken possession of my body years after that, and turned me into a murderer. Anael was there too, her spear flashing bright. This was the moment I had receded into my mind to battle the intruder. This was the moment I had fought my inner demon—literally—and won.

A pause. Reality broke, like static on a TV. The world became pixels, that then slipped out of alignment.

A boy made out of white, blue, and indigo energy. It called to me. It called me something...

My eyes sprang open and I was now looking at a very disheveled Ishtar. She was bleeding from her nostrils.

"Erik?" she moaned. "Erik, my head. It hurts." Her pallor had turned grey.

So now I knew what ailed her: a psychic parasite. Not unlike Wrath, but this one was not demonic. This was pure psychic power, a thought-form given an identity.

Again, there was something familiar about all this. I felt like a student ready for the test, knowing all the answers, only to have them slip out of my mind as soon as I looked at the blank sheet.

I helped Ishtar back on the couch.

"Here," I said. "Have some coffee."

She took it with shaking hands. "What are you doing here?"

"Checking on you," I said. "I was reading your aura."

She looked at me, her eyes broken. "You saw it?" She didn't seem surprised.

"You knew you had a psychic parasite on you?"

She nodded. "It's gestating," she said. "Growing, feeding off of me." She shook her head. "Something is agitating it."

I backed away. "Is it me?"

Suddenly Ishtar looked at the door and the buzzer went off. I motioned for her to stay put and silent, while I went to the door. My gun was in my hands, pressed against the door, ready to blast whoever was behind it through the wood.

I opened the door.

The vampire on the other side smiled. "Good morning. Are you Mr. Erik Ashendale?"

6

My finger tightened ever so slightly around the trigger.

"Who wants to know?" I asked.

The vampire tried to peer over my shoulder. He was a tall specimen, with a shiny bald head and small eyes with big whites. I noticed he was wearing a robe of purple so dark it could have been black, and his body was covered in purple tattoos. They snaked over his body like vines on a tree, some straight, others curling around, but all intertwined together.

The vampire turned back to me.

"We are the Brotherhood of the Vol," he said. "I am Bishop Sandor. And you, Mr. Ashendale, have something we want. We heard its cries and came running. It seems it is time we are reunited."

He never stopped smiling, that was what unnerved me the most. Sandor turned and left. I watched him descend the stairs, then shut the door behind him and rushed towards the window.

"Who was it?" Ishtar asked.

"Not who," I said, "but what. And what they are is trouble."

Outside, more of them gathered. I counted at least twenty, all dressed in some iteration of the robes Sandor had been wearing. I watched as the man himself joined them and spoke to the nearest two. His message was being relayed among the ranks.

"Vampires," I said. "But it's morning. How?"

"The Vol," Ishtar said.

"You know them?"

She nodded. "They are mystics, capable of a ritual that turns them into day-walkers for a few hours."

I swore internally. It all made sense now. One never expected a vampire ambush during the day. They knew my guard would be low.

"What ritual?" I asked. "The more I know the better."

Now I watched as Sandor removed his robe, left only with black linen pants in the middle of the road. Dark vine tattoos covered his entire body. He clasped his hands together. I couldn't hear the words he was chanting but I have been around magic long enough to recognize the beginnings of a spell.

The other vampires around him coiled and shuddered. Their tattoos glowed somewhere between black and violet. A car honked. One of the vampires punched the front and rendered it into pulp. In a blink he ripped the driver out through the window and sank his fangs into him.

"I don't know," Ishtar said. "All I know is that they've been after me too."

"You have *two* vampiric forces after you?" I sighed. "And I thought I had enemies."

"They hunt psychic energy," she snapped. "I don't know

why but it must have something to do with their physiology or that weird ritual."

I nodded. "And not only are you essentially a receptacle for sexual energy, but you're carrying that big psychic parasite." I exhaled. "Okay, okay. Think."

I watched as Sandor started handing out directions, pointing at me.

"The ritual is time-sensitive," I said. "And this place is warded. All we need to do is outlast them."

"Can't you portal us out?" she asked. "I've seen other wizards do it."

"No," I said, "you've seen my sister do it. I've only just gotten my full powers back, and I've never been any good with that sort of magic anyway. My powers are rougher."

She pressed herself against the kitchen counter, holding on. "Are you sure?"

I nodded. "Just hold on tight and-"

CRASH!

Two vampires crashed head-first through the balcony window. Before I could truly fathom what power level they had to possess to have just blown past my wards—which were admittedly much weaker than my office ones—they were already upon me. One of them found air; the other found a wizard.

We went rolling. The couch bit into my rib and the vampire wrestled his way onto me. I shifted my weight and wrapped my legs around him, tightening the lock. Djinn was sheathed horizontally against my lower back and pinned by my body, which left only my gun. I reached for it, grabbed the vampire's swinging arm and locked it against my shin. He screamed and reared up, giving me a clean shot to his face. Chunks of vampire brain matter flew.

Ishtar screamed and I heard her batting the second

vampire with a cast-iron pan. The vampire tore the metal away with one swipe and lunged for Ishtar. She shoved him, her palms snapping against his chest. Succubii were not the most powerful creatures around but they were still supernatural.

The vampire's chest caved in. He stumbled backwards. Tattoos glowed. They seemed to come alive beneath the vampire's flesh. He screamed for an instant and then rose, completely healed.

A bullet of hard red light shot through his head. I poured magic once more into the gun and fired another red bullet. The second one did the trick. The tattoos faded away and the vampire turned to ash.

I heard roars from the window and didn't even fully turn before switching weapons, my gun in my left hand, Djinn in my right. Yes, I had my magic back, but I had spent the better part of a decade using just my weapons.

A stream of blue energy trailed from Djinn's tip and punched through the wall panel beneath the window, just as the first vampiric hand reached the windowsill. The blast shredded the wall. The balcony and window frame warbled. Metal screamed as it was torn.

The entire thing fell down, a few thousand pounds of mortar, wood, iron and glass, plummeting six floors onto the vampires below. Most had the reflexes to avoid it.

Most.

There was a crushed car directly below, along with two very distinctive puddles of goop and ash.

"Whoa," Ishtar said. "You weren't kidding about the rough part."

I saw Sandor give an order and suddenly the vampires started scaling up the walls, like some B-movie special effect.

"We have to get out of here," I yelled.

At the same time, I focused my magic through my sword. I lowered the tip so that I stabbed four tiny holes in what remained of the wall. A trail of blue fire sped down along Djinn's blade and then separated through the holes, flowed down the walls. I saw vampires hiss as the fire burned their limbs, their progress halted.

Next I channeled magic through my gun and fired. The bullet was bright crimson as it shot down. Sandor scurried off but before the projectile met him, it split off into several smaller pieces, scattering like angry wasps.

Again, more vamps hissed, this time holding their legs and torsos.

None of my spells were powerful enough to kill, merely stall them. I sheathed my weapons and grabbed Ishtar.

"Have you ever seen Tarzan?" I asked her.

Without waiting for an answer, I tapped into my curse power.

My sister and I were born with massive reserves of magic, something to do with an ancient curse placed on our family. The details were still a mystery, given that exactly zero information existed on this damn thing, but it had something to do with the Seven Deadly Sins, and my supposedly predestined battle against them.

Living shadows coated my entire body, coiling around Ishtar and binding her to me. Then I extended my right arm and the shadows extended.

Like all my powers, there was a time this power had been used only to destroy. But I had been told that this was Life Magic, the ancient magic of creation, and while I was loathe to experiment with it now that I had my powers back (given that it had been used against me to give life to the Knightmare, a giant knight-like entity that had been Wrath's living embodiment), I could still use it much in the same way I always had.

The extended shadows latched onto the building opposite and held tight.

Ishtar realized what I had in mind and tried pulling away. At the same time, the vampires kicked in the door to the apartment, bashing through my wards, both physical and magical.

I tightened my grip around her, shutting her up, and leapt out the window. Vampires bounded off the side of the building in an attempt to catch me but the shadows around my body swatted them away.

For a long, long, *long* second we were free-falling. I could feel my cheeks hurting from grinning. Ishtar was screaming directly in my ear. The wind rush helped with that—a little.

Then the shadows on my right arm tightened and we swung like a certain Jungle Man. I whooped ecstatically as Sandor and his tattooed vamp freaks watched us make our daring escape.

And then he had to go and ruin it.

7

Sandor spread his arms and the tattoos pulsated. Two vampires came to his side. He touched one of them. The tattoos on the vampire glowed a painful purple and then he leapt, rocketing towards me from the pavement.

I braced myself for impact but the vampire overshot. The second vampire too, following the first. I glanced down at Sandor—the bastard was still smiling.

I hate it when other also have aces up their sleeve.

The vampires hadn't been targeting me. They had been targeting the building serving as my anchor point. The first vampire smashed headfirst into the wall where my shadows were bound. The impact turned him into goop and then ash as he fell. The second vampire smashed that same cracked wall, and died exactly as his predecessor.

And just before the wall gave and Ishtar and I plummeted down for real, I realized that I had underestimated whom I'd been dealing with.

This wasn't just some other group of bad guys.

This was a fanatic cult, where members were willing to kamikaze themselves for a mission.

We fell. I turned us around, hoping that my body could shield us from the impact. I had survived worse, and part of my curse was a healing ability that would put Deadpool's to shame.

But I couldn't say the same for Ishtar.

I used the remaining shadows to push her up and away at an angle. I had to take away her momentum. She would break most of her bones but she would be able to heal from that in time. The alternative...

You can't exactly heal a pile of squish.

As I pushed her away, something leapt over me, too fast for me to see, and tore Ishtar away from my grip.

I roared and turned, and then the ground suddenly rushed up to meet me.

The impact shattered concrete and most of my upper body.

Shadows retreated inside, my magic focused solely on healing the massive damage I'd just received. Within seconds I was able to turn, if not stand up.

And then I saw who had taken Ishtar.

The Asian man was tall, taller than me, wearing a Chinese suit of royal blue that caught the sun's rays at the edges. His moustache trailed down his chin and seemed unaffected by gravity, like whiskers of a catfish. Dark hair flowed behind him, with a balding spot at the very top.

In one of his arms he held Ishtar as if she weighed no more than the double-headed spear he held in the other.

I watched as he gently set the succubus down, and turned his gaze on an approaching vampire. The glare was powerful enough to stun the vamp, before a second Asian man came in and literally bisected the creature.

This other guy was shorter than the first, but built like a linebacker. His sleeveless black suit had orange lining and was held shut with a tan belt. His hair was a mane of dirty-blond the color of wet wheat, and he held a scimitar almost as tall as he was.

One-handed.

I watched as Long and Tiger turned vampires into ash, Long gliding in between them, stabbing them before they even knew what happened, while Tiger roared and turned his side of the battlefield into a bloodbath, hacking and slashing and laughing maniacally.

Sandor yelped in horror. Something in his eyes told me he recognized who these two were.

Which meant he—or potentially the one who had sent him—had done his homework.

Which in turn made him powerful, resourceful, *and* well-informed; the trifecta of dangerous.

By the time he backed away, his forces had been reduced to dust. Long and Tiger just stood there, watching him.

No, not him.

The third Asian man behind him.

He was short, and looked a million years old, but Sun Tzu was not someone you want to underestimate, ever.

His storm-grey eyes matched his suit, and he calmly raised one hand to prevent Sandor from bumping into him. I had no idea what he did next but then Sandor was on the ground and bleeding from his nose.

And if he was shocked that Long and Tiger had appeared, he nearly pissed himself when he saw Sun Tzu.

Thunder that hadn't been there a second ago rumbled. The ground shook, the tremors just about controlled.

"Leave now, foul creature," Sun Tzu said. His voice overcame the thunder. It was just an echo to the power he held in just a few syllables. "Your end will not be dealt on this day. Leave."

The sky roared and Sandor crawled away.

Fast.

Then Sun Tzu turned to me.

"Erik Ashendale," his voice boomed. I stayed my ground as he approached. "Whatever am I going to do with you?"

I stood up and grinned. "It's good to see you too, old friend."

The thunder raged for another second, enough to make me doubt if Sun Tzu was as friendly as I remembered him, and then it dissipated. The old man was grinning.

"And you."

We embraced. Sun Tzu and I went way back, to when I had been a bright-eyed, dumbass kid with more bravado than sense. In other words, a teenager.

Ishtar pulled away from Long and dusted herself off. "Can someone please tell me what's going on?" She glared at Long. "I would ask you to be gentle but I doubt you care."

Long ignored her. To be fair, he ignored most things.

"Hello?" She waved in front of his face. "Do you even speak English?"

Tiger chuckled and Long shot him a look. Tiger growled. Sun Tzu cleared his throat.

I pulled Ishtar away. "Can you please not piss off the Avatars? The last thing you need is more enemies."

Her eyes widened. "Avatars?"

I nodded. "Long means 'dragon' in Chinese. Tiger is self-explanatory."

Ishtar's bravado evaporated instantly. She looked at Sun Tzu. "Are you Phoenix? Turtle?"

He smiled. "Neither. I am... something else."

It dawned on her. "Oh..."

I chuckled.

It's not every day you meet God. Or even *part* of God.

To be honest I wasn't too clear on it myself. The way I understood it was that there were many gods, but they all formed part of *the* God. Some of them were closer to the pure source than others—Sun Tzu, or whatever his real identity (which he still wouldn't divulge—although if he did it would probably collapse a universe or something), was as close to the big G as I was going to get.

Sun Tzu waved his hand. I felt magic in the air and then again as it expanded. Whatever he did affected a five-block radius. I shook my head. It would have taken me about ten minutes to get the calculations right, and then twice that to make sure I didn't kill anyone by accident.

Guess being a god comes with some neat perks.

"I come bearing news, Erik Ashendale," he said. "This news requires time, therefore I took some measures to ensure we may talk without being interrupted by law enforcement."

I nodded.

"I have been asked to act as official emissary for the meeting to be conducted in Eureka between the Grigori and His Vampiric Majesty, King Rashid. I believe you have already received a similar invitation."

I nodded again.

"However I may not directly participate," he went on. "I am too volatile a being to be placed in such an open position. Therefore, I will send my messenger and he will enact my will in my stead." He glanced at Tiger and Long. "The Tiger and Dragon must remain at the opposite sides of the Balance. The Phoenix guards the Temple. Therefore, the Turtle shall accompany you to the meeting on this eve. A formal invite has been issued. I hope you find it acceptable."

I was getting tired of nodding, although this time I was happy with what I was hearing. I'd met Turtle before and had briefly worked with him. He was the most peaceful, the most diplomatic, and certainly the friendliest out of the lot.

Plus, I'd seen him squish zombies with his bare hands. So, best of both worlds.

"May I ask you a question, old friend?" Sun Tzu asked.

"Shoot," I said.

"Why are you safeguarding the very thing King Rashid is chasing?"

The question sent a chill down my spine. I felt Ishtar press closer to me.

I took a deep breath.

"I have no idea why Rashid wants her," I told him. "But she's Abi's mom. And she came to me for help. Greede did something to her."

Sun Tzu cocked his head quizzically, before giving me the "you-are-still-missing-something-obvious" look.

"Yet her crimes remain unanswered," he said instead. His grey eyes swirled, like thunder clouds roiling. "She is the cause of an imbalance."

He took a single step forward. The sky growled.

I stepped in between him and Ishtar, and tried very hard to ignore the fact that Long and Tiger had their eyes boring into the back of my skull.

"She is," I told Sun Tzu. "And she came to me to rectify that imbalance. This is also why you chose to side with me. I have never let you down, Sun Tzu, and I don't intend to start now. Give me time to fix this."

Sun Tzu's look seemed to pierce into my soul. He knew I wasn't lying.

First, because he was a god.

Second, because lying to a god always comes with consequences, and I had enough cosmic baggage to last several lifetimes without adding any more.

Finally he nodded.

"Very well. I shall transport you to where Turtle is."

"And where's that?"

"Your abode," he replied.

"Ah shit. You sent a cosmic being to my place?"

Sun Tzu raised an eyebrow.

"Amaymon is there," I explained. "And he's always itching to pick a fight with you guys."

Sun Tzu nodded. "Yes, I see. That might prove problematic."

I groaned. "Just take me there, please. Hopefully *before* they destroy my office."

8

Sun Tzu teleported me and Ishtar to my place just in time to see Turtle flying across the street and crashing into a thankfully abandoned building right across the street from mine.

He leapt out of the rubble, happy as can be, and patted down his dark-green Chinese suit. Like all the others he too was Asian, and stood at around six feet and change, with a shiny bald head, a big round Buddha belly, and a thick length of oak in one hand, as tall as he was.

"Hello, Erik-"

Amaymon crashed into him and took Turtle down, raining elbows and punches on him. Turtle brought his staff between them and Amaymon was thrown off.

And when I say thrown, I mean tossed high into the air until he was a tiny dot among the clouds.

The demon twisted in the air and nose-dived back to the ground...

Which parted and swallowed him.

He emerged behind Turtle.

"I'm gonna go inside," I said. "You guys carry on here.

Just fix the shit you broke before the council sticks me with the bill."

"Aye," Amaymon growled.

"Yes, Erik-"

Amaymon punched him in the face.

"That was quite rude of you-"

Amaymon did it again. Turtle picked him up with one hand and punted him into a building.

I kept walking ahead, ignoring everything happening around me, and found Abi sitting on the front porch, a beer in her hand. She opened a cooler with several more.

"They've been going at it for half an hour now," she said. "I thought I might as well enjoy the show."

I opened my mouth to say something, then shook my head. Ishtar went inside to grab some water and lie down. I cracked open a beer and watched my cat put a god in a headlock.

HALF AN HOUR LATER, Turtle was sitting in my office's living room.

My living space is a two-floor apartment. The top consists of two bedrooms, a bathroom, and a closet big enough for me to store the seemingly-endless supply of stuff that comes along with being a magic practitioner.

The ground floor is my office. Opposite the door is a desk with a laptop and various other gadgets that I tend to stay away from. That's Abi's realm. Behind the office to the right is the entrance to the kitchen. On the left are the stairs for the second floor. The walls are decorated with various trophies from my career—teeth, bones, weapons, crystals, statues, all placed on shelves or in glass cases.

The main area is a living space in front of my desk with

two couches opposite one another and a coffee table. This is where we all sat.

Once their sparring match was over, Turtle took me up on my offer of tea, while Amaymon turned into a cat and cradled himself besides Abi, who absentmindedly rubbed his belly. Ishtar sat beside me on the opposite couch and stayed uncharacteristically quiet.

"So," I said. "Any particular reason why you two decided to turn my street into an octagon ring?"

"Keep your pants on, dude," Amaymon said. "We were just sparring."

"Yes," Turtle said. "I arrived rather early, and was greeted with an invitation for a match." He sipped his tea contentedly. "I must admit, it has been a great curiosity of mine to gauge your strength, Amaymon, and by extension that of Erik Ashendale."

"Hm." I sipped my beer and pondered.

Sun Tzu and I often sparred. In fact, most of my sword proficiency was thanks to him. Apart from being a god, the guy had also written the book on warfare.

You can't get any more credit than that.

But if he really wanted to know my full power, he would also test out my allies. He knew what Abi could do—it was he who had set her a highly perilous test in order to obtain a weapon, the Sun Wukong staff which she kept as a keychain on her person at all times.

Now, thanks to Turtle, he had found a way to test Amaymon, who was the equivalent of a nuclear weapon, without any actual consequences.

Sun Tzu was observing me. Actively observing.

And gods don't take an interest in you unless they had something planned.

I found Turtle staring at me meaningfully. He had meant

to send me down that trail of thought. He could have come up with any excuse but he wanted me to know that he (and by he, I mean all four Avatars plus Sun Tzu, since they were essentially one being) wanted me ready.

But for what?

"Sun Tzu mentioned something about an invitation," I said.

Turtle beamed. "Indeed. I am the Avatar most suited for negotiation, and thus will be accompanying you to the meeting. Myself, you, and a third party will have the role of a panel to represent the various other interests of those whose voice cannot be heard."

"The underdogs." Now I understood why Gil wanted me.

A big bad vampire king wanted to initiate some kind of deal and he had gone to the leaders. But Gil wanted to make sure everyone was heard.

Which made me think that perhaps she wanted the option to sway the vote.

"Me," I said, knowing I represented the underdog. "You." Turtle, Sun Tzu and the rest probably had other contacts with beings beyond my pay grade. Him being there ensured that the voice of God (and who knows how many other deities) would have a say too.

Which meant if this went sideways, even *gods* would have to fight it out.

"Who's the third?" I asked.

"The current Captain of the Knights of the Order of the Grigori," Turtle said.

"That's a mouthful," Amaymon said.

"That's what she said," Abi said immediately after.

They both looked at each other, grinning like twelve-year-olds. I shook my head but hey, I was grinning too.

"That asshole," I said.

As you can tell, he's not a nice guy. He had arrested me and beat me when I didn't comply—and when I made fun of Mustafa's moustache. A few years later I coached Abi into kicking his ass and then stole a golem and *really* ruined his day.

But in spite of his epic levels of assholish-ness, the captain served the Grigori well. He was loyal, he was competent enough, and he always fought for what he thought was right.

And if they were giving the leader of their army a vote, then the Grigori was getting ready to throw down, as well as have one of three votes right in their pocket.

Which begged the question:

"What does Rashid want, exactly?"

Turtle pursed his lips and his already heavily-lidded eyes became hidden. He set his tea cup down slowly and deliberately, moving sinuously despite the massive belly.

"He claims he would like a peace treaty. The power vacuum left by Greede's departure is simply too big to contend with. I have spoken with your sister. She is barely able to hold on. Acquiring Ryleh Corporation into the Ashendale Estate meant that all those assets Greede acquired without consent brought forward claims for justice."

Ryleh was Greede's company and essentially the focal point of his criminal empire. If Gil was restituting most of its ill-gotten gains, then what she had acquired was debt and a massive headache, not an asset. But it was simply too big and too important to let someone else take control of it.

"She's in trouble," I said.

Turtle shook his head. "Of a sort. Financially speaking, the loss—while significant—is not an issue. The claimants to power, however... Greede kept most of the monsters in the city under control. Now their leashes are undone. Your sister, even with her familiar's formidable help, cannot contend with such volume. She is managing the stragglers but if, say, a well-trained battalion was to invade, her power would be in jeopardy."

"Like His Royal Darkness," I said, understanding. "Mr. Goth King's making a move. He's here to probe."

"You have encountered his scouts," he said, looking meaningfully at Ishtar.

I felt her recoil.

"Maybe," I said. "But no king brings an army to a peace meeting. That's why Gil wants me on that panel. I'm the guy who beat the last big bad bully. I'm the big gun she's waving at them."

"Indeed," Turtle said. "But deterrents are not always effective. There are multiple instances in history when they merely incited more violence."

I grinned at him. I caught the same look on Abi's face. Her fingers stopped stroking Amaymon, who was now sitting up, glaring at Turtle.

"That's the thing about us," I told him. "We're always ready for war."

9

There was to be a party.

I didn't know that until I was knee-deep in tactical plans and picking out various forms of ammunition, when Turtle reappeared in my foyer wearing a fancier version of his usual forest-green Chinese suit. Even his staff had been polished and waxed.

"Why do I smell perfume?" I asked, sniffing at him.

Turtle cocked his head. "I have been told this fragrance suits me."

"You smell nice, Turtle," Abi said, elbowing me.

He beamed at her, then frowned at the weapons. "Erik, this is a peaceful gathering."

"With vampires," I added.

"They want to ally themselves with us."

"They being the aforementioned vampires."

"It's a peace talk."

"With vampires." I sighed and put the gun down. "Look, I'll wear the stupid shirt and put on the stupid fancy clothes-"

"And a tie," Abi—who had done me the kindness of helping me avoid any fashion faux-pas—interjected.

"No tie."

"You're impossible."

"No, I exist, therefore very possible, and also not wearing a tie."

She sulked. "Why do I even bother?"

"As I was saying," I turned back to Turtle. "I'll wear the fancy stuff but I *am* getting my coat because I look great in it-"

Amaymon made a noise.

"Shut up, you," I snapped. "I look great in that coat and it's shielded and charmed, and also, did I mention the vampires?"

"I see." Turtle gave Abi an apologetic look. She smiled back and then they both looked at me like I was a painting in a modern museum—not quite sure where to begin to unravel me.

Thirty minutes later I was ready (and armed) for whatever this meeting was to entail, while Abi and Amaymon took Ishtar to another safe house. This time, I instructed them to take it in turns guarding her. Amaymon also agreed to place a few mud golems around the perimeter as extra security. They wouldn't be much in a fight but they acted as sensors so if any more vampire cult whackos came at her, Abi and Amaymon would have plenty of warning.

Turtle extended his free hand, I took it, and a portal swallowed us.

TRAVELING by portal is not fun. My stomach used to be more sensitive, but since regaining my magic I've been revising all

I had learnt in my childhood, including spatial magic (i.e. teleportation).

I did not throw up. Which was good because no one had told me we were having this shindig inside my old house.

The Ashendale Mansion is likely older than most American cities and is a literal fortress of magic. Far below it is a dungeon for some of the most dangerous creatures this universe had hacked up when it was busy birthing planets and solar systems.

But above those horrors, Alan Ashendale, my father, had built a mansion that would one day inspire a certain white building in Washington. The first sixteen years of my life had been spent here, learning magic, learning about monsters and how to fight them, as my sister and I became the next generation of warlocks.

I hated every second of it.

It might have something to do with my father wanting to offer Gil and I as sacrifices to a ritual that would have enabled him to maintain all his powers. Long story short, I killed my father, and then I left, never to return.

Gil had stayed behind to rebuild the ruins.

Now, more than a decade later, she sauntered towards her brother.

"If you throw up in my foyer, I'm going to be very annoyed at you."

I grinned at her. "Fancy party. Chandeliers and all. And what looks like a good spread."

My sister rolled her eyes. "Have I introduced to you to the other members of the Grigori?" She motioned behind her and half the population of the room glided towards her.

Some, like Luke, Mustafa, and Evans were not new faces. Luke, tall, blonde, handsome in a would-like-to-repeatedly-punch-your-dimples kind of way, offered me a grin and a hand.

I kept staring at it. "Smells like barbecue."

Luke chuckled and retracted his hand. It hissed as he rubbed it on his expensive-looking black jeans. I wasn't about to fall for that.

Again.

Gil shot him a look. He winked at me.

"Hey, at least he's learning," he said, actually reaching out for a pastry. It was charcoal by the time it made it to his mouth but he munched happily.

Behind him, a massive hand fell on his shoulder. The monster it was attached to clapped him twice, in a way that Lenny might have petted the rabbit. Evans was wider than he was tall, bulkier than a WW2 tank, and wore a suit that was struggling to the last stitch to remain around his body.

His expressionless face moved with the rigidity of an automaton. Which made sense given that the Evans before me was not human.

"How are you, Erik?" he greeted me.

"Peachy," I told him. "Got yourself back in shape I see."

The last time we had met, Evans was in pieces and I had to hijack him. I was also a ghost.

Long story.

He nodded, his smile plastered soullessly on his face. "Of course. You too, I see."

I returned his nod.

Mustafa was next. He was around my height, with a small pot belly and beady black eyes. His moustache had grown twice as much, making him look like an Arabian version of Yosemite Sam. His turban matched his silken suit, an off-white and cream number with gold lining and pearl inlays. He looked like a million bucks and was probably wearing that too.

He didn't offer me his hand. Mustafa was an Abjurer, someone who specialized in the meta-tinkering of magic and energy. Barriers and runes were the basics, but more advanced levels could literally drain a person of their life force, or amplify it to a point where they made regular Adepts into Specialist level.

"Mr. Ashendale," he said.

"Mustafa."

"Is your familiar in attendance?"

I suppressed a chuckle. The last time I had met Mustafa he was the judge to my trial. I set Amaymon on him. Clearly, he remembered.

"No," I said. "We are going to keep this civil, aren't we?"

He didn't miss the threat. "Of course."

His two assistants, both dark-haired caramel-skinned beauties with light-blue and pink veils covering the lower part of their faces, glided along with him as he left.

Greg the Kresnik came to my sister's side, with drinks in hand for all of us. I gladly took mine, while Gil damn-near downed hers. My sister could manage a few multi-billion dollar empires at the same time, but set her brother on a diplomatic treaty and she was pounding drinks like there was no tomorrow.

Greg, bless his heart, was gently rubbing her shoulder. Turtle, I noticed, had set his drink down and switched to water. I offered him my empty glass and he smiled in thanks, before offering me his.

"Emrys just arrived," Greg said. "Seneschal needed a bathroom break."

"Again?" Gil asked.

"You know what slimes are like."

"No, actually I do not. I never met one before Seneschal."

"I'm sorry," I interjected. "A slime? What the hell is a slime?"

"Living Slime," Greg said, shrugging. "You know... squishy. Goop. But looks like man."

"He's a sentient sub-species that escaped the dark wizard who created him," Gil explained. "Slimes are incredibly difficult to animate, much more so to turn into servants who are worth anything. Seneschal is even more incredible in that he was created using his master's blood and therefore has access to magic. He's been working with the Grigori for the last fifty years, right after he reported his master for trying to recreate the black plague."

"So, a talking slime dude?" I asked. "Okay, I gotta meet this guy."

"He's... hydrating," Greg said.

"He's getting drunk?"

"No. He's in toilet, tapping into plumbing system," Greg said. "Please do not ask more detail."

I shuddered. "I won't."

Something set my warning bells off and I spun, coming face-to-face with a guy who stood inches behind me. He was exactly my height, wearing a black suit and a black shirt, which only made his white tie stand out more. His hair was graying and neatly combed, while his goatee was neatly trimmed and came down to a tapered point. His complexion spoke of the outdoors and he smelled...

Well, he smelled like a whole forest.

Like mildew, crushed leaves, wet fur, and blossoming flowers all rolled into one. He smelled like bark off a tree, ripe berries, and blood from a fresh hunt.

Slowly, the others turned to look at him. He had taken

everyone by surprise, excluding Turtle who was now examining an egg roll at the buffet table.

"Hello, all," said the newcomer. He kept his green eyes on me. "Sorry about the fright. Couldn't help myself." He extended his hand. "Emrys."

I shook his hand. His grip wasn't hard but I could tell he was hiding his strength.

"Erik," I said.

"I know," he said. "I've heard quite a bit about you."

"Neat trick."

"Camouflage," he explained. "But you sensed me."

"Only when you snuck up right behind me."

"That's the funny part."

The grip was now iron-tight. I pressed back. He winced. I heard teeth grind.

"Let me guess," I said. "Druid?"

"Indeed." He slackened the grip and rolled his shoulders. "Do you feel as uncomfortable in this monkey suit as I do?"

"You have no idea."

Emrys chuckled. "Finally. A kindred soul. A fellow wild beast." He glanced at Greg. "Sorry, Greg."

"I can be wild beast." He gave Gil a look.

"Ew," I said.

"Not like that," Greg said.

Gil let out something very strange from her mouth. It sounded like a giggle. Greg turned red and smiled sheepishly.

"Awkward," Emrys said. "So, Erik. Where do you stand with this whole vampire situation?"

"About as far away from them as I can," I replied. "You?"

The Druid smiled. "I see a few wards around the place. A good section of the surrounding forest is enchanted too.

Nice place to gather the big boys of the fanged community... And set them on fire once and for all."

"Emrys," Gil snapped. "We've discussed this before: this is a peaceful delegation. We will treat them with respect." She lowered her voice. "And I just paid a fortune for those drapes. If anything, we poison them. No fire."

"But fire is fun," I said.

Emrys clapped me on the back. "I like your brother, Gil. He makes some good sense. Erik, let's get you a drink. None of the champagne shit—a real drink. Something Irish."

Okay, so maybe the Druid wasn't that bad.

Whatever I was about to say next froze in my mouth. I turned to look at the main doors. Everyone else did too.

Mephisto opened the doors and announced:

"His Vampiric Majesty, King Rashid; Princess Carmilla; and Prince Valen. Welcome to the Ashendale Manor. We greet you in peace, honored guests."

10

The vampire contingent consisted of over a dozen soldiers, all dressed in a similar fashion to the trio I had faced a day ago. In the clear light of day—or rather, fancy chandelier—I saw that their armor was grey with a purplish hue, and dull gold trimmings. The helmets were sleek and medieval, along with the two-handed longswords that were strapped to their sides.

I counted at least sixteen, though I was sure the king would have more soldiers at his call should all of this turn sour.

Rashid himself was taller than his soldiers, closer to seven feet tall, with a long neck, long arms, and a jaw-line that could have been chiseled out of dark marble. His skin was a deep chocolate brown, complemented by the vermilion suit, a red so rich and deep it looked like red wine. His hair was black and tied back with a matching black bow that I would wager cost more than my house and car put together.

What really struck me were his eyes. Molten gold, somewhere between dark yellow and the color of flame.

His demeanor, his walk, his clothes—they all spoke of a predator that knew exactly the extent of his power and how far-reaching it could be, without directly flaunting it.

Behind him were two figures that stood out from afar.

The first was a stunning woman with skin of alabaster and eyes matching that of her father's. Princess Carmilla wore her black lace in a way that was equal parts seductive and uncaring. She smiled at me. The tips of her fangs brushed against her bottom lip.

I kept my eyes steady.

Or tried to.

At least the clown on Rashid's other side was a familiar beast. Prince Valen strode in with two scantily dressed vampire floozies at his side. He walked like he owned the place and looked just like his father, except shorter and leaner. As he sauntered by, I noticed for the first time that part of the buffet table did not have food but rather was stacked with blood bags, just like the kind one would find in a hospital. A golden punch bowl was filled with the same dark-red liquid, a few petals of white and pink floating on top.

As he walked by, Valen snatched a goblet and dunked it in the punch bowl, before throwing it back and gulping loudly.

He too met my eyes but I had no trouble staring this asshole down.

"Careful, Erik," I heard Emrys mutter beside me. "You might end up making more than your share of friends today."

"Just have the gasoline ready," I muttered back.

He chuckled into his whiskey.

Gil went over to greet Rashid. The latter bowed and formal introductions were made.

"I thought you'd at least provide some mage's blood," I heard Valen interject. His floozies giggled, as floozies are wont to. "So many options here. The least one of you can do is open up a vein for your guests."

Emrys muttered his excuses and rushed to Gil's side. He was beaten there by Greg.

"We keep things civil here," Greg told the prince.

"Yeah," Emrys said. "I mean, I've been told not to say anything rude. Play nice. That sort of thing."

Both Valen and Rashid regarded him. Druids have a certain aura. If they are strong enough they are essentially extensions of the land itself. That made vamps uneasy. The earth is their coffin, and the ash they become upon death is welcomed into the earth.

Rashid nodded at him.

"Master Druid." His golden eyes narrowed towards Greg. "Master Kresnik. We were once mortal enemies. Our kinds hunted one another."

"That is past," Greg said. The ice in his voice made me shiver. "Let us leave it there."

"Indeed we shall," Rashid said. "Valen, behave yourself. Our guests have esteemed us beyond our expectations. We will be nothing short of respectful."

Valen muttered something fast in a language I did not recognize. But clearly Emrys did because he chuckled and said,

"So many words," he said, casually sipping his drink. "Makes you wonder how come you never bite your own tongue."

Valen would have sprung on him. I knew he would have, I've seen that look plenty of times.

But his father laid a hand on his shoulder and spat out half a syllable and the asshole prince quieted down. He shuffled off with his sluts and went off to torment some other poor soul.

"What an asshole," I heard from behind me.

I spun and came face-to-face with Carmilla.

She grinned. "You should see the look on your face, Mr. Ashendale. Don't worry, I won't bite." Her voice lowered. "Not at first."

In my mind I said something suave and cool. In fact all that genius was so epic, it came out as:

"Uh huh."

Carmilla turned, giving me a wonderful peek at her bare shoulders, and picked up a pastry. She set it on her tongue and chewed, slow and sensual.

"Oh, it has been ages since I ate something human," she said. "Did you know vampires have different tastebuds? We are geared towards blood of course, so most food is horrendous to us. Only the richest human food will sate us."

"That explains the castles," I said.

Carmilla looked at me, and then burst out laughing. "From the movies you mean? Quite so." She gestured with her hands. They were amazing hands. "Speaking of castles, have you even been to Prague? I make my home there."

"Can't say that I have," I said, drinking more. I reached the end of my drink. So much for liquid courage.

Carmilla snapped her fingers. A waiter appeared from thin air, a whiskey glass poured and ready. A goblet of blood rested next to it. I felt something akin to electricity when Carmilla brushed her fingers against mine, relieving me from my empty glass and handing me a second.

All the while I kept looking into her golden eyes. To be honest, I think the ceiling could have come down and I would still have looked at her.

"You should come," she said, breaking eye contact and

sipping her drink. "Prague is wonderful, especially when seen at night from the topmost spire of my castle."

Okay so let's recap here:

Our hero has just been propositioned by a *vampire princess* to visit her castle—and yes, that includes all possible euphemisms—in freaking Prague. And while my head was being filled with wonderful images of her perfect physique and mine intertwined in a variety of X-rated ways, a small tiny, cock-blocking fact burrowed its way into my mind.

Carmilla was hot. Smoldering hot.

Carmilla was also a deadly, *old*, vampire, with powers that far outclassed those of any vampire I had met up until this point. The woman was a predator and worse, a politician.

And here's the thing I had learnt from Abi, her mom, and pretty much every sexy supernatural lady in my life:

They are hot. They know they are hot. I know they know they are hot. And if they have half a brain, which most do, they would also know that I know that they knew they are hot.

Confusing? Let me clear it up.

Sex, seduction, beauty, sensuality—these were all just tools for them. I had no doubt Carmilla would have taken me to her castle and banged my brains out.

And then, as I was grinning like a dumb idiot, she'd drain every last drop of blood and toss my carcass off that tower.

But I had to give her props. Her seduction mojo was perfect. I didn't even know I was being enthralled until the very last second.

She must have felt me pull back.

"Sorry, I'm not one for much travel," I said.

Her expression soured for a moment before she replaced it with a smile. Before I knew it, she was gripping my arm and leaning in, and her lips brushed mine.

"Shame," she said. "You are a legend, Mr. Ashendale. I will have you yet."

And just like that, I was watching her glide away, watching her as she strode further and further away, and then came the cold shower of having Greg and Emrys right in my face.

"So," the Druid said. "She try to bone you?"

"Huh?"

"The princess," Emrys said. "She was the first one here, you know. Came to town about a month ago to set this whole thing up. You were the first one she asked for."

"Apparently, you are legend," Greg said. "Is not good to be legend with vampires."

"They do tend to rip your head off," Emrys said with more joviality than that statement merited.

"Or they take you to bed and rip off other head." Both of us frowned at Greg, who shrugged. "What? I can tell joke too."

"Okay, big guy," Emrys said. "Let's keep you away from the vodka. Meeting's about to start anyway. His toothy highness wants to see you."

Sure enough I saw Gil beckon me over, with Rashid standing statuesquely behind her. His eyes were fixed on me.

"Want some back-up?" Emrys asked.

"Nah," I said. "I'll handle him."

"Erik," Gil said when I approached. "Meet His Vampiric Majesty, King Rashid."

He nodded at me. "You need no introduction," he said.

"Yes, I heard I'm a legend," I said. "Pleased to meet you, King Rashid. Are you here to start a war?"

The entire room fell quiet. Gil was practically vibrating next to me.

I kept my eyes on the king.

Rashid smiled, fangs bared.

"On the contrary, Mr. Ashendale," he said, speaking loudly enough for the room to hear. "I am here to bring peace between our species. Violence begets only destruction and poverty, wouldn't you agree?"

Now everyone was nodding at him, and generally loving his Gandhi impression and now I was the asshole.

Point, King.

As the buzz of the room grew louder, Rashid leaned in closer and whispered,

"Our friend Greede sends his regards."

I froze. My heart thumped loudly in my chest. Magic threatened to spill out.

Greede—what did he have to do with all this?

Was Rashid working with him? Was this all another plot?

Or was Rashid just messing with my head? Further throwing me off my game?

"Madam Ashendale," Rashid said. "Shall we commence?"

Gil nodded. She must have heard what he whispered to me because she had her battle face on.

She clapped her hands once. The room quietened again.

"I, Gil Ashendale, second seat of the Grigori and interim leader, hereby declare these peace negotiations begun."

11

The atmosphere inside the hall went from cordially cool to absolutely frigid.

After Gil's announcement, tables and chairs began moving of their own volition, rearranging themselves into a courtroom-like design. In the middle of the room stopped a massive round table, with high-backed chairs marked in Roman numerals. Gil had even gone to the trouble of personalizing the seats.

Hers was a black no-nonsense number with the Roman numeral 'II' etched at the top. I caught glimpses of flowers and vines chiseled along the sides. Beside her was a plain brown chair with 'III' that remained empty—that one was supposed to be my reward for doing a good job. I wondered if I could set it on fire—maybe that would finally indicate to my sister that I had no interest in joining her annoying book club.

Greg sat on a grey chair with 'IV', while next to him was the strangest chair in existence. It looked like a cross between a divan and a fish tank, rounded and high-backed but the seat was akin to a bowl.

Seneschal, the human slime, wore what looked like a neoprene rubber suit, with a comically large zipper running along his front. Several other smaller zippers ran haphazardly all over his body. His head was the only part of him that was visible. The skin was pale and almost transparent, with a tuft of black hair sticking out from beneath an old school biker's cap.

And he had no facial features. No eyes, no mouth, not even so much as an edge to mark were his face started and the back of his head ended.

Emrys sat on a throne made out of ash and thorn wood. The vines and leaves around him were very much alive.

Next, at number 'VII', was Mustafa, sitting on a throne of velvet and gold.

Evans' seat was a steel-reinforced chair. It looked more like scaffolding than furniture.

Luke the Pyromancer occupied a throne made out of plastic. As soon as he sat, the material smudged and smoked for just an instant. Something told me it was a fireproof chair.

Two seats were left at the round table. The one next to Gil was just a plain black chair marked with 'I'—the ever-elusive first seat of the Grigori, supposedly the most powerful magic-wielder on the planet.

The chair marked 'X' was also vacant.

The Grigori sat at an angle, all the better to watch King Rashid, who stood behind a pedestal with a screen behind him. One of his aides handed him a remote.

At his sides, Carmilla and Valen sat on thrones of bones and skulls. The princess waved at me.

I shifted uncomfortably. I and two others were situated adjacent to the Grigori on a table of our own. A much smaller table. I thought we looked like the kids table at Thanksgiving.

I sat on the furthest right, with Turtle next to me, munching on a plate of samosas. On his other side was the Knights captain, who wore his party outfit. That is, he had added a cape of mauve with gold trim to his usual medieval armor. His sword rested against the chair, while the one-handed mace he favored hung from his belt.

We did not make eye contact.

See? Keeping it peaceful.

"Thank you all for your welcome," King Rashid began. He walked slowly to the pedestal, the picture of a politician about to wow his audience.

"As you all know, I seek peace between our fiefdoms," he went on. "In recent years, a certain individual turned this city into a Nexus of power. Beings that once slumbered have now awakened."

He clicked the remote and aimed it at the screen. Greede's face appeared on the wall.

"This is Alan Greede, the man responsible for the destabilization of both your and my hubs of power. I believe it was one who sits with us today who eliminated this most prominent of threats."

Slowly faces started turning to me. I kept my eyes on Rashid, still trying to figure out his game.

"But with his demise, a great power vacuum formed," the king went on. "The Grigori are doing an excellent job, but you are outnumbered. You do not possess the resources needed to maintain such a level of excellence." He pressed the remote again. A line graph appeared on screen. "Behold. Do you see this rise over here? This represents the onset increase of vampiric activity in the city. Many of you have already encountered them."

Another click, another image change.

"This, is your new threat."

The image showed a desiccated vampire, clearly dead but somehow preserved from turning into ash. His body was marked from head to toe with tribal, swirling tattoos.

The same tattoos as the vampires that had come after Ishtar in my safe house.

"They call themselves the Brotherhood of the Vol, but they are better known as the Vol Bloodletters," Rashid explained. "They are a death cult that for millennia has been in search of a panacea for the vampiric condition that prevents us from walking under the sun. In short, they seek to become Daywalkers."

A collective murmur from the humans. I knew what they were thinking. Vampires were bad enough just at night—if they could hunt by day, they would overwhelm us. This wasn't just some power-hungry maniac.

This could spell the extinction of mankind as we knew it.

Emrys raised his hand. Rashid frowned, clearly not used to being interrupted.

"You said they've been attempting to find this cure for millennia," he said. "How come they have not succeeded?"

The king nodded and smiled. "That was my next point, Honored Druid. Observe."

The next picture was of a scepter. It looked like an ankh, the ancient Egyptian cross with a loop at the top, one of the oldest symbols of life and magic in existence. Embedded in the loop of the scepter was a solid black gem. Even through the picture, I could tell it was dull, as if the stone absorbed all light that touched it.

"This is the Scepter of Osiris," the king said. "It is an heirloom passed down from the time of the first vampires, when we were just whispered shadows in the night. The gem in the middle is an Astral Shard, cut from an Astral Stone."

Rashid switched off the presentation. His eyes glowed in the sudden darkness.

"What I am about to tell you may not leave this room. To do so would violate my decree as vampire king. And extermination would follow."

Well, that was one way to make everything tense again. Everyone gripped their weapons tighter but no one drew. No one wanted to ignite this tinderbox.

Rashid raised his right hand. "As such, I would like to request that all non-essential personnel be removed from the audience. Is this acceptable to the Grigori?"

They all looked at Gil. She nodded. From his position near the main door, Mephisto clicked his heel loudly enough for it to echo around the room.

"If you please," was all he said.

And when a primordial demon tells you to fuck off, you get out, vampire or otherwise.

He waited until the last of the servants was ushered out and closed the door behind him.

"Thank you, Madam Ashendale," Rashid said. He looked at the main table and then at the smaller panel I sat behind. He nodded again.

"Let us continue. I shall now reveal one of the most paramount and closely guarded secrets of the vampire. I do this as a show of faith, and to extend peace between our kinds."

He took a deep breath.

"Vampires are not of this world. We were not birthed by the Old Mother, nor were we blessed by the Ancient Father. We were made, by the very black stone you see embedded in the Scepter of Osiris. The Astral Stones connected the

Astral Realm to the Earth, allowing for the possibility of new species. We, the Vampyr—as we were known back then—were the first.

"But the Astral Stones have more properties. They also allowed the creation of a sub-species of our kind. An *abomination.*"

The passion and hatred in his voice made my teeth clatter. This was not something he had just come to believe. This was sentiment that was carried on from generation to generation, a culmination of years of indoctrination. An iron-clad belief, as real as gravity or the fact that the sun comes up every morning.

Faith like that has a real, primordial power.

"Some of my kind took to experimentation," he went on. "We determined that due to the astral nature of our condition, we could not walk the physical Earth when the sun was at its peak. The sun gives strength to those of the Old Mother, and we are not of her. We are of the Dark. But some were not content. They experimented. They sought those who were birthed by the Old Mother, and finally found a species that would be the ancestor of the were-creatures roaming the earth today. They found the Shape-Changers." He cocked his head. His fangs were eerily visible in the gloom.

"Today, you call them Lycans."

I had to give it to Rashid, the guy knew how to capture an audience.

Lycans were the ancestors of werewolves. Or, as he explained, any were-creature. They had roamed the earth thousands of years ago, shifting from one beast into another. How exactly had they settled on one shape and passed that singular lycanthropic gene on was uncertain. Maybe turning into so many shapes was unstable. Maybe it was the climate or the temperature. Hell, maybe they chose to stay in one form.

Either way, as far as we knew, they were extinct.

"Vampires and Lycans merged," Rashid went on. "The resulting creatures are the reason why genetically superior species do not conquer the planet, yet the weaker humans do. These abominations nearly wiped us all out, vampire and Lycan alike, as well as anything that could be used to sate their thirst.

"And that is why I have collected every last Astral Stone in existence. The Scepter, and the Astral Shard inside it, is the only object that contains this power outside my reliquary. Kings of old used it to keep their subjects in check."

He snarled and clicked the remote.

Ishtar's face filled the screen.

"Until this accursed harlot stole it from it me five years ago and gave the Scepter to Alan Greede."

OKAY, so, let's recap:

King Rashid just admitted that someone—Ishtar—had stolen his precious magical Scepter (and somehow that was *not* a euphemism, even if she had metaphorically cut off his balls).

Ishtar had given the Scepter to Greede who had done God-knows-what with it.

The Scepter was being hunted by a vampire cult who wanted to use the magic inside it to turn into Daywalkers.

And somehow I had ended up being shafted due to having already promised Ishtar my help.

"That's one of Greede's partners," Luke said, breaking the silence. "She's not some errand girl. She's also a succubus. Not someone you can control."

As soon as he said succubus Gil's eyes turned to me without moving her head. I kept my gaze plain and steady, the picture of casual ignorance.

"What do the Vol want the Scepter for?" Gil asked Rashid. "I assume there is a ritual involved. If we can find out the parameters of the ritual, we might narrow down the location they are in."

Rashid nodded. "Exactly what I was thinking, Madam Ashendale. I am glad we are of one mind. The Bloodletters take their name from the fact that they kill these hybrids—usually freshly created ones. They will undoubtedly attempt to find a Lycan descendant, commonly a werewolf in this part of North America, and capture a pureblood infant. They will turn it into a hybrid and then slaughter it. This ritual will help them gain more resistance to the sun until they become immune to it."

Gil turned to Evans. "Make a list of all known werewolf colonies and send a twenty-four-seven security detail."

He nodded.

I must have growled a bit too loudly because they all turned to look at me. Wordlessly I wanted to communicate to Gil how stupid her order was. If she showed Rashid the werewolf colonies, he was bound to just slaughter them as a precaution.

"Vaewolves," I said. "I heard that these hybrids are called Vaewolves in media circles."

Rashid took a step towards me. "And tell me, Erik Ashendale: as a hunter, do you think yourself capable enough to kill one of these… hybrids?"

"Never faced one, so I can't tell," I said. Then I grinned. "But I can hold my own against regular vampires and werewolves."

If the threat bothered him, Rashid did not give me the satisfaction of showing it.

"Be that as it may, Mr. Ashendale, you do stand a higher chance of stopping such a creature should it go rogue," he said instead. "But for now, the Vol Bloodletters are our priority."

Greg shifted in his seat. "Then I go, too."

Rashid nodded in agreement.

"This is what I ask of the Grigori," he said. "Help me eliminate this threat. Help me ensure that no one has to suffer because of these abominations, and I promise you that there will not be another vampire attack in North America. I will personally manage my brethren and ensure that we work together, not in opposition."

Ah, there it was.

Carrot, meet stick.

This is why I hate politics. What Rashid was basically saying was that if we didn't help him, he was going to loosen the reins on his people here. It would become a free-for-all. No one would be safe once the sun set. He could destabilize the Grigori and the system that kept us safe in less than a month.

And what's more, his people would already be here. All he would have to do is catch a first-class flight to his new castle.

On the other hand, if we *did* help him, we would be eliminating his rivals. Their methods aside, he had said this cult had been around for millennia. Which meant that until now they had been some sort of counterforce to the vampiric expansion. They had kept each other in check, or at least preoccupied enough to leave us alone. Eliminate them and there was going to be nothing holding Rashid back.

Not to mention that having the Scepter back would only serve to reinforce his seat of power.

Which only left one loose end.

"What about the woman?" I asked. "The succubus. The one who robbed you. You need any help finding her?"

His mask broke. Rashid's fangs grew larger and his eyes bore on me like a tsunami.

"No," he said, speaking in a very calculated manner. "I will find her myself. And I will endeavor to make her regret her decision to steal from me." He turned to the Grigori now. "After all, she was a partner to Greede, you have said so yourself. Eliminating her would be in our best interest, no?"

No one answered. Because no one wanted to condemn Ishtar to her death by agreeing.

"It is settled then." Rashid stood up. "As a show of faith, I shall leave my daughter and emissary, Carmilla, in your care."

At this point a smile slid up onto Gil's face that reminded me a lot of an alligator. She waved her hand and the chair marked with an 'X' slid away from the table.

"Of course," she said. "And it is my pleasure to welcome Princess Carmilla into the Grigori to occupy our tenth seat, where all probationary members sit."

I was pretty sure my blood turned to ice at this moment. Carmilla, a vampire-freaking-princess, had just been given access to possibly mankind's last defense against... Well, her own goddamn *father*!

I watched in horror as Carmilla slithered out of her throne of skulls and sauntered over towards the Grigori table. She gave them all a bow and sat down. The chair morphed into a replica of her skull throne.

"It is my honor," she said. "Let this be the first of many steps towards peace between us all."

"Indeed," said Gil. "But until such time as new rules are put in place, you—and by extension any vampire left behind by your father—must adhere to the common law set by this table. This will also include any hunting or dispensation of justice that you might feel the need for. We will work as one unit. Won't we, Princess Carmilla?"

I mentally screamed *YES*, and flipped the vampire lady off. Gil had outplayed them all! She let them go on and on, and then effectively neutered Rashid's progress with one move. True, Carmilla had a seat of power, but there were nine—well, seven—more on that table, plus the three of us stooges sitting back here.

Carmilla smiled venomously. "Of course. I am looking forward to it."

I half-expected a lightning bolt to go off between them. They had each outmaneuvered the other, taken an advantage, and to be honest, I had no idea how they'd done it.

All I knew was that I had to stop a vampiric death cult and prevent Rashid from culling the entire werewolf population this side of the Atlantic, while simultaneously hiding the succubus that was being hunted by both vampire parties.

Oh, but I had to play nice with said vampires or risk an all-out war.

I'll say it again:

I really, really, *really* hate politics.

12

After that whole debacle with the politics and the manipulation I was looking forward to some straightforward carnage. Not that I don't appreciate a good session of watching someone screw over delegates and be all Machiavellian. But there is something utterly serene about the directness of battle. It made things simple.

And you know me, I like things simple.

Fellow simpleton Greg asked me to come along to one of the known vampire nests in the city, one that had been cleared out years ago, but now neighbors had reported activity in. We suspected it was being squatted by the Vol.

The place was a downtrodden club that had seen better days, maybe working plumbing, and certainly less rats and roaches skittering all over the place.

I made a noise. Greg raised his eyebrows.

"Is not so bad," he commented. "Usually bigger rats. Good that it is still winter."

"Lemme guess," I said, putting on a thick accent. "In Russia, rat eat you."

Greg looked at me with a mixture of disapproval and amusement. "I lived nomadically for most of my life. Made good training. Adversity breeds power."

I shook my head. "So you're not Russian then?"

He shrugged before prying apart a rusted padlock that held the doors to the club shut.

"Define Russian."

"Um... I'm trying not to sound racist but I guess: vodka, Red Square, communism, USSR. Bad guys in movies." I shrugged. "Sorry, I've never been."

"Is okay," Greg said. "That is new Russia, though. I am from old one."

"So some Tsar before that? I'm rusty on my Russian history."

"No, before that," Greg said. "The man with pointy hat and lots of horses. Conquered China too."

I stopped in my tracks. "Hang on, are you referring to Genghis-freakin'-Khan?"

Greg beamed. "Yes, that's the one. Sorry, after few centuries all those memories get muddled."

"But... but that means..."

"I am older than you expect," Greg said. "This shocks you?"

I nodded. I mean, can you blame me? Usually the creatures I meet that are centuries old are just that: creatures. Sun Tzu might have looked human but for him it was just a necessary guise.

Greg *is* human. He was not a vampire—even though I doubt anyone knew what a Kresnik really was—he was not a demon, he was just a regular dude you could grab dinner and a beer with before going to slay some monsters.

"Does Gil know?" I asked.

"Of course," he said immediately. "There are no secrets-"

He snapped his head around suddenly. "We are being watched."

I reached back and drew my sword. Djinn's blade glowed faintly but it did nothing to illuminate the open area we were in. This was once a dance floor; now it was a lair.

I heard nothing but I could sense something was off. Like an itch at the back of your head, informing you that something that should not be there was.

Greg whipped his hand outwards. I never saw the dagger. There was a thud of flesh, a hiss and then a vampire was launching himself over us.

A glass ball rolled lazily between it and Greg, before exploding and showering the area with light. The vampire screamed and landed as a pile of charred flesh.

Suddenly we were surrounded. I didn't hesitate.

The first streak was large and wide, and largely a distraction. I held Djinn with both hands despite the handle being only large enough for one, and applied my magic. A twin sword emerged, made out of pure energy but identical to the real one.

Like I said, I'd been experimenting with spells I would have never thought of in the past.

Trailing my swords around me, I left tails of light that formed into phantom copies of Djinn. They hung in the air, lazily spinning around me until I was enshrouded with blades.

The first vampire struck. I swung. Seven swords cut a trail over his body. I ducked a swipe and struck with the left blade, embedding it deep into the vampire's thigh. Two more blades speared him before emerging free when the vamp became ash.

Behind me light seared my back even through the reinforced coat I wore. Greg was holding a seven-foot spear with a thick cruciform blade at the end. It glowed painfully and made a whistling noise as he cleaved through the denizens of the undead before him.

Then something hit my senses. Greg may be good at picking up motion—he was a predator after all, a hunter. But I'm a wizard. I've lived around magic all my life, honing my senses to it.

As Sandor drew closer, I sensed the Vol spell he used to empower the new vampires he brought with him. These were proper Vol, unlike the ones we had already faced. Their tattoos were glowing painfully, and most of them shuddered and shivered in agony.

"Go, my brothers," Sandor declared. "Eliminate the heathens who've disturbed our rituals. Go and test out the power I have bequeathed upon thee."

Seven of them rushed Greg, and four came at me.

I shot the floating blades at them. Two were struck down but did not stop. Their flesh was instantly sealed once Sandor spread his arms and began chanting. His own tattoos wriggled and danced on his body.

I charged towards the attackers, both Djinn and the copy in my left hand now pumped with energy that doubled the size of their blades, turning them into longswords. Both met the closest vampire and cleaved through his chest. I ducked, but was not fast enough to avoid a swipe at my neck. A talon gashed open the left side of my neck, a blow that would have been lethal were it not for my magic.

But it did slow me down enough for one of them to grab me. You never want to grapple with something that was bigger, stronger and faster than you. I felt him pull and reversed the grip on my left sword, plunging it into his stomach as he dragged me back. I managed to spin us around so that he was facing me but his back was to the other vampires, and released all the magic I had accumulated into the energy blade.

The resulting blast atomized the impaled vampire, tore another in half, and knocked both remaining vampires onto their asses. I was knocked back too, and that's when the normal vampires reached out to grab me.

Twin daggers shot into them, and I caught Greg using the momentum from his throws to swipe his glaive around, forcing the vampires back.

One vampire clutched my shirt. I stabbed Djinn into him and then shot myself forward…

Towards Sandor.

He caught my movement at the last second. His tattoos swirled on his body, forming a whirlpool which fired a beam of thick purple energy at me.

I hugged myself and pushed my magic. A dome of azure energy—the same color as Djinn's—shielded me from the blast. Sandor was looking at me, uncertain.

Like the other vampires, I was sure he knew about my condition. He must have also known that I never used shields. Now he was trying to figure out if the shield spell was channeled through my sword or maybe the information he had on me was wrong.

He raised both hands. Twin lasers shot at me. I rolled to one side, and intercepted one of them with Djinn, deflecting it towards the ground. A cloud of dust billowed up. Once it cleared I saw the little vampiric weasel running away.

"Don't lose him!" Greg yelled. "I will finish them off."

Sandor had the advantage in speed but he was no wizard. He did not know spatial magic; then again neither did I.

So I used something more basic: vectors. I focused on my trajectory and felt the wind rising around me for a second before it all compressed and became one single movement:

A single step that catapulted me the entire distance to Sandor.

I crashed into him, slamming both of us into a wall. My healing magic instantly began repairing the broken joints, while his vampiric biology did the same. I was the first one on my feet but nowhere near ready to fight.

Sandor rose and spread his arms. And that was when I realized he wasn't running to hide. He was running to recharge.

The sigils all over the walls of the small room, which had once been an office or a private party room, glowed. Energy flowed into him. Those tattoos swirled and glowed. His eyes became purple and hazy.

"I will not be defeated a second time."

I cocked my head. "Third time."

"What?"

"You will not be defeated a third time," I insisted. "Because you were defeated twice already. So a subsequent defeat would make it a third."

He chuckled. "Do you always jest this much in the face of death?"

"It's practically on my résumé."

"It does not matter."

"Oh, but it does." I swept my sword up, unleashing a beam of energy. I caught him right between the legs and Sandor was slammed into the ceiling. "It gives me time to charge up my spells."

As he fell I released my hold on the floor beneath him. Metal and linoleum withered and warbled, and began wrapping around him. Sandor ripped himself free but the spell was stronger. I just had to hold out a bit, maybe weaken him a little more.

And that's when Greg screamed,

"Erik, RUN!"

I looked out but did not see him. "Why?"

Half a second later my question was answered when a werewolf the size of a bus ripped a hole in the wall and roared in my direction.

13

In the course of my long and checkered career as a monster hunter, and part-time supernatural punching bag, I've had the misfortune of encountering not one, but *two* werewolf alphas.

One was when I was just starting out, a fresh-faced wizard with hopes and dreams. That werewolf was an angsty teenager who had managed to tap into anger-fueled magic and let loose on his bullies.

The second was Greede's personal guard, Ubatu. That guy had been huge, laced with muscle, sinew, and silver fur, and more power than I had ever faced from one of his kind.

So when the *third* preternaturally large werewolf caved in half the office and slammed into Sandor, I thought I knew what I was in for.

The shriek that came out of Sandor was primal and bone-chilling. As it hit me I remained there, my legs suddenly jelly. No matter how powerful you are, how adept you are at slinging around the forces of nature, when faced with something that *is* a force of nature you Know (with a capital K) just how far down the food chain you truly are.

So I just watched as the werewolf clamped down its massive jaws on Sandor and bit down with a thousand pounds of force. Teeth the size of daggers sheared through the vampire's flesh and blood spewed everywhere. The werewolf gave one shake and Sandor's screams became squelches that abruptly stopped when the werewolf got his heart. Ash fell past the werewolf's teeth.

It turned to look towards me, yellow eyes of hate bearing down on me.

I've always said that when you get right down to it, there are two types of people in this world: those that go down cowering from the nightmare, or those who take the viking route. Those crazy bastards that look upon an oncoming horde, grab their axes, scream something towards Odin, and just resolve to die grinning.

"Good doggie."

Hi, my name is Erik and I'd like a first-class ticket to Valhalla. And I'll take my mead in a horn. Like a boss.

Doggie wasn't amused.

I never saw him strike. I just felt something sledge-hammer into my side and then I was airborne. On my flight, I saw a blur of grey and white, and Greg was swiping at the werewolf, who dodged and did something I had never seen a werewolf do.

It chuckled.

My journey came to an end when I crash-landed (because Erik Airways does not believe in commodities likes smooth landings) into a wall and slid down. My legs took a while to respond but my hands were fine so I held out my gun.

The werewolf's eyes trailed my movements and dodged behind a wall.

Huh. Since when did werewolves play the tactical game?

They were the powerhouses (well, one of) of the supernatural world. Especially a werewolf that big. It would be able to tank just about anything I threw at it. And yeah, I knew there was a human brain behind all that, but "human" was a loose term with transformed werewolves. They were capable of the full level of intelligence—but the act of transforming into an animal was a willful choice. You *chose* to let go of your humanity, and that choice started with your consciousness.

Greg yelled something in a language with a lot of guttural sounds, and stabbed the tip of his spear into the wall where the wolf had taken cover. White light sheared through the mortar, and the werewolf emerged. He pelted Greg with rocks, catching him unawares, and managed to get a set of claws between them. The end result was Greg on the ground, two of those claws digging into his chest. I had heard the chainmail beneath his baldric as he fought earlier, but that mail was meant for the relatively weak vampires, not a hulking werewolf.

"Bad doggie," I yelled.

He turned to look at me. I shot him in the face. My bullets were not silver but Jack, former student of mine and professional blacksmith, made them out of melted crosses and church bells.

The wolf dodged at the last second. The bullet—angry red thanks to the magic I had pumped into it—sliced into his neck. On a regular person it would have been game over, bye bye artery. But this wolf had a neck the size of a car tire, so all I got was muscle and a whole lot of angry canine.

The wolf leapt at me. I made my legs motor and off I ran. As I retreated I fired some more, and then a silver lance shot through, embedding itself in the wolf's back.

The werewolf reared up and roared. I swapped my gun

for Djinn, slicing as I drew the blade in a reverse grip. It was not a particularly powerful strike but I needed speed. The blade cut a nice gash that distracted the werewolf and made it roll forward. I fixed my grip and gave him a proper strike.

Claws intercepted the blade. I pumped more magic into it. The wolf snarled, his snout close to my face. I could see a deep scar running down one side of this face, a hair away from his left eye.

He could be injured. It was just a matter of power.

Good. Now we were on Erik's turf.

"Bad. Fucking. Doggie."

My voice changed as shadows emerged all around me. One of them snaked behind the wolf and wrapped around Greg's lance, still embedded inside the wolf. I wrenched it out, while also blasting magic along Djinn's blade. The wolf stumbled and flattened on the ground.

The magic slash tore a deep gash in his shoulder.

I faced up to him, sword in my right hand, lance in my left.

Then, something *burned*.

I mean, burned me on a primordial level.

I screamed as I dropped the lance, and looked at my left hand. My palm was scorched. Half my shadows wrapped around my hand, healing it fervently.

What the hell was up with that lance? I knew it was bane to anything unholy, but that's a really subjective term in my world. We tend to think unholy means demons or vampires, which isn't too far off the mark, but my shadows were Life Magic. The primordial stuff of creation.

The realm of gods supposedly, though I thought it prudent to keep that bit of information to myself. People tend to get all uppity when you tote around that kind of power. Mortals would want to kill you as a contingency, and gods would want to kill you just to eliminate a potential threat. Read: competition.

The wolf took a step towards me. Something round exploded between us. I felt the explosion in my gut, and was flung backwards. There was no shrapnel: just a very loud bang, and then I went blind.

When my eyes worked again, the werewolf was gone.

"What the hell was that?"

"Silver chaff grenade," Greg said. He was holding his lance again. A black handprint marred the polished silver shaft where I had grabbed it.

He cocked his head at me. "Do you want to explain something to me?"

I picked up my gun and held it to my side. "Sure."

"This lance is warded off against beings that are not of this world," he said. "Why did it hurt you, Erik Ashendale?"

I shrugged. "Beats me."

Greg seemed to consider the answer for a second. "I have seen your powers. I have also seen the white smoke your sister emits when in a similar state to yours."

"So now you're trying to figure out which wins," I said. "The hunter or the boyfriend."

"Do not be so ridiculous," he said, casually wiping the scorch mark off the lance. "I was merely suggesting finding out the nature of your ability. Both of you." He shook his head. "You can be so stubborn."

I'm no expert in reading subtext but I had the distinct suspicion he was not talking about me. Greg and Gil were not seeing eye to eye.

But then again their relationship was not my business.

Unless he hurt her. Then I would make it my business. Starting with shoving that fucking lance up *his* business.

I shook my head.

"What was that thing?" I asked. "The werewolf. Where the hell did it come from?"

Greg sighed. "He is a mighty beast. I have encountered him before." He pointed at his eye. "I gave him that."

"Nice."

"It was not."

I shrugged and started walking. "Let's have a look around Sandor's place. I saw some markings I want to examine. It might give us a lead as to how the Vol ritual works."

We walked in silence for a while.

"So you have a werewolf problem then?" I asked, as I inspected the walls. None of the markings made sense to me.

"I suspect he is from a lost tribe," Greg answered. "He loathes vampires with a destructive passion."

I looked back. "And we know the Vol are looking for a werewolf baby to experiment on." I turned back to the markings and followed them to an altar.

"Oh, hello," I said, picking up a dull item.

I turned to show Greg the Scepter of Osiris, sans black gem.

"Is that…"

I nodded.

"And it's missing the Astral Shard," I said. "I think we're too late. We're no longer looking for the Shard now. We're looking for the Vaewolf it created."

14

A knock on your door at midnight is never a good thing. Some might call it an omen. An optimist might call it opportunity.

It wasn't.

I opened the door to find Carmilla, vampire princess, and Turtle, a demi-god emissary.

"Hello, Erik," Carmilla said, her tones all silky smooth and cordial, and taking me completely unawares. I saw her eyes glide down my body—I was half-naked and freshly roused from bed.

Turtle waved at me, his massive palm windmilling behind her. "We have a message for you."

"And of course you had to deliver it now," I said, trying to hide the sarcasm from my voice.

I didn't try very hard.

In my line of work you get few hours of sleep, so whenever, say, one gets done hunting vampires and getting slammed by werewolves a little earlier than anticipated, one goes the hell to bed because one is usually sleep-deprived.

Carmilla shrugged. It did wonders for her shoulders.

"Sarcasm does not suit you, Erik. Besides, the night is so young."

Vampires. No respect for us diurnal creatures.

I stepped back and walked a little further into my office, intent on making coffee.

"Erik..." came Turtle's voice. I turned. "While I have no issue with your threshold and the defenses thereof, I am afraid that we still require your permission to enter your home."

I blinked several times at him until my brain went online.

"Right, right, sorry. Come on in," I said.

The two of them sauntered in, headed straight for my couch and sat down.

If movies have taught us anything, it's that inviting vampires into your home is a bad idea. But in reality, that invitation comes with a whole bunch of clauses and conditions, primarily the negation of maliciousness towards the host (me).

Which meant that Carmilla couldn't just decide she was bored and rip my throat out. Likewise, she couldn't leave and then come back. Invitations are a one-time pass.

But that also meant that she was my guest and I, her host. I had to abide by the old ways of respect and decorum. It's not exactly something you learn in schools anymore, much to the detriment of society.

Essentially it all boils down to "no violence under any circumstances".

Does that mean that these rules were always observed? Of course not. The world is filled with assholes, supernatural or otherwise. That's one thing you can count on.

But I had invited them in, so I was responsible for them

while they were under my aegis. And that was enough for me to take said responsibilities seriously.

I found a shirt and put it on, and then went to the kitchen to make some coffee. Turtle walked next to me, wordlessly taking over the beverage section. He was here just as a witness, because those were the rules of the peace treaty. Whatever message the vampire princess had, it was for my ears.

"What brings you here, Princess?" I asked her, taking the seat in front of her.

Carmilla pursed her perfect—and lethal—lips and glanced towards the stairs leading to the bedrooms. "I do not sense anyone else in this building," she said. "Yet my intelligence sources inform me that you live with a succubus and a demon."

"They are taking a sabbatical," I replied. "Something about me being a handful."

In reality I had sent the two of them on guard duty with Ishtar, while also having Amaymon check out known werewolf tribes around the city. Most of them were friendly and I wanted a heads-up if Rashid, the Grigori, or the Vol moved against them.

"Plus," I said, "with them around where would I be able to fit in all the extravagant orgies?"

I have no idea why I said that. Men have this thing where sometimes we think with our downstairs head. Then again, I was fairly sure what, or who, could have inspired such fantasies in me.

Carmilla was dangerous, she was seductive, and she was a bad idea. Going by my past relationships, she was just my type.

Let that sink in for a second.

My last relationship was with Gil's predecessor, a woman

centuries old, possibly the most powerful magic-user on the planet, and someone with whom messing about had not been recommended. She had died in my arms.

Before her there may have been one or two fleeting encounters, going back to the time I faced the Leviathan, the Sin of Envy, on an island of its own making and had a romantic encounter with a witch stranded there. Who then chose to defend the monster who had kidnapped her in the first place.

So yeah, Carmilla maybe be ticking all my boxes but that didn't make it a good idea to give into whatever she was offering.

She leaned forward.

"You jest but you needn't be lonely tonight," she said.

Sometimes having both a penis and a brain is really, *really* hard.

(Hah, get it?)

"That's alright," I said. "No need to trouble yourself. I was just headed back to bed."

Her eyes were positively smoldering. "That *is* where I intended to lead us."

Turtle mercifully appeared with what was a pot full of coffee, and set down three cups. He offered me one—as well as a withering look. I took the cup. I drank. I shut up.

Carmilla seemed amused even as she sipped her coffee.

"To business then," she said. "My father has returned to Egypt, along with Valen and the rest of our entourage."

"Sans army of course," I added.

She nodded.

"And you have been invited to visit," she said. "My father wishes to impress upon you the importance of eliminating the Vol Bloodletters. He has already heard of what you and the Kresnik did earlier today." When she smiled her fangs poked out. "And he was most impressed. So impressed in fact that he has given you license to hunt on his ground."

I considered that for a moment.

If I took the fight to the Vol's home turf it would definitely spell trouble for me. They were at home—I was not. They had all their power hubs ready while I would have to build mine from scratch. It wasn't necessarily a lost battle, but I would be fighting uphill.

But on the flip side, it would force the Vol's attention behind them. Hell, if all the fighting was taking place in Egypt, then there would be no reason to get America involved. I'd be clearing my home from invaders.

It seemed like a good idea.

Which is why I said, "What's the catch?"

Carmilla smiled. "You would be doing my father's bidding. With you fighting the war on the Vol, he would have no issue expanding his territory." Her eyes darkened. "Including into mine."

Ah. The plot thickens.

"I do not wish to have my father rule any longer," she said with a long sigh. "Have you ever been to a place where there is nothing but sand and heat? It is a miserable place for a vampire."

"Then why does your father stay?" I asked.

"Because of *tradition*." She spat the word like it was poison. "That was where the original Necropolis was built and all of my ancestors buried. It is there that our legends have taken root, where our names are spoken only in metaphors and children's stories. That is a form of power, as you well know."

I did. There was only one way to defeat immortals: forget about them. Over the decades, beings like the Roman and Greek gods had lost influence. They didn't die out, of course, which is why their legends survived. But now they were not even a fraction of who they were a thousand years ago.

Deities feed on belief, and immortal creatures like vampires, while not technically on the same scale, required that belief for their way of life. It's what kept the torches and pitchforks at bay.

Hell, magic-users operate under the same guise. What happened in Salem should never be allowed to happen ever again.

"You struck out on your own," I said. "You started all over, in your own territory. Inevitably, you created a new world order."

Carmilla nodded. "I chose to be happy under my own terms. And to that end, I was content with the king's rule. The distance proved beneficial for our... relationship."

Translation: Carmilla was an independent child and no one was going to tell her how to live.

"And if I help him out," I summarized, "he's free to deal with all the other issues stopping his plans for world domination. Including his daughter."

She shook her head.

"Not domination," she said. "Subjugation. My father is a king, and he understands that a king of nothing is no king at all. A king requires people to willingly accept him. The first few generations will be slaves, but eventually, maybe in five hundred years, a vampiric monarchy will become the norm." She sighed. "My father is over six thousand years old. I myself remember the pyramids being built when I was a little girl. We have time, Erik Ashendale. We are used to simply waiting for our opposition to die out."

"Which means we need to act now," I said. "Which also means that you're here with a proposition: to join you."

I glanced at Turtle. He sipped his coffee, looking at the table the entire time.

"Yes," said Carmilla. "I find myself in need of power if I am to depose my father. And lest you think me tyrant, consider this: I have not kept a single soldier in my retinue. All troops left in the city owe their fealty to my father. It was only thanks to Turtle's abilities that I managed to sneak out unnoticed."

It was hard to imagine Turtle, with his massive gut and size, sneaking anywhere but I had to remind myself that I was dealing with an avatar here.

"Unlike my father, I believe that peace is begotten through mutual agreement," she went on. "Perhaps even pleasure." A smile. "If both parties are satisfied, no one fights."

"Make love, not war," I said. "Literally."

"Of course," she said. "The purpose of life is to live it to the fullest. My father was right about peace bringing prosperity to our respective species but he is willing to get it through fear. I am not. He rules via tradition. I have proof that if one rules with openness and kindness, one is loved more as a monarch. I do not exaggerate when I say that my people love me, Erik."

"This sounds a lot like a pitch," I said. "And I have learnt not to take sides in matters that I don't understand." I leaned forward and set the cup down. "Look, Carmilla, I wanna believe you. But what you're saying sounds too good to be true. You sound freaking perfect. Which leads me to believe that either you're lying or you're delusional."

She bared her fangs at me. It wasn't a snarl or a gesture of violence. She was just showing me our primary difference.

"I am what I am, *human*," she said. "I am a huntress, a predator. Of course, you will fear me. Of course, you will question your sanity around me, and by extension the validity of my existence. I will shed blood and feed on it." She shook her head. "But I do so in a controlled fashion. My kine comes to me voluntarily, wizard. I have no need to take what is freely given."

I watched her in silence. There was a lot to unravel there, but essentially she wasn't hiding who she was. Carmilla had just told me she was dangerous, but in a controlled way. She was a ruler like all others, and rulers were killers in some fashion or another. It was part of the job.

"Say I side with you," I said. "Let's pretend I throw in my lot with yours. What happens to your father, the current king?"

She cocked her head and gave me a look as if I was the stupidest person she'd ever seen.

"He would be dead," she stated plainly and emotionlessly. "King Rashid will never give up his seat. It must be taken from him."

Well. That was that, then.

"And Valen?"

That one actually got a laugh out of her.

"My brother? Yes, he is next in line but he is no ruler. Frankly, I am more threatened by your teapot than I am my brother." She chuckled. "I will give Valen the option to rule as my vassal. He likes Egypt—he can have it. But I will make my lands the new capital."

Her look turned feral.

"Or he can choose to die, along with all the elders who will inevitably oppose me. I intend to cleanse the old world of our presence and focus only on my territory. There, at least, I can smell the mildew and wet grass, and not be miserable under the scorching heat."

She leaned forward.

"This I swear," she said. "I will rebuild the vampire kingdom under my aegis, far away from you and yours—unless you prefer us be a little... closer," she added seductively. Then she straightened up. "I will not interfere with mortal affairs nor will I seek to conquer more than my own lands. I am quite content with what I have. Like you, I seek peace. And my first act will be to sabotage my father's attempts at robbing you of yours."

Her hand reached out and grasped mine. It was cool to the touch but not unpleasant.

Not in the slightest.

"Will you help me, Erik?"

There it was. The plight of a damsel in distress. Princess or not, she was a woman who needed my help. I am old-school like that.

More than that, she was trying to do the right thing. Or at least she believed she was.

Part of me knew she was painting too pretty a picture for it all to be true. But she was offering a solution against Rashid and there was nothing pretty about that.

Survive today to fight tomorrow.

"Okay," I said. "What do you need?"

Carmilla glanced at Turtle. He nodded. "We will not interfere with this course of events," was all he said.

"The Scepter," Carmilla told me. "It is a ruler's symbol. Give it to me and I will depose my father. I know you have it."

I stood up and retrieved the Scepter of Osiris. Carmilla practically drooled but then her face slackened when she saw it was devoid of the black jewel.

"This is all we found," I told her, offering her the Scepter.

She took it reverently. "This will appease my father temporarily. But it is the Astral Shard I need."

I shook my head. "Too late for that."

She smiled. "It is never too late. The Vol have learnt how to mine for Astral Stones."

"But I thought…"

She held up her hand. "My father told you he has all the samples in existence. My father is a ruler and a tyrant. In truth, these Stones have always been available to those with the correct means to obtain them."

"The Vol," I surmised. "That's why you want me at their stronghold."

"Come to the Necropolis, Erik," she said, gently standing up. Turtle likewise stood up.

They had started walking out when she turned back. "Who knows? Maybe it won't be so miserable with you there."

15

Needless to say, I did not go back to bed.

Instead I waited for a few hours and cast several detection spells. Once Carmilla was no longer there to do wild things to my hormones I could think clearly again. It struck me that one way to play me more efficiently was to spy on my every move and I didn't want that.

Twelve detection spells later I had found three basic surveillance spells. They were hidden beneath several concealments, which meant mortals had cast them.

Humans.

The Grigori.

Which made sense. Rashid wanted Ishtar, who in turn was linked to Abi, who in turn was linked to me. Besides, I knew my sister. She was that paranoid.

I dismantled the spells, doubled up my wards, and then set to work on a golem. Mine was slightly different than Amaymon's. He was intimately linked to the element of earth. I had to do it the old-fashioned way. Kiln, pottery, sigils, the whole nine. Luckily, you only need a lump of enchanted clay, and we had plenty of that. The golem grew into a clone of me, and I made it sit in front of the TV watching sitcoms (my typical stay-at-home routine). Hell, I even put in a call for a pizza an hour from then.

To anyone observing me, it would look like I was having a lazy day off.

But when I made my clone open the door to check the mail, I slipped out under a camouflage spell. Once again, I thanked the stars for my training with Abi. My camouflage spell was nothing to write home about. I know mid-level wizards who could do better. But it was enough.

I couldn't take my car either. That would have been a dead giveaway. So I jogged.

I jogged right until I felt my lungs on fire and then hailed a cab. I gave the driver the address and then sat back the whole way there, grinning like an idiot.

THE SECOND HIDEOUT we had put Ishtar in was a boat.

Not a big boat.

More like a barge.

A really tiny barge.

Hey, *you* try renting marina space in this economy and see how well that floats your boat! (Pun intended.)

It was still early morning but Eureka had a thriving fisherman's business, so I did not go by unnoticed. Hell, the security guy even recognized me, and watched me with nothing short of suspicion when I inserted the little key and made my way inside.

My part of the dock was old. Very old. Yeah, it was cheaper, but more importantly, it was remote.

Which was good, because Ishtar was having a fit.

I climbed on the boat to find Abi wrestling her mother. Ishtar was halfway over the railing, attempting to scream but the railing was cutting off her oxygen. Abi's face was covered in a sheen of sweat. She was in her underwear which lead me to believe that Ishtar had had a fit, and her daughter had jumped up to rescue her straight from bed.

But from what?

"Erik, help me," Abi snapped when she saw me.

I reached over and hauled Ishtar back on the deck. She struggled and kicked me in the shin.

"No! Let me go." Her voice echoed loudly. "Let me end it."

I blocked another wide swipe for my torso and held onto her arm. "End what?"

"She wants to kill herself," Abi said, wrestling her mother's body to the ground. She settled her weight on her. Ishtar was taller than her daughter but Abi had gone from a super-slim cover-model physique to that of a fighter. She had more mass and, more importantly, she knew how to use it.

Ishtar was going nowhere.

"Stop," I said, holding Ishtar's head in place to stop her from accidentally snapping her own neck, she was thrashing so hard. Tears streaked down her eyes. "What's going on?"

"The pain!" she wailed. "It won't leave me. There's something inside me that's tearing its way out."

I didn't have time to focus my aura vision but I recollected the way that parasite had hung onto her, slowly sucking her life-force. How long had she had that thing? If it had been there the last time I'd seen her, then Ishtar had been carrying that thing inside her for about three years.

Even the most powerful immortal creature would eventually run out of juice. In fact, I was kind of impressed Ishtar had lasted this long.

Of course, that also didn't take into account how much the parasite would have grown.

And just like any infant, it would start to kick.

I winced and waited until Ishtar's struggles ceased. She got rapidly exhausted and then, like a narcoleptic attack, she fell asleep, snoring softly.

"What the living fuck?" I began.

"She's been in pain since last night," Abi said, leaning back. Her breathing was heavy. I tried hard not to stare. "I gave her some painkillers but it didn't take."

"She's not safe here," I said. "She's calling attention to herself."

"Just let me catch my breath," she said. "I can mesmerize any onlookers."

"That's the least of our problems," I said. "Your mom's got a psychic parasite inside her. And when it cries, the Vol hear it."

To her credit Abi took all of three seconds to digest that information and summarize it in one word:

"Shit."

"We have to move," I said, getting up. "We need to get her someplace they will never find her."

Abi shrugged. "Underground?"

I shook my head. "No. It literally can't be a place on this Earth. That thing inside her can tap into the material frequencies of this plane. We can put miles between them but it's still a game of cat and mouse. And I don't know about you, but I don't like running."

She nodded. "Erik. You said this was a parasite." She bit her lip. I knew what was coming next. "Is there a cure?"

I shook my head. "I don't know. I've never encountered anything like it before. But I do know that you can kill anything that's living." I gave her a hard look. "Or you can extract it."

She understood. "Just like…"

"You can say it, Abi," I said. "Just like me when I had the cacodaemon inside me. I managed to push Wrath out and face him."

"But you're you," she said.

"I had help."

"You had an angel."

I looked up and grinned. "And I can get her something even better. Tell me, does your mom like Chinese?"

16

We drove—or sailed, I suppose—the barge a few miles out from the coast. I had never tried making this kind of long-distance call before, and if the being I wanted to summon turned up, or even if something else did, I wanted to make sure no one got swallowed up in the accidental tsunami they might cause.

Water is the element of change. It represents patience, logic, alchemy and science, but it is also linked with psychological instability. Being sane usually means having some form of routine, something to anchor you to reality. Water does not have that. It is ever-changing.

Now imagine that inside a monster and you know why it was wise to take precautions.

From what I knew about Sun Tzu and the Four Guardians, each one of them was linked to an element. If my theory was correct, then Sun Tzu was the balance, the aether, the Center. Phoenix would be Fire, no doubt, which would make him south, cardinally speaking, and Summer in terms of seasons.

Now here was where it got tricky. My magical education

was western. We had four elements plus the spirit, whereas eastern magic is usually divided up into five elements, and a central being that might or might not also be part of the five-element sequence.

Yeah, it's confusing.

Lucky for me, I wasn't summoning Tiger or Dragon, or Sun himself. I wanted Turtle, and him I knew would be the water element. Water is opposite Summer and south, making it Winter and north.

I was simplifying a lot but it wasn't as if I could show up at Sun Tzu's front door. Not without alerting every vampire in the damn city.

I had Abi stop the barge smack in between the harbor and one of the islands, thinking that if I got super lucky we would be able to swim to either location, and set about chanting.

I don't speak Chinese. I don't read Chinese.

Luckily, when you are summoning something that you've had a connection with before, you can substitute the words. Words by themselves have no power—it is we who give them meaning, who shape them into something real.

So I chanted the only Chinese I knew: the ghost-banishing chant that Uncle uses in *The Jackie Chan Adventures* cartoons.

Racist? Debatable.

Desperate? You bet your ass it was desperate.

I stood on the prow of my barge, bobbing on the waves, recalling a chant from memory without any clue of what I was saying, and hoped for the best.

My life in summary, ladies and gents.

I really did hope. Turtle was, at least so far, one of the good guys. He had come through for me on multiple occasions. I mean, if it weren't for him slipping me a stake made out of peach wood one time, I would have been torn apart by a Jiang-shi, a subtype of vampire.

The sun beamed down in my eyes and I closed them.

"No!"

I winced when a wooden staff struck me in the shins. "Ow!"

"Bad Erik," Turtle said. "Summoning me is not a good idea."

I rubbed my eyes and gasped.

Turtle was sitting cross-legged on a turtle's shell in the middle of the ocean, just a staff's swing away from the barge. His jolly face had a frown marring it, which made him look more like a fussy child than a scary elemental being.

Turtle stood up on the shell and hopped on board. The barge creaked and groaned and tilted a bit too much, but it held and Turtle sniffed the air.

"I see why you called," he said. He waved and I saw the turtle in the ocean raise a flipper and wave back, before sinking into the depths. "The woman Rashid is seeking is here."

I gritted my teeth.

Sun Tzu had known about Ishtar when he saved us from Sandor and the Vol's first attack, but that was *before* the peace treaty.

Now that we were all playing nice, having ties with Ishtar basically meant I was openly defying the terms of the treaty.

Terms that Turtle and Sun Tzu, and possibly a host of other deities, had agreed on defending.

"You were there yesterday," I told him. "You heard what Carmilla said."

He said nothing.

"Ishtar is under attack by something psychic," I pressed.

"She needs help. Now, whether she will be useful in aiding us with Carmilla's plan, or whether she will be given to Rashid for justice, that remains to be seen."

Turtle's grip tightened around his staff. "And will you, Erik Ashendale, mortal wizard, be the one to pass judgment on her?"

I forced down a gulp.

"No," I said. "I'm the one saying that no matter which direction this goes, Ishtar needs medical attention. She needs to be alive. And I do not have the necessary means to aid her. You do."

He cocked his head. "I am who I am."

"You're a guardian to a temple," I said. "We've been there before."

He glanced at Abi. "Yes, I remember. How is the trickster?"

She glanced down at her weapon, now a keychain hooked to her belt loop. "He is what he is."

Turtle nodded. "Apt." He turned his attention back to me. "You ask of me a great deal, Erik Ashendale. You ask me to take sides."

"You came to me," I told him. "Before the treaty, before Rashid even showed up, you came to find me. You didn't have to but you did. That tells me that you're playing a long game with people you do not trust. And maybe the decision we make affects not just one god but many." I took a deep breath and released it. "You want to know who you can trust. Because you are not human. But you're forced to play with us."

Turtle held his stony gaze for a second.

Then he threw his head back and laughed.

It wasn't just a laugh. The water rocked the boat. A

million seagulls took to the air. The winds picked up, howling along with him.

"Yes," Turtle finally said. "Perhaps you are not as wrong as we originally anticipated. You are still misinformed and you make assumptions based on the limited scope of your training and humanity." He chuckled again. "But you are not wrong. And that is most marvelous."

He raised his staff and slammed it forcefully into the barge. I half expected him to sink us into the abyss.

Instead, when I opened my eyes, we were in a dark room, I'd been in before.

Sun Tzu appeared with a tall Asian man wearing a scarlet Chinese suit. His nose was long and hooked, and his features were sharp as a lance's tip.

Phoenix wordlessly came over to us and scooped up Ishtar from the ground next to Abi's feet. He placed her on a divan and glided over—yes, literally glided—towards a medicine box. When he opened it, the smell of a thousand ointments wafted through the air.

"Come," Sun Tzu said. "We must let him work in peace."

We walked up to the Chinese food restaurant in chilling silence. Sun Tzu sat us down on a vacant table and provided us with tea.

"Drink," he said gently. "This tea will help clear the mind."

I sipped. It was leafy and grassy and tasted like a meadow, but a look from Sun Tzu made me finish the whole cup.

"Abigale," he said. "I wish you to remain here. Your mother's health will greatly improve if she knows her family is close."

She opened her mouth to speak but he held his hand up.

"Where Erik is going next he cannot take you."

She looked at me.

"I've been invited to check out Rashid's place," I said. "And he's right. Your mental powers will either piss them off or will make them hunger after you. I'll take Amaymon. He should be back at the office by now."

She nodded. "I'll head back there as soon as I can. Will call you if there are any changes."

She didn't mean about her mother. With Amaymon gone, Abi would take over watching out for the werewolf clans and monitoring the Grigori, as well as Rashid's—and Carmilla's—vampire forces here.

Sun Tzu didn't say anything so I took that to be acquiescence.

I stood up. "Thank you," I told him.

He smiled. "Just remember what you are, Erik Ashendale. In days to come you will be challenged on that. You must remember."

Well, if that wasn't ominous...

I walked outside and found Turtle accompanying me.

"Sorry about before," I said. "The summoning."

He beamed at me. "You mean the cartoon chant?"

"Yes."

"It was funny," he said.

"Not racist?"

"Oh no," Turtle said. "You did not mean it to be racist. So why should it be then?"

"Oh, okay."

"Very millennial of you," he said opening the door for me. "Worrying about racism and cultural appropriation. We are meant to share what we are with others. Such is the nature of improvement and growth."

And then I remembered something I had read about the turtle guardian. How he wasn't just the element of water. He was the aspect of growth and nourishment.

He was the life dwelling inside a forest.

In that split second I understood why no matter the mythological pantheon or culture, there was always a thunder god, always a sun and moon god, always a fire and rain, and war, and nature god.

These are aspects and one god representing that aspect usually meant he or she was also the other aspects. Turtle could also be Cernunnos, or Ceres, or…

Holy shit.

Turtle's smile was motherly.

He handed me a tub of sun lotion. "For the desert. Some places even Mother Nature cannot fix. Goodbye now. Enjoy your trip. Try not to start a war with the vampires."

And he shut the door in my face, leaving me there with an aghast look on my face and sun lotion in my hands.

17

We emerged from the portal straight into King Rashid's throne room.

Amaymon held my shoulder, his gaze bored and observant at the same time. With good reason, since about four million spears were thrust in our direction.

I held my hands up. "Um, we have an invite?"

The soldiers parted for their king, lowering their weapons in the process.

"Erik Ashendale," Rashid said. "Welcome to my palace, spanning beneath the Pyramid of Khonsu." Then his gaze fell upon Amaymon. "You've brought a troublesome guest."

Amaymon grinned. "Don't worry, pal, I'll keep it in my pants." He winked at a few female retainers at the back who hissed at him. I spotted Carmilla in their midst, an amused smile painted on her face.

Rashid stepped up to Amaymon. Power hummed between them.

"We have not forgotten your actions, Stoneweaver," Rashid said. "We have not forgotten the smell of blood from when you haunted the night. We have known you by many names, Shadebreaker. Prowler From Beneath. Devouring Abyss. Many are the mountains and valleys you have rendered and shaped, just for the sport of hunting my kin."

I glanced at Amaymon.

The demon was older than the Earth's first rotation but I had no idea just how old. All I knew was that he was so dangerous that it had taken the entire Ashendale clan at their peak to contain him, and even then, it had been the equivalent of locking him up and throwing away the key. No mortal could kill something like Amaymon.

"I am what I am," Amaymon said. Same words Turtle had uttered. That seemed to be the theme of the day.

"And what he is," I interjected, "is my familiar."

Rashid turned his gaze at me. His eyes were sharp enough that I felt something hollow in my stomach.

"Indeed," he said. "The world has changed. We no longer need to fight one another. You may enter my territory, provided that neither of you incites violence against my name or my people."

"Thank you," I said.

Then I elbowed Amaymon.

"What? I may get bored."

Another elbow.

"Fine." Amaymon gave an overly-theatrical bow. "Happy?"

"Ecstatic," I said. "Now play nice." I raised an eyebrow at Rashid. "We *are* here to play nice, aren't we?"

Rashid's lips curled into an amused smile that made my lower intestines curl.

Carmilla appeared by her father's side. "Come now, father. You have preparations to oversee. Let me show them around instead, as per my duty."

Rashid glanced at her, then nodded. He turned around and just walked away.

"He's in a good mood," Carmilla said once he left.

"That's him in a good mood?" I asked.

She laughed. It rang about the whole place. "Of course. Do you see any blood? No? Then he's in a good mood."

She slipped her arm into mine. We walked outside and through a vast corridor. I couldn't even see the ceiling. The sides were illuminated by LED lights covered in a casing that made them look like crystals.

"My idea," she said, following my gaze. "Fire and vampires do not go well together."

"So I remember," I said.

"Hm."

"Carmilla, why am I here?" I demanded.

"Because King Rashid asked you to be."

I stopped, forcing her to swivel and turn to face me. Her features were soft and sharp at the same time, beautiful to look at, but it was her eyes I wanted. They were mesmerizing and enrapturing, and for just a split second when I surprised her, predatory.

I cocked my head.

"Very well," she said. "I want you to see for yourself that which we spoke of yesterday." Her voice fell to a whisper. "I dare not say anymore, not in this place. But there is something you need to see. Urgently."

Her hair flared, whipping past my face and filling my nose with a delightful aroma of rose and lavender as she kept walking ahead.

Amaymon let out a soft chuckle as we followed her.

"Oh, shut up," I muttered.

18

Carmilla led us to a guest room and left us there. And when I say guest room, I mean a suite the size of a freaking submarine. You could fit a football field in there and have room for an after-party.

The walls were gilded in gold leaf and designs reflective of the part of the world we were in. Dainty hieroglyphics ran down the walls and columns, unreadable both due to their size and my lack of Egyptian linguistic knowledge. Around the walls, a wavy cerulean pattern snaked around the room.

I turned to ask Carmilla why she had brought us here but she was long gone. Amaymon shrugged at the empty space.

"Let's just have a look around," I said. "If this was where Ishtar stayed, then maybe there's a clue to find."

The demon sighed. "You think? If I were the king I would have scrubbed this place clean."

"Why?"

"What's Rashid really concerned with?" Amaymon asked. "He wants her found, but from what we know, he ain't exactly lacking in the whole magic stone department. He can make a new Scepter whenever he wants. Get where I'm going?"

It took me a second to figure it out but I did eventually get there.

"Saving face," I said. "He would have retraced her steps and then he would have hidden any potential evidence of *how* she did it to prevent further attempts. Possibly from someone in his court getting ideas."

"Like the hot piece of ass that's currently serving as our guide," he said. His grin hardened into something of a warning. "Careful around her, Erik."

I sighed. The bed was nice and thick, and it was immaculate, with fluffy-looking gold-colored sheets. I sat down.

"You think I'm gonna get in bed with the crazy vampire chick?" I asked him. "I'm not that desperate."

Amaymon shrugged. "You've been on this self-discovery crap for a while now. I haven't seen you dating anyone. That's bound to give a guy pause when someone like *that* gives him attention."

"Which is precisely why it's suspicious," I told him. "She wants something."

"Yeah, she does."

"Dude. Get your mind out the gutter."

"Hey, all I'm saying is, you're a tasty meal, vampirically speaking."

"What?"

He raised his hands and frowned. "Have you learnt nothing? Your blood, dumbass. It's magic. She ingests blood. If it's got magic, it makes it stronger." His tone indicated that he was speaking to a slow child. "Now throw your sexless existence in the mix-"

"It's not sex*less*," I complained. But not very loudly.

Hard to argue with the truth.

"And Hell forbid you actually move in on that hot secretary you got in your office," he went on.

"Dude, she's also my apprentice," I said. "I'm not doing Abi like that."

"You're not doing her at all."

"You're a child."

"And you're not seeing what's in front of you," Amaymon said.

"Abi's got her own life to live," I told him. "Besides, she dates around because of her succubus heritage. I'm not exactly cut out for that sort of thing."

Amaymon laid a hand on my shoulder. "I hereby award you first place in the Most Clueless category," he said. "Have you noticed any guys around her recently? No? Because the last time she had some was when you were dead. Hell, she had someone new every day back then. Had to keep 'em on a roster."

I stood up. Abi and I were not an item. Yes, she was important to me, and she was beautiful, and being with her would not exactly be the worst thing in the world…

But there were boundaries.

Or maybe you don't think you can handle it.

Shut up, brain. We're in Egypt. I can be in denial—get it, the Nile, denial.

Oh, yeah, you're real clever.

Okay, so I was scared of jumping into something with a woman I saw and worked with every day. There was a lot of risk, and I did not want that. Yeah, I was a coward. So sue me. My life was a rollercoaster. I had *died*. That's not something you could just walk off.

And something so emotionally heavy—and risky—could undo all the work I had done on myself.

In that regard someone like Carmilla was better. At least

with her I knew where I stood. Sex and hunger. I could handle those, and like she said, so long as both of us get ours all was well.

Besides I've never been to Prague.

Amaymon must have sensed my thoughts—likely, since he and I are connected by a deep magical connection—but whatever he had in mind was cut off.

A blood-curdling scream erupted from outside.

Amaymon and I rushed out, bursting through the door.

"Where?" I asked.

Amaymon pointed to one side and we sprinted in that direction. More and more vampiric retainers crowded this side of the palace, but most of them saw us in the nick of time and glided effortlessly out of our way.

When a demon and a guy holding a blazing sword come running, that was the usual reaction.

The smell of blood hung heavy in the air. Not just a tinge. This was enough to clog the back of my throat. It was nauseating.

I snuck a glance at Amaymon. The demon's eyes were glowing with the sort of bloodlust that meant something terrible was about to go down. The last time I had seen him geared up this much was just before taking on the former Emperor of Hell.

Amaymon was a hunter by nature. Blood was a trigger for him, just like for sharks. It drew him in, turned him on, and made him damn-near impossible to control.

"Erik..." he began. "This is not good."

"Stay here," I said.

"I can't," he replied. "Not with what's in there."

He was glancing at a pair of mahogany doors. Two armed guards stood by the door. A few feet from them was a gaggle of women, most of them too young to have a drink, clasping a girl.

A girl who was losing a lot of blood.

I ran up to her and recognized two things: first, the rip on her throat had been made by a vampire, one who had little care or control.

Second, she was a normal human, as were the rest of the women. She wasn't going to heal or recover.

"Erik," came Amaymon's warning from over my shoulder.

I looked up and saw the soldiers glaring at me.

"Make sure they don't interfere," I said.

Amaymon grinned. "*That*, I can do."

One of the soldiers recoiled.

"Who did this?" I asked one of the women, as I cradled the wounded girl in my arms.

The woman just stared at me.

"English?" I asked.

She shook her head.

"Dammit. Step back please." I held up my hand and lightly pushed her shoulder. She instantly recoiled, like a startled cat.

I ignored her and pressed my hand on the girl's wound. Blood soaked my clothes as I channeled magic through my hand.

I had meant to hide my trump card—the fact that I could use magic normally—but there was a girl too young to die doing just that. I couldn't sit by.

Healing magic is not easy for me to do. My powers naturally looped around me to create an automatic healing factor but that didn't mean I knew how it worked.

Also, healing magic is precise, it's controlled, and most importantly, it requires a lot of medical knowledge. Mend the wrong place and you ended up with a blood clot. Fix a fracture at a slight angle and your patient ended up bow-legged.

Luckily, the body is naturally very good at healing itself. All I had to do was accelerate that a little. And if you broke it down to one of the four elements—which I had to do since my healing magic was *that* basic—healing was closest to fire.

I know, it sounded weird to me as well, but essentially it boiled down to the body consuming energy to create new cells. *That* was what I needed. No need to use water to get blood flowing, plenty of that happening. Or earth to replenish her lost minerals—just get her some food and a good, long rest.

But I needed her body to mend, and mend now, which meant she needed a blast of energy.

And that, I was *very* good at.

The outline of my hand actually glowed as energy transferred between us. Her blood hissed and fizzled, sputtering in places before hardening instantly and ruining both our clothes. The smell of blood was permeated with another stench: burning flesh. I wasn't cauterizing her wound. Rather her own flesh was so energized, it was searing part of itself.

Whispers from the other women echoed around the corridor, and I caught words like "*magi*" and "*majinnun*". I knew the first one meant "magician". I was too distracted to ask them to clarify the second.

Two minutes later, the wound had closed and a scar the size of my palm ran along the side of her neck. It was likely going to remain there for the rest of her life.

The girl was unconscious but she was breathing. She

needed an IV and at least two days of bed rest before she could even get up to use the bathroom by herself.

At the back of my mind, I knew I could rope Carmilla into helping me out. Bully her, if I had to.

But first...

I stood up and faced the doors. I knew I was on the right track because one of the women gasped and the soldiers stiffened.

I took a single step. One of them lowered his lance. And then the two of them were ripped apart. I never saw Amaymon move. I just heard their bones squelching and the clang of metal.

The demon stood there, his clawed hands sopping in blood which he then scooped into his mouth.

Then with a mighty kick, he literally blasted the doors in.

PRINCE VALEN'S private quarters were large, drenched in blood, and filled with fear.

Proper, thick, tangible, palpable fear.

A fear that was alive, feeding the bloodlust in the air.

Prince Valen was on the bed.

He was naked. He was hard. He was having sex.

With a girl.

A girl whose legs and arms had been ripped out and who had bled all over the bed, and was now very much dead.

Other women, maybe girls too, were whimpering around the bed. Some of them had wounds ripped open in them. Some of them shivered in a way that some logical part of my brain recognized: they were being transformed into fledglings, newborn vampires.

That same part of my mind, the logical side, told me that vampires were no longer made this way. That this was an ancient practice that had a high mortality rate because not everyone was strong enough to survive the process of being bled out and then fight death's oblivion before it consumed them forever.

That was the logical part of my mind.

The rest of my mind had only one other emotion: rage.

Anger.

Wrath.

19

I've always had an anger problem. Even before the literal embodiment of the Sin of Wrath was placed in my head, I'd had issues with controlling my temper.

Now that I had defeated my inner demons—literally—and gotten my magic back, I had a better grip on my emotions.

Now I could choose when to let go.

And when I saw Valen, I let go.

Hell, I practically poured gasoline over my anger and tossed the lighter.

My aura blazed to life.

Most wizards can do an aura blast, and nine times out of ten, it's nothing more than a show of force. It's Gandalf yelling at the Balrog.

A battlecry.

My aura threw Valen off the corpse and slammed him into the wall.

And the pressure did not let up.

I threw everything at him without even casting a single

spell. The walls shook. I heard screams from outside. I knew more soldiers had made it to the chambers. They were flattened to the ground under the sheer pressure.

Only Valen could stand up. He was a prince after all, and his royal blood would have endowed him with certain advantages.

But certainly not enough to contend with the likes of me.

"What. The Fuck. Are You. *Doing*?"

The pressure increased with every syllable. Now Valen was bleeding.

Amaymon suddenly spun, claws extended, and the ground rumbled for an entirely different reason.

I glanced over my shoulder.

Carmilla stood there. She was not alone. Vampire women were all around her. They were scantily clad and each bore a curved dagger in both hands. Most of them were on their knees due to my aura.

Only the princess was on her feet, her smile now venomous.

Amaymon hissed.

I could sense him asking me—begging me—to give him the command. One thought was all it would take for him to unleash Hell over this whole pyramid.

We could kill them all, every last bloodsucking fucker and make history. Get rid of a scourge.

But then what about my home?

What about Gil? And the Grigori?

What about the power vacuum?

There is something you need to see. That's what Carmilla had told me.

And then it all clicked.

I wasn't here to look at Ishtar's room, or a part of peace treaty, or to help with the hunt for the Vol.

I was here as a bomb.

What she wanted me to see wasn't Ishtar's room. Amaymon had been right about that. She wanted me to see Valen. She knew her brother was a junkie. Having us here would send him into a frenzy, and his only recourse would be to fuck, break, feed and rape as per his usual manner.

Which would attract the attention—and subsequent firepower—of a certain wizard with a history of helping people who had a monster problem.

She wanted me to blow things up. To kill her brother, who was next in line for the throne she coveted. My actions would incite war.

With the Vol and a war campaign, Rashid's forces would be divided, which would give her a perfect opportunity to strike.

Fuck me.

She had even told me herself that she was good at playing the long game.

A *centuries*-long game, if she had to.

Hell, I wouldn't be surprised if she had even provided the girls herself.

My aura died down with such force that Valen hacked up blood and vomited all over his bed. A cacophony of groans came from the vampires who were still conscious.

Amaymon inclined his head and kicked away the hand of one of Carmilla's retainers when she weakly tried to swipe with her dagger. The blow tore off her arm. Amaymon scooped it up and took a bite out of the flesh like one does a drumstick.

I caught Carmilla's eyes as I walked past and muttered,

"Never gonna happen."

As I walked away I heard her throaty chuckle. "We shall see."

I kept walking.

20

I did not need directions to the throne room. Simply follow where the largest amount of vampires were collected.

They glided out of my way as I steamrolled in front of King Rashid and a few other soldiers. Their gilded pauldrons and burgundy capes suggested they were generals in the army, which made sense given that they surrounded a large table with what looked like a scale model of the city we were in.

"Erik Ashendale."

If my bursting in bothered Rashid, he did a good job of hiding it. In fact, he seemed almost amused.

Which meant he had known exactly what I would find. The bastard was likely trying to incite me to do something and that would give him the perfect excuse to invade.

Games, upon games, upon more fucking games.

"I'm done playing," I told him.

The shadow of a smile crept up his lips. "Whatever do you mean?"

And at that moment—because what is my life if not a

series of dark dramatic moments?—Valen and Carmilla came in.

The princess glided in smoothly, her black dress trailing behind her like a living writhing shadow, while her handmaiden slash assassin-bodyguard women stealthily swarmed the edges of the room.

Valen was still half-naked, covered in blood, and his face looked like a punching bag.

Was that all me? Was that the effect of my aura?

Damn. I guess I was stronger than I imagined.

"You!" he snarled at me.

Amaymon stepped in between us, and even if he was slightly shorter, he managed to stare the prince down.

"What is the meaning of this?" Rashid snapped.

"Him," Valen said. "He attacked me."

Rashid's eyes turned wide and golden, and very, very hungry. "Is that so?"

"Oh, hardly, Father," Carmilla interjected. "The wizard never even touched him."

She stepped forward, her stilettos clicking softly on the marbled floor that echoed the sound into something thunderous.

"Valen was being his naughty self again," she said. "Our guest here demanded an explanation for what was, in his *human* opinion, abhorrent behavior. And rather than calmly provide an explanation, Valen thought he would show up the wizard."

I tried not to wince. That wasn't exactly how it went down but the way Carmilla told the story, her tone all bored and casual, made it seem like it was no big deal that I had basically done the equivalent of shoving Valen into a wall in his own home.

It was bad form on my part and it would be the trigger that incited a war.

I started reaching for my sword, slowly, stealthily.

"Untrue!" Valen was saying. "He attacked me unprovoked. I demand blood. *His* blood." He turned his eyes—and fangs—on me. "It's been years since I drank magic."

Rashid was about to say something but then he found himself face-to-face with Amaymon. And when I tell you that the room fell silent, I don't mean silent enough to hear a pin drop.

All the sound, including my breathing, was sucked in. Nothing existed anymore except the two primordial beings facing each other. Forget heavyweights—these two were *planet*-weights.

"King Rashid," Amaymon begun. "Do you remember what we used to do to pups who yapped as much as yours? We brained them, alleviating them of an organ they clearly had no use for."

"My son is a prince," Rashid said.

They both spoke in whispers and yet were clearly heard.

"Your *pup*," Amaymon said, "is behaving like a petulant toddler that must be disciplined. Perhaps it requires to be broken and reforged into something appropriate."

He smiled. The act was so menacing it could be considered an act of war in itself.

"I would happily assist you. Perhaps I could even show him my trophies. You remember those, do you not?"

"You made trinkets from the fangs of my fathers," Rashid said coldly.

"And armor from the bones of your brothers," Amaymon finished. He altered his gaze slightly towards Valen.

The prince recoiled. If I were a betting man, I would put

money on him soiling himself. There certainly was a waft in the air.

"That will not be necessary," Rashid finally said. "I will see to it that Valen is removed so that we may proceed."

That last part did not sit well with His Petulant Highness because he immediately resumed his griping.

"But Father, I was attacked. I *demand* blood!"

And in response Rashid turned on *his* aura.

I've already told you about the force an aura can have when someone powerful enough throws it around. Mine was strong. It was a direct emission from my magic, a force of light and love and creation.

Rashid was neither of those things.

A gravity filled the room. Dread pumped through my brain. I felt a sour taste in my mouth like rot, and screwed my eyes shut as the sound of a thousand nails on a thousand chalkboards permeated my mind. It was hard to breathe, to *live*.

Rashid was a creature of death and darkness and shadows, and all that drove people to fear or madness, and often both.

"You *demand* nothing," he said. His voice was like shattered glass that was being pressed against my skin. "Leave, before you embarrass this court and your title any further."

Valen did not argue. He scampered off, his feet quick and his eyes wide with fear. Even Carmilla seemed uneasy. She gave her father a courtly bow and departed.

Rashid lowered his aura.

"Now then," he said. His yellow eyes were still wide and full of bloodlust. "It seems your presence here has stirred old memories, ones we have fought long to forget."

"Hey, you invited us here," I replied. "So let's get this over with."

Rashid's jaw twitched but instead of arguing he motioned towards one of the men behind him.

"This is General Karim."

I hated him on sight.

His face would not have been out of place on a marble statue, all perfect lines and chiseled jaws. His eyes were yellow and cat-like as well, but in a darker hue than those of Rashid's. His fangs were elongated and poked at his lower lip.

The broadsword he wore at his hip was about as wide as my entire face, a weapon that required both hands. I sensed a faint whiff of magic coming from it.

An enchanted weapon then. I made note of that in case I needed to take this guy down.

Karim gave us a nod. "We have a strike team ready," he said. "Five of our best warriors including myself, will be attacking the Vol's basecamp which we discovered this morning five miles from the central oasis in Sector D."

As he spoke, he pointed at the map.

"Our sources tell us this is their most recent location," he went on. "We must know why they constructed a new base. You are to accompany General Karim and his men on a raid."

My guess was they needed somewhere to gather the ingredients for the ritual. Cells like this were excellent foraging grounds. You sent each one to retrieve one ingredient, and then had them all gather at the ritual site when the time was ready. That way, if you were struck by the enemy, you only lost one or two ingredients, not the whole batch.

But I kept my mouth shut. I did not want to help Rashid or his crazy psycho kids any more than I had to.

Also, I knew that one of the ingredients was an actual living person, a hybrid child. So I made that my priority:

rescue any hybrid kids, learn all I can about the ritual, and stop the bad guys.

Simple, right?

Yeah.

Right.

21

Here's something Hollywood never tells you about the desert:

At night, it's freaking *freezing*.

I pulled the hem of my leather coat around me in a useless attempt at keeping the bone-chilling cold out while trying not to break an ankle as I crunched sand.

The desert is not a nice place to be. It was downright shitty when you had to traverse it with a team of five vampire soldiers who barely upset a grain of sand as they slithered through it—while carrying weapons and armor no less—and who could turn on you at any moment.

Amaymon was not having an issue. The demon was an earth Elemental. Sand hardened as a platform beneath his feet and simply hovered him up.

He grinned at me and stuck his tongue out teasingly.

I threw a fistful of sand at him.

We found their hideout just south of the oasis, a little closer than the spies had informed but the numbers were right on the money: thirty vampires of the Vol Bloodletters.

General Karim was ready to roll. I saw him nod at his men and they dispersed.

I hissed at him. We should have sent one of his men to scout, probe their defenses. Karim glanced at me with an expression that told me he couldn't give less of a shit about my tactical opinion and dashed forward.

Sand rose at his wake and I swallowed half the damn desert. When my eyes and throat stopped burning, I was choking and hacking and all of a sudden, I saw two Vol vampires coming towards me from the left. We had missed them. Why? Because *they* had scouts.

Fucking Karim.

Amaymon's arm reached out and wrenched the closest vampire's head from its moorings. By the time he dropped it, he had already torn the second in two.

"Get to Karim," I said. "Stop them from killing any innocents."

The demon nodded. He took a step forward and the sand swallowed him.

I made my way towards the enemy on foot, and I was faced with a lot of opposition.

Fortunately, I was very much in the mood to destroy something.

"Come on, you fuckers!" I screamed.

Here's another thing Hollywood doesn't tell you: sound doesn't bounce or echo on sand. It gets absorbed.

So only about half a dozen vampires from the Vol's horde heard me.

"Mother-"

"*Die!*"

I swept my sword out before I even registered the attack. Djinn's blade cleaved through the first vampire, eliciting a scream. And I guess I was angrier than I expected because a thick azure beam of energy shot along the arc of the blade and punched through another vampire.

Another one turned to dust immediately.

A few dustings later and I had reached Karim and his men. Even together, we had a massive numerical disadvantage. But reality and math rarely ever work that neatly together. What actually happened was that two of the vampire soldiers ended up biting the dust (literally, in their case) and then I had ten Vol on me.

"Bring it, bitches!"

My war cry was epic and powerful, and in my mind I was a viking on a mound of corpses clambering for glory. In reality, it looked like a tangle of limbs and shorn flesh. Battle, true battle, is ugly and terrifying. And no matter how strong you are, numbers usually tend to win.

I killed three of them, and then I stumbled. One of the Vol, their tattoos active, raked a deep gash in my shoulders which made my next strike slow. Djinn went sailing when another disarmed me by... Well, disarming me.

I screamed.

Black shadows rose from me. I reached out to my severed limb and activated a transmutation spell. All matter is energy if you mess with the frequency of the molecular and atomic vibration. The severed limb turned into a bomb that tore two more vampires in half and sent a third my way where I impaled him on several shadow spikes.

A shadow arm formed over my severed stump, because while my healing was busy regrowing a new limb, I needed that limb *now*. A shadow fist—*my* shadow fist—punched through flesh and bone.

Two vampires pinned me down while a third shoved a dagger into my belly. I screamed again and enchanted the sound to a decibel level that made them bleed from the ears. I found my gun and fired, once, twice, thrice.

I grabbed the knife-wielding vampire and literally shoved the barrel of the gun into his stomach and kept pulling the trigger until the gun clicked empty and all that I held onto was a bloodied spine adorned with gore and entrails.

Something raked at my back. A vampire with a sword. The Vol soldier swung the broadsword again, only for a mound of sand to climb up and swallow him whole.

I roared—someone had taken my kill—and felt Amaymon's powerful arms around me.

"Erik!"

His voice cracked through the fog of battle. I could see clearly again, and feel the agony on my body. Magic fixed the life-threatening injuries but it did nothing for the pain.

Pain was something all wizards knew something about. Fantasy stories would have you believe the trope of the squishy wizard, the caster who slung fireballs while others clashed with swords and spears. But I'd wager magic hurt just as much as any other form of training. You literally channel the primordial forces of the universe through yourself.

Not to mention that whenever something went wrong, it was your body on the line.

I grasped Amaymon's arm. What the fuck had just happened to me? I was trembling and shaking. I wanted to fight, I wanted to kill and destroy.

I wanted to give into the wrath. This was how they had gotten me. This was that rage that the cacodaemon had fed on to turn me into a serial killer.

And I *wanted* it.

"You need to see this," Amaymon yelled. He pressed

Djinn—how did he get it? Oh right, he could call it through the sands—and then the two of us disappeared underground.

Nothing like a bit of underground traveling to cool the head. Or any body part really, since the sands were freezing cold and Amaymon could not feel the temperature difference.

When we emerged I was cussing over the cold and the sand all over my body.

I heard the sounds of battle and kicked in the door to the hut just in time to find Karim standing over a Vol priest, broadsword raised.

"Wait," the Vol was saying. "I can tell you where to find the child-"

Karim chopped down.

"*No!*" I screamed.

The Vol turned to ash and the general wiped blood off his weapons with bloodlust in his eyes.

"What the fuck is wrong with you?" I snapped. "He was confessing. They have someone."

He brushed past me. "Our orders were to destroy everyone. That Vol was lying," he said. Then to his men, outside: "Burn the hut."

I looked around me. There were several pieces of parchment and papers, along with a scroll or two. All of it was information I needed to see if I was going to get to the bottom of this.

I pulled out my gun and shot at the ground, inches before the closest vampire soldier with a tubular device in his hand.

"No," I said. "I need time to collect this information."

Karim grasped his sword and pulled it out in one languid movement. "Our orders are clear."

Amaymon stepped up to him, his body language even lazier. "And when either of us gives half a shit about your orders, we'll let you know. Until then, sit, bitch."

The general twitched—just *twitched*—and suddenly Amaymon thrust his arm out. Karim flew.

"Whoops," he said. "This sand is mighty slippery." He squared off against the other vampires. "Erik, why don't you go have a look while we wait here until the general makes it back?" He bared his fangs at the rest of the vampires. "Funny thing about a big 'ol empty desert like this one. Loads o' ways to get disappeared."

None of the vampires moved.

Amaymon nodded. The sand rumbled around me and rose into a protective dome over the hut. Darkness swallowed me.

The first thing I did was raise both hands and focus on a pair of light globes. I had to be careful and regulate the heat coming off them. To do that I had them hover around me, moving in slow undulating movements. Their movement meant that they were losing energy through kinetics and not heat, while also providing a nice ambiance.

What can I say? You make the best of a lousy situation.

I ignored the sounds of battle outside, and picked up the first notebook. It was written in plain English, clearly meant for the Vol expats on the American continent.

One of them had an entry I recognized:

Alan Greede.

My heart sank as I began reading.

And then I understood. The pieces all came flooding together.

The psychic entity that Abi and I had fought, the creature he had killed an angel over, and for whom he had built an indestructible body out of the bones of the creatures that I had brought over from Envy's island.

The reason he had Ishtar steal the Scepter of Osiris, and the Astral Shard within. He needed something that was already activated.

It all made sense now, especially the parasite inside Ishtar.

I knew who had created it: Alan Greede.

With the aid of his sponsor, King Rashid.

I gritted my teeth and packed up the notebook with all the evidence.

"Let's see you get out of this one now, you son of a bitch."

22

I did not go to Rashid. I did not even go outside the hut. I called Amaymon over, who popped out of the ground, and had him portal us straight to the one person who could shed light on all this and hopefully a thick beam of sunlight onto the king himself.

GIL WAS PACING around her study the way she did when she was nervous. She had that in common with our father.

The journal sat open at her desk.

"Are you *sure?*" she asked for the umpteenth time.

I sighed.

Gil sat down. "Who else have you told?"

"No one," I said. "Just you."

She looked at me, silent.

"I don't trust them," I said. "The Grigori. I don't trust them. Not even Greg. He's too invested in this. It's personal now."

Gil pursed her lips. "He hasn't tried to kill Rashid."

"Not that," I said. "He's invested in you."

"Erik, if this is about my relationship-"

I held up my hands. "That is your business, I know. But hear me out: Greg is old school. Emphasis on the *old*. Guys like that won't let things like politics get in the way. I know, because I'm like that, too. The only reason I haven't opened up on Rashid is because I have something to lose. Greg, too. But with this, that may all change."

"We all have something to lose, Erik," she said. My sister's shoulders sagged. Not for the first time it seemed to me as if the weight of the world was resting on top of her slender frame. "And an alliance with Rashid... it won't be the worst thing ever."

"It'll only cost you your soul," I told her.

"But it would save countless others," she said. "Besides, I've already had to dirty my hands. What's a bit more?"

And right then it dawned on me what acquiring Ryleh and the Grigori, and running the Ashendale estate had really done to Gil.

Power like that always has a price and when it comes to those dark deeds, you begged for a physical sacrifice. But the price is never so overt—it's always paid in small dividends, in the twisting of singular decisions that slowly alter you until, one day when you look up, you find you have diverted so far off your course you are well and truly lost.

I didn't have to ask her why.

My sister and I are cursed by something other than a literal curse. We are cursed with the stupidity of being heroes. Not everyone swings swords and casts spells.

Some offer up their sanity so that others may live peacefully.

Gil stood up again and poured herself a drink. A big drink. My sister is not a drinker.

"How much?" I asked.

She sipped. "How much what?"

"How much money did you lose?" I asked. "That's why you signed on with the Grigori and that was why you made that deal with Greede when he first came into the city, and now that's why you've lapped up Ryleh rather than burn it to the ground."

"Oh, that. Yes, we're in the shit," she admitted. Perhaps a bit too nonchalantly. My sister and I had had very different upbringings. People like her don't see money the same way I do.

"Do you remember when someone hacked into our accounts?" she asked. "This was round the time Lilith was still a thing."

"Eight years ago," I said. I closed my eyes. "Christ, I feel old."

"You're telling me," she said. "Anyway, that hack was part of something. Maybe it was Greede screwing with me but we never found out who took it."

"So how much are we talking about here?" I asked her. The Ashendale coffers are large. As in Fort Knox-large.

Let me put it in perspective: my clan built an island.

Yes.

Built.

A whole freaking nation. Out of magic (and a shit-ton of materials for those rituals).

During the freaking *Age of Discovery*.

Compound that by a bajillion years, and you get one very rich family. Hell, I think we owned like half of New York at some point when the British first came over.

Gil gave me a look.

"Six, seven figures?" I pressed.

She raised an eyebrow.

"Eight?" I let my jaw drop. "Nine?"

"Try eleven."

My jaw left a dent on the floor. "E- eleven?" I squinted really hard as I tried to do the math.

That's right. That was so much money my brain couldn't comprehend it.

I knew eight figures meant ten million, nine a hundred. Ten, a thousand million, or a billion. That meant that eleven was...

"You let someone steal *ten billion* dollars from you?" I was practically yelling now. "And you're somehow *not* bankrupt? How, Much, Money, Does this fucking family have?"

"Your family too," Gil said. "Before you threw a tantrum and ran away."

I would have argued—at least scoffed—but Gil just waved me off.

"The money was never the issue," she said. "We have too much to go bankrupt, anyway, even at our lowest. Last time I checked, I was personally worth somewhere around two or three billion." She frowned. "Which doesn't mean much when you can't expand your operations."

"You keep yourself hidden and you're worth that much?" I fished out the change in my pocket. "I am worth..." I said, counting the money, "four dollars, sixteen cents, and one coupon for a free sub. God bless the one percent."

Gil chuckled for the first time since I came to see her.

A servant came bursting in through the doors.

"Madam," he said, in between hyperventilations. The mansion is huge. (As you'd expect when it was built by kajillioners.)

"It's Sir Mephistopheles and your brother's familiar, Madam," he said. "They are fighting something outside. Something that just breached through our containment field and headed straight for the mansion."

. . .

THE ASHENDALES HAVE ALWAYS BEEN warlocks. We had explored lands, pushed the boundaries of magic, broken and reforged laws, and captured and experimented on thousands of magical beings.

If there was one thing we could do very well, it was a containment field.

Whatever it was that Amaymon and Mephisto were fighting had just knocked it over like it was a goddamn fencing post.

Outside, a small earthquake was happening. Literally, since my familiar was involved. A tornado gathered a few yards outside of the front gates. Armored vehicles were sent flying.

I sensed both demons in their elemental forms beating at a lone figure that oozed more power than I had ever seen.

No, wait. I had.

This was an ocean of power but it wasn't metaphorical.

"Erik, careful," Gil said as I approached the chaos.

I raised my hands and yelled, "Guys! Stop! That's Turtle!"

They ignored me.

Like, completely.

And then Gil stepped up and reached out with her magic. Those three might be God-tier beings but they were on Gil's turf.

And in her castle, Gil Khaleesi wasn't about to be ignored.

The word from her lips was deafened by the roar of the wind and the cracking of the earth, the surging waves and winds and roiling trees, as vines the size of telephone poles whipped at the two demons, but I saw white smoke billow out of her.

Instantly my shadows reacted, and we reached out.

Our demons appeared next to us.

"Turtle!" I roared.

There was power in my voice, power I would not have elicited were it not for my sister.

The Chinese deity appeared in his human form.

"What's the meaning of this?" I asked. "Why did you attack us?"

"I simply walked through your doors," he explained.

"You broke the damn field," Amaymon countered. "And you kept saying you had business with Erik here. And you didn't stop. That don't jive with me."

"Me neither," Mephisto coolly added.

"I am not bound by your rules," Turtle said. And then gave them the cold shoulder.

You had to admit for a big chubby guy, and purportedly a peaceful god, Turtle had a big pair on him.

"Erik Ashendale," he said, looking gravely at me. "I have once answered your summons. Now you must answer mine in great haste. The temple is under siege."

"What?" I asked. "Who in their right mind would raise a hand against Sun Tzu?"

"He who believes himself a god already," Turtle said. "The king of the dark ones. You must answer the call to aid." Then he turned to Gil and threw her a dark look.

She actively recoiled.

"This is not our mess," he said. I could feel something pulsing in the air when he spoke, like a distant chord being struck. "We have not begotten such mortal affairs, yet it is our temple that is being destroyed. The vampire king's army marches upon us. The first wave is at our doors."

He leaned in, towering over Gil.

"You know whom we represent," he said. "I speak to you now as a friend of your people. This is a test. Should our temple fall, our aid will be rescinded from the war to come." He looked at me. "Answer the call, Erik Ashendale."

Turtle stepped back and disappeared into thin air.

"Shit," I swore. "Abi and Ishtar were there as well."

Gil snapped herself out of her daze. "Likely why they attacked," she said. "That, and Rashid knows more about the gods and their motives. Mephisto!"

"Ma'am," he acknowledged.

"Send a strike team to intercept the rear of the army," she ordered. "And have the Grigori assembled. We shall strike at them from both sides."

"They will be expecting that," Mephisto said.

Her eyes were practically on fire. "Then we shall show them why we are the ones in charge of protecting our kind from theirs." She turned to me. "Erik."

She tossed me a set of keys. "You can't portal or tunnel to Sun Tzu's place. Pick something from the garage and have Amaymon channel magic through it. It should get you there in time."

I nodded.

"Be careful," I told her.

"You too."

I grinned. "No promises."

23

Gil has a lot of cars.

A lot.

I strode past Lamborghinis and Ferraris and Rolls Royces and a million other brands that would have made a car guy salivate.

I'm not a car guy.

So I stopped next to a dull-silver motorbike. Amaymon turned into a cat and sat poised in between the handlebars.

"All this, and you go for a bike?" he asked disapprovingly.

"We're going through the forest," I told him. "Taking a shortcut."

"Ah," Amaymon said. "The direct approach." He tilted his cat head to look at me. "And you know the bike will not last."

"Just get me there."

Some cats look evil, some cats *are* evil, and then there's Amaymon, who is downright sinister.

"Will do, boss."

Magic coursed through the bike, and some through me.

It was like he captured lightning and placed it inside of me. The engine whined. Angry red light glowed around the edges of the bike.

I twisted the throttle and we rocketed out like a comet.

And yes, I was grinning the entire time.

WE TORE through the forest like a shot arrow, speeding over rocks and roots, zigzagging in between trees and bushes, and pretty much every other form of terrain that was *not* designed to host a motorcycle.

I only realized we hit the city when the blur around me became lighter, more grey and unnatural. It took us seconds to get to Sun Tzu's place.

Amaymon did not stop the bike.

"Shit," I yelled, propping my feet up and vaulting off the bike.

Below me, the bike kept going, an unstoppable missile, and met the front door of Sun Tzu's Noodle Shop.

Half a second later there no longer *was* a Sun Tzu's Noodle Shop.

The explosion rocked the ground. Soldiers from Rashid's army fell on their asses. I landed and managed to slash at a couple.

The ground rumbled again and from it emerged Amaymon in human form. He screeched in ecstasy and proceeded to…

Well, he did what he always does. He cut loose on the enemy and doused himself in gore.

I pulled out my gun and sword, and cut a swath through what was left of the ranks in order to get towards the pile of rubble. A quick spell removed enough debris to uncover a set of steps that led to the basement.

A basement full of vampire soldiers.

"I'm only saying this once," I said as they all turned to look at me. "Get the fuck out of my way."

They did. And then we all went for ice cream.

Yeah, right.

The area worked to my advantage. It was a narrow corridor leading to a kitchen. Not a lot of maneuvering space, especially if you're wearing armor. Their longswords were not really a problem for them though. Sure they couldn't swing them around but swords had pointy ends and usually that's enough to ruin your day.

I blasted my gun at them, sowing chaos, but they formed ranks, two men side by side, swords out, while the other two behind them poked their swords out in between the gaps.

In response, I put away my gun and placed my left hand on a metal countertop. Transmutation magic wasn't complicated, at least not the basics, which were just about the only thing I had studied. The metal twisted and folded, and soon I was holding a shield before me, while Djinn changed with magic.

"Viking time, bitches," I commented.

They charged.

So did I.

Their swords struck and pierced the shield, but then got stuck. And that, ladies and gentlemen, is why the Romans and Vikings used short blades and axes along with shields. You were getting up close and personal. Range is a good thing, but it went out the window as soon as someone sandwiched you between two slabs of metal.

I thrust, finding the gut of the closest vampire and then released the spell.

The blast of magic wasn't my best work, the aim was for

shit, and frankly I could have gotten more bang for my buck with a bit of refinement. But it worked.

Vampires were blasted in every direction, some smoldering and turning into ash, some with crippling injuries and in the process of healing, others still running at me.

I stumbled into a kitchen and, with my shield gone, I grabbed the closest thing to me with my left hand. A meat tenderizer.

Then I got to work, hacking and smashing, shoving and pushing. Djinn and the improvised mace hewed flesh and bone and hammered skulls. I felt shadows ooze out of me, sometimes pressing vampires against the narrow corridor wall, allowing me to kill them with ease.

I got cut and hacked up too, but my healing took care of that, while the shadows around me made sure I never stumbled or fell. Trust me, you do *not* want to fall in battle—there's a reason it's analogous to death.

"Erik!"

I turned and found myself in the temple. Abi had her golden staff out while Ishtar—who was apparently feeling much better—had gotten her hands on an actual mace and was swinging that thing around with enough force to rend armor.

Off to one side Sun Tzu was annihilating vampire soldiers. He wielded a Han-period Chinese sword long enough to be two-handed, but he was agile enough to wield it with one.

I often sparred with Sun Tzu. Hell, I said he had been the guy who taught me how to fight.

And now, watching him, I realized just how much he had held back.

A vampire came at him with an axe. Sun intercepted the strike and seemed to sluice off to one side. The axe head sliced along the neck of another vampire, killing him, while the wielder gasped. Sun held his blade over his shoulder, the tip emerging from the vampire's mouth.

He stabbed it forward, diverting a spear coming at him. I never saw him strike, the thrust was so fluid that all I saw was the vampire stop, freeze, and explode into dust.

Sun was already grasping another vampire by the breastplate, tripping him and impaling him on another's sword, while he bifurcated a third. Another came at him with a mace. He never got to swing down. One second his hand was up, weapon poised to strike—I blinked, and then the vampire was holding up a stump while Sun was dancing off against two other soldiers.

Heat blazed from the middle of the temple.

Ash piled all around Phoenix, who held out a pair of jian swords, their slender blades glowing yellow from the heat of his phoenix fire.

He snarled. "Out!"

That word had enough power to turn an oncoming vampire into ash.

The *word*. Just a word!

Then he turned to look at me, and I felt all the heat aimed straight for me.

No, not me.

Behind me.

I ducked and the sword caught my shoulder instead. The last three inches of the sword jutted out of my shoulder. It wasn't a stab. Someone had *cleaved* through my shoulder. Djinn was sent skittering from my grip.

Phoenix threw one of his swords at whoever was behind me, instantly manifesting another in his hand. I heard the thrown sword clang against a wall.

A flock of bats whipped past my face. I caught a series of

fangs and claws, ripping at my face. Several of them were clustered around a medieval longsword.

Like a movie special effect, the bats melted into a humanoid shape. King Rashid held the sword at my throat.

I chuckled.

"What's so funny, Erik Ashendale?" he asked.

"You can actually turn into a flock of bats," I said. "That's so cool. And so cheesy."

"I'm glad to entertain you in your last moment," he said.

"I'm glad to distract you."

"What-"

CLANG!

Sun Tzu shouldered Rashid and their swords clashed. I never saw them moving. I only saw sparks raining from their weapons and caught their conversation.

"The great Emissary," Rashid said. They circled each other. "I have long awaited to meet you in battle. Even if with just a fraction of your power."

"The time has not yet come for my kin to fight together and awaken the Yellow Dragon," Sun Tzu replied. "I'm afraid you'll have to contend with me in my current form, O King of Shadows."

Rashid stopped pacing and raised his sword. "It has been a while since I heard someone mocking me."

Sun Tzu offered him a grin that made my blood run cold. "You are a mere child, Dark One, and children who behave badly deserve a spanking. Come, then. Time to put you in your place, King of Nothing."

Oh snap. Sun Tzu never threw shade like that. I had caught a fraction of the anger Turtle had let slip when he mentioned that Rashid considered himself a god's equal.

Sun Tzu was humble, yes, but he *was* a god, so pride also hung around him. Unadorned perhaps, but ever-present.

And punish Rashid he did.

Their match resumed, a flurry of strikes too fast for the human eye to see, when suddenly Phoenix let out a screech. Behind him, the tapestry and walls were cracking.

Dark energy leaked from the cracks, seeping into the vampires. I felt physically ill. Even Sun Tzu and Rashid had slowed down.

A *presence* emerged as it grasped the vampires and possessed them.

And that's when I remembered that the temple was not really a temple at all.

It was a maximum-security prison.

A prison so dangerous that beings like Rashid wouldn't even be considered a threat.

And these idiots had just battered the door to one of the cells.

"Phoenix!" Sun Tzu yelled. "The Outsider."

Phoenix released a blaze that momentarily blinded me. I heard a scream that was most certainly *not* human—not even something resembling our reality—and when my sight returned, Abi and Ishtar were at my side.

Phoenix was still going on with his tantrum.

"OUT!"

Reality bent around us. I recognized the workings of a portal opening around me, and suddenly we were falling.

And falling.

And falling.

24

I woke up with the mother of all headaches. Wiping my brow, I noticed the wet stickiness of sweat on my palm. I ached, and then pain began flaring from my shoulder.

I shifted my position and heard my coat scraping against gravel. Red spots flashed before my eyes as agony shot from my shoulder. Instantly I grasped it. The wound was still there, albeit not bleeding. Or at least not as profusely. My shirt was wet and sticky with blood but I did not know if that was from when Rashid had struck me or more recently.

The room was illuminated only by a single torch, the fiery kind. Firelight cast shadows all over me and made it impossible to really ascertain the extent of my surroundings.

I sat up, grinding my teeth against the pain, and tried to stand up. It took me several tries but I was finally upright.

Okay. Step two:

Where the Hell was I?

The smell of mold and blood was heavy on the air. And

not my blood. This was a place of butchery and death, the kind of smell you'd expect in a morgue.

A crypt then.

I walked closer to the torch to get a better look at my injury. The wound was not as bad as it looked. Most of the flesh had knitted back, but blood still sluiced out when I moved too much. It was the sort of thing I wouldn't usually worry about, given my healing magic.

So why wasn't it healing?

The last thing I remembered was being at Sun Tzu's place, fighting Rashid and his forces. I glanced around me. I was alone, I was injured and unarmed, and I was in a place I would certainly not have freely chosen to be in.

Which meant we had been captured. Someone had messed with or hijacked the teleportation spell that Phoenix had used. Or maybe he'd done it on purpose—those gods often work in mysterious ways, the devious dickheads—and here I was.

My ears picked up something. A slight scraping, the kind you'd miss if you weren't completely spooked and standing still. It was barely more audible than the hum of the torch but I was looking for it.

If this was a jail then there would be a jailer.

I considered unhooking the torch and holding it before me. That would have been smart. But instead I grabbed it and chucked it a few feet ahead of me. Creatures that lurk in the dark do so for a reason, usually speaking of a sensitivity to light. In battle they relied on spooking their opponent into falling for a trap or hit-and-run tactics. All indicators that whatever it was, it was not powerful enough to out-muscle a fully-grown man.

So I stuck to the shadows and threw the torch.

Sure enough, the torch sailing through the air cast light

over the shadows and elicited a hiss from a creature that had been suddenly exposed.

It looked like Gollum's uglier, gym-going buddy. Four feet of ropey muscle that was designed for quick springing and scurrying about. Its claws, three for each of its spidery limbs, were thick and straight. Not something designed for hunting, but a tool for digging out food. Its teeth were pointier than a human's, and it had a face that a mother would have to be severely medicated in order to love.

A necrophage.

Or as it was affectionately known, a corpse-eater.

It confirmed the crypt theory. Necrophages were scavengers and ancient civilizations used them to clean up their gravesites. They preferred to live underground where sunlight would not disturb them, and feasted on dead flesh.

And they were pack hunters.

This one must have been a scout. I glanced down. Of course, the blood.

I crouched down, my hand feeling in the gloom for a weapon, when I heard a whoosh no louder than breeze. Instinctively, I ducked to one side, and the necrophage found an empty wall. It rebounded just as I stood up and we went rolling together.

Usually, taking on something that was not a predator was not too much of a struggle. Fully armed, or at least fully healed, I could have wrestled this thing no problem. But I was wounded, I was dazed and surprised, and it was determined to eat.

The necrophage raked those fingers along my shoulders. My coat took the brunt of the damage and the nails barely scratched the leather, but the blow made my shoulder flare up again. I was only pushing it away with one hand now and the phage knew I was weak.

Strange yelps and clicks escaped its throat and echoed all around us.

Shit.

One I could just about take, but if it called its buddies, I was screwed. I grimaced and called for my magic. I felt a presence, the power still within me, but nothing came out. It was like trying to sprint through snow and mud.

No magic then.

I gasped in pain when I reached out with my injured arm towards the torch. We had rolled dangerously close to it. The phage raked at my weakened side again. I roared this time, and swung my elbow in its face. The blow struck home and I felt very satisfied by the sensation of its face cracking. The phage screamed, its cheek partially caved in. They weren't particularly tough creatures. Guess rotten bones don't give you enough calcium.

I reached for the torch and swung it. The phage yelped like a wounded dog but I struck it again. Tossing the torch away, I knelt over the phage and grabbed a piece of stone lying around. I began to savagely slam the stone on the phage's head, cracking the skull and only stopping when my hand went all the way through its head.

I staggered back and felt my head bump against something. I reached out and felt the familiar shape of a table.

More hissing behind me.

I seized the torch and held it before me. Three more phages had appeared and they stood there watching. I glanced at the table and picked up something that had once been a hatchet. Half the head had rusted away now but it would serve.

With a roar, I threw myself at the phages.

. . .

I WAS DRAGGING myself across the walls, torch held out before me. The passage was endless.

As I walked, I tried to force my magic out, but every time I tried I felt my body shake and go numb. The most success I had was when I sat down and meditated for a few minutes.

After some healing time and meditating enough to calm my frenzied state of mind—and listen some more—I kept on going.

I tried my magic again. This time I felt the vibrations so deeply that I thought they were coming from the walls.

How the Hell were they blocking my magic? What was this place? What sort of prison kept necrophages?

I stopped and looked at the wall. I called for my magic while placing a hand on the wall. It vibrated.

Not me.

The wall.

I set the torch at my feet and pulled out my hatchet. It took a couple of swings but a thick layer of mud and dirt came off. Little peaks of light came through from beneath the first layer of the wall. The hatchet shattered but I had enough leverage to expose a section large enough to see the faintly glowing hieroglyphics.

And then I knew where we were.

I had heard tales of such places in holy sites. Places that were essentially the equivalent of Faraday cages, barring all outside magic but their own. I had used a version of the spell on a rogue angel that had gone on a genocidal spree. My version was rough-and-tumble. It basically cut out *all* forms of magic, which turned it into an endurance match.

But this…

This was centuries of work. Magic that took lifetimes and generations to create. It would likely negate only those that were designated prisoners by the one who controlled the location.

I sighed. There was no way to strong-arm my way out of this one, at least not without locating a fracture or a weak point.

A scream.

I spun my head and grabbed the torch. That was not a human scream. Suddenly I saw a stream of necrophages scurry away. I tucked my torch into a corner and stood over it.

I needn't have bothered.

The humanoid creature chasing the phages was in such frenzy it would not have noticed anything. It grabbed one of them and literally tore it apart, draining it of its blood.

A vampire then.

Worse, a blood-starved vampire.

He roared and tossed the necrophage carcass away. Then he reached down and picked something up. He stayed there sniffing for some time—I was too far away to see what he had found—before dropping whatever he had and went off in a hurry, scaling walls like a spider (or a bad vampire movie) and bolting further into the darkness.

I picked up the torch and examined what he had dropped.

It was a shoe. A boot to be specific.

I had seen this boot before.

On my apprentice's foot.

My blood ran cold.

Abi was also trapped inside this crypt, also without magic and likely injured.

And a starving vampire had just caught her scent.

25

I tailed the vampire, watching it skittering from one side to the other.

It had once been clothed, but only tatters remained now. It was a guy. Don't ask me how I knew that. His hair was clumped with blood, his skull adorned with big raw patches where he had torn his own hair out. He walked hunched and emaciated, alternating between bipedal running and crawling on all fours.

The vampire stopped. I froze and hugged the wall. I wasn't worried about the torchlight anymore. There were crystals embedded in the walls that provided some illumination, though the entire place was so dark the light served only to distract you from the things scurrying in the dark.

The vampire sniffed and snarled. It took off, now in a straight line. I had spent some time living in a forest. I knew what that meant. He'd caught Abi's scent.

I had to sprint to keep up with him, and it wasn't as if I had magic to enhance my physical abilities. Still, good diet and regular exercise enabled me to keep up. That, and enough mental discipline to block out the aching shoulder.

The vampire turned into a corridor.

I heard a snarl and loud clang of metal against stone. I turned the corner and came face-to-face with the vampire.

I knew him.

It was Prince Valen.

He had been blocked by a portcullis and was slamming with all his might against it. The mortar held but I saw cracks snaking. Valen wasn't going to be trapped for long.

He roared.

Something tackled me from behind and the torch went sailing. I rolled on my back just as someone swept my legs aside and landed heavily on my stomach. I slid aside, redirecting their weight, and heard a yelp as their knee found stone. Having learnt my lesson with the necrophages, I kicked out.

The opponent caught my legs. Almost as if they knew what to expect. I knocked again and swept, and flipped us over. The opponent wrapped their legs around me and I recognized the triangle choke just before they applied neck-crushing pain. I slipped out but she had trapped my arm and extended her legs out, crushing my windpipe.

I threw my weight forward, breaking the lock, and came face-to-face with Abi's snarling face.

"Erik?"

I hacked and wheezed in response. "Hey."

She slackened the lock without releasing it. Good on her. There were a number of creatures that could change their shape.

"What are you doing here?"

"Chasing the vampire chasing you," I said. "Why am I still between your legs?"

Her eyes widened and then she let go, scrambling up. She picked up my torch.

"He's been following me since we got here," she said, pointing the torch at Valen.

Who was no longer behind the portcullis.

"Where did he go?" I asked, ready for a manic vampire to come out at any second.

Abi shrugged, maybe a bit too casually. "You missed the precious seconds when Phoenix threw us into a pyramid somewhere beneath Rashid's palace. They tossed us down chutes, except for my mom. One of the generals said something about extracting the Astral Shard." She nodded at the door. "Valen's here for some reason."

That didn't make sense.

I told her so. "Why would the king send his son to die down here? And Valen's an addict. Deprive him of his fix and he goes insane."

"I noticed," she said. "Hence the trap. What about you?"

"Necrophages," I said. "A whole squad of them."

She swore.

"Exactly," I said. "Which means there's more lurking down here. This place must have thousands of years-worth of dead bodies in it."

She nodded. "I got no magic. And judging by your shoulder, you're not getting any either." She sighed. "We have to get out of here."

"I'm all ears," I told her.

Abi turned to illuminate the path ahead. "Look at the walls. See the bright-white corners?"

I nodded and smiled. "Good on you for noticing that. You're following the path of the airflow."

"I do pay attention, you know," she said with a self-satisfied grin. "Now we just have to follow its way up."

26

"Fuck."

My exclamation was soft and whispered but it did not deter from its impact in summarizing our predicament.

We had followed the airflow on the way out, walking for what seemed like hours. Twice we had come upon necrophages. The little shits were now armed with swords and daggers. One of them had a small axe, the kind that could be swung one-handed.

One short skirmish later and now *I* had an axe.

Which was going to serve jack-shit in our current situation, because we had found the next major obstacle.

It was a pit, perhaps thirty feet deep, with a ledge on the sides barely big enough for one person to pass. We'd have to go through single-file and hug the walls, and be comfortable with the fact that we'd have to shimmy on the balls of our feet because the ledge was too small for our whole foot to fit.

But that wasn't the issue.

No, no. That was just the icing.

The cake was the metric fuckton of necrophages that

swarmed all over each other like cockroaches. There were snarls and crackles, and the snapping of bones, scrapes on the walls, and the clinking of weapons from a variety of eras.

On the other side of the pit was a door with a platform. It looked to me that this had once been a dumping ground for corpses. Vamps would toss the carcasses of their enemies over and let the phages do what they did best.

For every phage we saw there must have been ten more. A series of tunnels had been dug around the bottom of the pit, leading to the windows that appeared around the ledge (which was just wide enough to fit a necrophage, I noticed), and likely kept going all around the whole pyramid.

Just like an ant-hive.

Abi and I went through, and instantly backed away. Only a few scouts spotted us. We ran all the way back, turned a corner and then picked the stragglers off.

"We need a distraction," I told her.

"Are you sure we can make it through?" she countered. "That ledge seemed awful skinny."

"We don't have a choice," I said. "That door must lead to the palace."

"I hear a lot of maybes there," she commented.

I shot her a look. "Sorry, I left my creepy crypt map in my other pants."

She actually laughed. It wasn't a ha-ha laugh. I heard her shudder at the end. "What are you thinking?"

"Valen still has your scent," I said.

She added up the rest. Wordlessly, she stood up and hefted a cleaver she had stolen off one of the necrophages. In the other she fisted a sharp piece of rock.

She took a step towards the corridor we had come through, then paused.

"This can't be it, right?" she asked.

I found myself shaking my head. "No," I told her. "You're too pretty to die, and I'm too stubborn."

She barked out another laugh and took off, running towards the crazed vampire hunting her.

In the meantime, I made my way back to the pit. Necrophages scurried about, in and out, unaware that a lone wizard was observing them. I made note of the nearest tunnel, then started looking for the largest ones. Abi and I would need to fit in. I saw one and nodded to myself. It was wide enough that I could go through, albeit a tight squeeze, and it would emerge close enough to a series of rocks that once had been steps. Abi and I could scale them towards the ledge and shimmy our way across.

A foul smell struck my nostrils. Well, a *greater* foul smell, something other than the necrophages and the corpses.

Methane.

It was a good thing we hadn't brought our torch along, otherwise we'd have lit the whole place up.

Wait... hold on...

Since when was I against lighting things on fire?

A scream erupted from behind me, followed by a snarl. Abi!

The necrophages below stopped still and then started scurrying all over the place, like agitated ants. I had to do something. They were converging around the main tunnel, the one Abi would come running out from.

So I did the only thing on my mind:

I set things on fire.

I tore off a strip from my shirt (it was ruined anyway) and struck my hatchet against the wall. Sparks flew. Some fell on the bits of tinder I laid over my shirt, bits made out of wooden scraps I found on the ground. A small flame licked at them, growing as it consumed my shirt.

I waited a few seconds until it grew, and then swung it gently. The toss was languid, but it sailed over a few phages and tumbled lazily into the pit.

Nothing happened.

Several of the phages now converged towards me, the arsonist wizard, while Abi emerged from behind screaming "ERIK!" at the top of her lungs.

She sprinted in my direction and then Valen appeared behind her, sprinting on all fours like a hound after his kill.

BOOM!

Fire roared out from the pit. Air expanded rapidly as heat jettisoned out of the tunnels. A whole load of Necrophages crashed into me. I swung my hatchet and knife, slicing and cutting at anything that could be sliced or cut, while charging towards Valen.

"Get to the ledge," I screamed at Abi. Without waiting for her confirmation I barreled into Valen and heaved.

The vampire was strong and he ripped at my back, but strength and mass were two very different things, and I had the advantage of momentum.

Valen's feet were off the ground as I heaved him up and carried him forward.

Over and into the flaming pit.

IT HAS BECOME something of a running joke now that I'm always throwing myself off of high things. Buildings, helicopters, dragons (that was so cool)—my resume of things I could toss myself from or into was steadily growing.

Now I could proudly add "flaming pit of necrophages, add one vampire" to the list.

We fell hard. Luckily, corpses and necrophages make for

good cushions. Still the impact was jarring and bone-shattering, and I was lucky to still be conscious.

Valen however, was not. One of his arms was bent at an awkward angle. His left leg was broken, the bone sticking out from beneath skin.

I had broken at least two ribs, maybe three, and I braced myself when I crawled onto my knees. Something tore inside of me. Maybe it was a lung, but I was breathing okay.

Relatively.

I walked awkwardly and realized that my hip was broken. My right leg was dragging behind me. I willed my magic forward on instinct, but nothing came out. I was on my own, having to survive on just adrenaline and willpower.

A phage closed in. It shuffled in a daze, the knife in its hands old and dulled. I was somehow still holding my hatchet. My swing was wild and mostly I just threw myself forward. The hatchet head buried itself inside the necrophage and he fell dead. The momentum carried me towards the tunnel.

Behind me, I heard bones snapping.

I dared a peek. Valen had a phage wrapped in one arm, draining it of blood. He shuddered and shook, and when he was done he turned and vomited. But blood was still blood. His bones started healing.

Shit.

I winced as I pressed myself inside the tunnel. The fire had died out, the heat killing most of the phages, and those still alive were more concerned with their survival than fighting the invaders. I was all the way through the tunnel, pushing past asphyxiated phages (the fire had robbed them of oxygen), while Valen reached out to grab another mangled phage to drain.

I crawled and crawled, ignoring the pain, ignoring the

screaming panic in my head. I crawled even when the walls tightened around my shoulders and pressed against my spine, and crawled still when dead phages blocked my path, forcing me to push them forward.

I felt something give. I pushed the phages before me and they dropped back down the pit. The tunnel had come to an end.

I poked my head out and found Abi pressed against the ledge, almost at the door. Below, Valen was now standing upright.

The ledge was just a few scant inches below me. I would have to crawl very carefully, and balance myself just right—an impossible feat given my condition.

Valen looked up. He saw me. Then a rock went sailing as Abi tossed a small boulder at his head and struck true. Valen staggered.

"Hurry, Erik," I heard her call.

Never one to leave a lady waiting, I forced myself down on the ledge. I grabbed some of the jutting rocks to steady myself on as my weight dropped from the tunnel and into...

Nothing.

I slipped and reached frantically, found the ledge. I held on for dear life. Valen was moving beneath me, out of range from Abi's missiles. My shoulder screamed, my hip, dangling in the air, screamed too, and my ribs...

Well, I was literally breathless.

"Erik!" I glanced towards her, sure I was going to drop at any moment.

Abi stood just before the door. She cupped her mouth and shouted, "Too stubborn to die."

The words echoed eerily around the pit, followed by my laughter. I didn't know how I could laugh, or why. I was just doing it.

"Too stubborn to die," I heard myself say.

I reached out and grabbed the ledge with both hands. I swung my hips to get momentum and shimmied to the side. One hand at a time, I shifted along the ledge, occasionally finding a foothold. I could not hoist myself up, but I could slide one hand at a time towards the door.

I had no other choice. I was in pain, it was impossible, but I had no other choice.

I had to do it.

I didn't think about the pain, or how I was moving, or where the hand- and footholds were. I just thought about living.

Suddenly, Abi's arm was grabbing mine in a vice grip and she was grunting in effort. *Now*, I hoisted myself up, and then I was over the ledge and on solid...

Well, Abi.

I was on top of her.

It would have been a moment, were it not for the snarling vampire beneath and the sudden onslaught of agony that hit me now that I was relatively safe.

I could barely stand up, but Abi hoisted one of my arms over her shoulder and carried me through. The door gave easily and light hit our faces.

27

The first thing that hit me was a wave of soothing heat and light. Abi set me down against a wall, which was lined with more sigils than I had ever seen before.

In the middle of the room was a pedestal with a crystal formation that was darker than black. From around the formation, sigils glowed and spread out, forming a spider web of some seriously eerie ambiance.

I felt my body heal as soon as my hands brushed against the sigils. I took my hand away and the agony returned.

I grunted and started removing my tattered coat and shirt. Abi turned to find me half-naked and pressing myself against the walls.

"Um... Erik?"

"Magic," I croaked. "Healing."

I closed my eyes. The healing was quick and effective, but not instantaneous. I had too many injuries, and even if I was healed, there was nothing I could do about the pain.

I woke up startled.

"Shh, shh," Abi said, calming me down. "Don't panic.

You were out for about ten minutes." She checked me out. "You seem okay."

"I don't feel okay," I answered through clenched teeth.

But I could move, and reasonably well, which was more than I could do a few minutes before.

"We've got a problem," she said as soon as I was on my feet.

I groaned. "No magic? Because I can't feel it back yet."

She shook her head. And then I heard it for the first time. A bone-deep shuddering coming from the door.

She didn't have to tell me who it was. Valen had recovered, just as I had.

"One way in, no way out," she said. "And that door won't hold for much longer."

I stood up and reached for my weapons, before remembering I had none. The rudimentary arms I had wielded just a few moments ago were lost when I had nearly plummeted down the pit. Abi had a long knife with more chips and clips on the blade than a saw, but it would do in a pinch.

And this definitely qualified.

"I'm done running from this guy," I told her. "We're trapped. Which means this is our last stand."

She looked at me weird. It was an expression I had seen once or twice on her face before but never quite so intent.

So resolute.

Before I knew it she had pulled me in and was kissing me. At first, I thought it was magic transference (succubii have a kinky way of helping you out) but I felt nothing. Just her soft perfect lips and about ten thousand butterflies in my stomach.

A dozen emotions ran through my system. Fear could make a person do some stupid things. I've always kept things professional between us but you can't help but get intimate when you live with the person. There was nothing romantic, not yet, and I couldn't exactly say I hadn't thought about it.

So I closed my eyes and leaned into it, and a second later it was over. Her eyes were glimmering with a fire that artists could only hope to replicate one day.

"Open the door," she said. *That* growl I recognized.

I walked towards the door—which had been barred with a panel of wood—and watched as Abi stood in plain view. I kicked the panel. The doors flew open.

Valen was a blur but I was waiting for him. He was on Abi in a heartbeat. She moved but left the knife poking out, letting it sink hilt-deep into his chest. Valen swiped at her and found air.

I wrapped my arms around his neck, tightening the choke, and drove him away. This was a fight I could win. It wouldn't be easy, and he was stronger and faster and a bitch to kill—but I had been fighting battles beyond my weight class ever since I was eleven.

I pressed Valen face-first into the wall and went low, punching his kidneys. Valen twisted from the sudden pain. I shot knee after knee into his spine, but then he heaved and levered himself off the wall. We spun, and he slammed me into the wall. My choke slackened.

Abi swooped in, all fists and elbows, wreaking havoc on the vampire's already-mangled face. She pulled out the knife and tore open a gash on the inside of his right arm. She stabbed. Valen extended his left hand and the blade punctured through his palm. He twisted and wrenched the blade from her hand, then slapped her with enough force to send her flying.

But she had bought me enough time.

I grabbed the extended arm and snapped all of my

weight on his shoulder. Valen fought back and I slid backwards. My back pressed against the giant black crystal in the center of the room. I winced and doubled my efforts on the arm lock. With a massive grunt, I managed to change our positions. Valen pulled his hand back but I had the knife in my hand now and I slashed at his chest.

Blood splattered all over the crystal. I felt something shift, magically speaking, but nothing actually changed that was important to the battle. Every last microsecond mattered. One fault and I would be dead. Abi would be dead.

Valen snapped his jaws at me. I punched him in the mouth, something that vampires never expect you to do. His teeth were brittle and gave way too easily. Guess it doesn't lead to good dental hygiene when you switch your diet to rotting necrophages.

I slashed across his eyes, blinding him, and then again at his throat. None of these were death blows to a vampire, and I did not have the right weapon to saw his head off.

So I did the next best thing. I stabbed the knife into his chest and slashed downwards, eviscerating him. The knife snapped halfway through but the gash was wide enough for me to stick my hand in, elbow-deep, and literally grab his heart.

Valen screamed and swept his claws at me. I roared back and shoved him into a wall, stopping suddenly. His back kept going—his heart stayed in my hand.

But instead of slumping against the wall, Valen fell *through* it.

I dropped the vampire's heart and stomped on it. It turned to dust, and from beyond the wall I heard a similar sound.

"Through here?" I pressed my hands on the wall. It was solid as ever.

Abi mirrored my movements. She slid her hands along the wall, no doubt thinking there was a switch.

I turned to the black crystal. Valen's blood was all over it. Maybe I had hit my head during the battle (a likely possibility) but I instantly figured out the puzzle.

I grabbed Abi's hand and found one of the several cuts.

"Hey," she protested.

I pressed her hand on a clean section on the crystal and smeared a little of her blood. Then I pointed at the wall.

"Try it," I said.

"I'm gonna run into the wall," she replied.

"That's kind of the idea."

She shot me a look. "And here I was thinking the *Harry Potter* bullshit was over with." But she took a deep breath and briskly walked forward, not stopping but definitely screwing her eyes shut, and then she disappeared through.

I saw that the top of the crystal was jagged and pointed. I slammed my hand over the point, grunting softly, but to be honest, the pain was nothing compared to just twenty minutes ago.

I felt that magic again and walked through the wall.

"This is..." Abi said, kicking a pile of ash that had once been a vampiric royal member.

I also recognized the place. "Yep. We're still in Egypt," I said. "Only now we're inside Rashid's palace."

28

We had a good-news, bad-news situation.
    The good news: magic was fully back and I couldn't wait to start burning things down.
The bad news: it was the dead of night.
Inside a vampire stronghold full of screams.
Not a good place to go for a stroll.
It didn't take long for a couple of palace guards to show up. It took even less before they were dust piles and we had taken their weapons. The sword I now wielded was nothing compared to Djinn but I had lost that somewhere in Sun Tzu's temple. Djinn was not just a weapon. It was an object of great magical power, a channel made using lost Druidic techniques, and more importantly, it was the only physical object linking me to my mother.
I would have to talk to Sun Tzu about getting it back, but for now, I had a weapon and a boatload of "pissed off" to unload.
Abi took off towards the direction of the screams. She was obviously worried about her mother and it showed in

her fighting style. No quarter, no flourishes—just rapid violence, just like I had taught her.

Reaching the guest chamber, we found several vampire soldiers standing between us and Ishtar, who was not holding back on her screaming.

Abi screamed and five vampires were shoved into the wall, telekinetically blasted. But these weren't vanilla humans. Vampires, though not the most resistant species of magic, were strong nonetheless. Those five stumbled backwards while the other half-a-dozen just ambled to the side, out of harm's way, and raised their weapons. Before any of them could take another step forward I held my sword out horizontally in front of me and used the edge to shape a beam of plasma. Red-hot fire magic burst out in a horizontal line, searing through vampires like a laser cutter. The sword warped and curled into a tight ball of metal. I dropped it as it seared my flesh, and bent over to pick up one of the many fallen halberds. The vampire I thrust it at moved to the side, his reflexes faster than anything I could ever hope to have, but in doing so he built up momentum and could not stop from crashing into a force blast I released towards where I more or less guessed he would end up.

Meanwhile, Abi had projected a couple of illusions of herself and was keeping her targets occupied that way. In a normal setting the vampires' heightened senses could pick up the real Abi no problem but the adrenaline of battle must have dulled their senses long enough to give Abi that small edge she needed to swipe a sword at their heads.

Without breaking her stride, she shouldered the door. It gave.

General Karim turned around. He had the Scepter in one hand, while the other was wrapped around Ishtar's throat, claws perilously tight against her jugular.

"Do not approach," he ordered.

Abi and I dropped the weapons but made no effort to leave.

"Let her go," I said. "It's over. Your soldiers are ash, and there's no way you can take us on your own. Even if you do kill her, you won't make it out of here alive."

"My life has no meaning," he shot back. "I live only to serve the king and execute his will." He pressed the Scepter against Ishtar who writhed in clear agony. "The Shard yearns to come out of its host. It shall not be long now."

"And then what, you fanged fuck?" I asked.

Karim's smile unsettled me. "Then you bow down as the natural order is restored."

It's rare that good things happen after the bad guys say something like that. I watched another spasm hit Ishtar. The way she was moving, there was a good chance she might rip open her own throat on Karim's claws by accident.

I needed a plan.

Something... Anything.

And then the cavalry arrived.

You can always tell Amaymon is close by when the building shakes. You can tell he's pissed when the roof starts coming down.

The mortar above our heads snapped in protest but it was forced to give. I leapt back without thinking when a massive piece fell through and landed on the spot I had occupied less than half a second ago.

"ABI!"

Ishtar's scream came with a force of power. Karim's claws ripped at her neck but his feet came out from under him. Still, blood rivered down from Ishtar's neck as she slammed into her daughter and pushed her out of the way from falling rocks.

Karim snarled. "The Shard is *mine!*"

He leapt.

A cannonball slammed into him from the other end of the room.

There stood a man made out of metal, dark grey and powerfully built, as if a linebacker and Colossus had had a love child. He had his hand extended, the palm morphed into a barrel of sorts.

Jack, a metal Elemental and one-time apprentice of mine, turned his hand back to normal and beamed at me. "Good to see you again, boss."

"Jack," I said. "Perfect timing."

"Your cat is grouchy," he said.

"I can tell."

We traded grips and Jack was about to say something, but then Karim was on him, fangs extended, arms interlocked around his neck. The vampire bit down.

His fangs snapped off.

Jack, completely unconcerned that a bloodthirsty ravenous being was trying to suck his blood, cocked his head at me.

"You were right. They are not the shiniest light bulbs in the chandelier."

"I've never used the word chandelier to describe anything," I said.

"Yeah," he said. "I may have embellished a little. My boyfriend may have taught me that."

"Boyfriend?"

Karim moaned over Jack's shoulder. The latter casually punched backwards, a knife appearing over his knuckles that stabbed neatly into Karim's head. The vampire let go. It was not a mortal wound but who among us can take a knife to the head and walk away?

Jack shrugged. "Don't make a big deal out of it."

I was going to say I didn't really care who he dated, but Ishtar had other plans.

"It's coming out!" Her screams managed to dull out the sound of the entire damn palace falling apart, so that'll tell you what level of hysteria I was dealing with.

"Quick," Abi said. "We have to get her out."

But Ishtar was on the ground, and she lay there. "It's too late for me," she said. "The parasite... It wants you, daughter. You are its original mother, not me. I simply took the burden."

"What are you talking about?"

More rocks fell. Walls caved in. I spotted a large hole in the ground that just kept growing.

"We need to move," I said.

Amaymon appeared out of the hole, as if to answer my prayers. He stomped over to me, grabbed me by the shoulders and half-hugged, half-crushed me.

"You smell like corpses."

"Necrophages," I grunted before the last oxygen left my lungs.

He wrinkled his nose. "You need to learn how to keep better company."

I was about to point out that my current company was literally crushing me to death, but Amaymon used his powers to suddenly lift us up.

And I don't mean us, as in the people.

I mean us, as in *the building.*

Rashid's palace was an underground pyramid. That didn't seem to bother Amaymon.

We rose from the ground, and suddenly we were in cold,

starry, Arabic air, above a hole the size of a... Well, a palace, filling up with sand. By all accounts we should have been sucked right back into that vortex.

Again, that fact did not bother Amaymon. The earth was under his firm grasp.

"Mom." Abi cradled Ishtar's head in her lap. Ishtar looked old now.

No, old was the wrong word.

She looked withered, shrunken into nothing more than skin and bones.

"I've kept it at bay for as long as I could." Her voice was barely a whisper, but it seemed to echo around the desert surrounding us.

"I don't understand," Abi said. "What do you mean, *my* parasite?"

Ishtar closed her eyes. "You will see, daughter." Her hand grasped Abi's. "I was happy to have met you again, Abigale. Despite our differences, you made me proud. You've inherited all the best qualities a mother could hope for her daughter. You are far stronger than me, child, and I am grateful for that. I love you, Abigale."

"Don't say that, mom," Abi said. She shook over her mother. "Please don't say that."

"Hush now," Ishtar said. A smile crept on her face. "Thank you. I was once told I would die in a land unknown, but I never imagined it would be under such a beautiful starry sky. Why... look at it... it is so... so...beautiful."

The effects began as soon as Ishtar took her last breath. I fell to my knees as something pulled at the insides of my head. Abi similarly contorted in the sand, her hand still clasped on her mother's cold one.

My aura vision popped on automatically. Whatever it was, it wanted me to see it.

That blob of bluish, purple, white mass of psychic energy—the parasite—slithered from Ishtar and onto Abi. It seemed to sigh contentedly as its aura merged with Abi's and I heard one word echo in my brain:

"Mother."

29

Abi fell unconscious right away and I could tell that she wasn't about to wake up anytime soon. The parasite had taken over, put her in a dormant state and there was jack-shit I could do about that fact.

Or anything I could do to remove it.

Dammit.

Dammit all to Hell.

I had just watched one succubus die, and I was hours, if not minutes away, from watching a second one. My apprentice. My friend.

My Abi.

Amaymon took us back to the States, but it was not a pleasant homecoming. I had Abi prone in my arms, while rushing up the stairs to an apartment building I did not recognize. That didn't surprise me. This part of town was not somewhere I tended to hang out.

Jack took the lead. Somewhere along the journey he had shed his metallic form, but even as a regular human, there was still something unnaturally solid about him.

He fished out a key from underneath a welcome mat and

let us inside a moderate, if well-furnished apartment. Everywhere I looked there was black furniture, lacquered with metallic paint. The scent of jasmine hit my nostrils, along with a variety of other spices coming from the kitchen.

"We're home," Jack announced.

Then—and I say this in all sincerity *and* taking into account my weird-ass life leading up to the events up until a few minutes ago—the most bizarre thing I had ever seen walked out of the kitchen.

Luke, Pyromancer, Grigori member, one-time enemy of mine, jury-still-out-on-ally—Luke, the wanna-be tough guy —emerged from the kitchen wearing an apron with the words *Hot, Handle With Care* stitched on the damn thing.

Needless to say, my jaw hit the ground. Luke just snickered, walked past me, and pulled Jack in for a kiss that would have rated NC-17 on a good day.

Holy shit.

"Holy shit," Amaymon echoed. "Look at 'em go."

Jack, bright-red, turned to me. "So, um, I know it's not under the right circumstances, but... Luke and I are sorta dating."

Luke chuckled. "I'm making curry," he declared, sauntering back to the kitchen. "Sorta dating," he echoed with a chuckle.

"Erik." Gil emerged into my vision. Greg was sitting on a couch in the living room. He and Gil must have been there the whole time, but I had been obviously distracted. "Put her here."

I set Abi down on the couch as Greg got up and placed a pillow under her head.

Luke came back with a bowl that trailed a long billow of smoke. "Out of my way," he said, half-pushing me aside.

Before I could do anything, he started waving the

smoking bundle inside the bowl over Abi, who whined and groaned.

It was the first sound she had made since the parasite overtook her.

"What are you doing?" I asked Luke.

"Cleansing her aura," he said with a straight face. Then, when he noticed my look, he added, "You remember my father was an Ectomancer, a ghost wizard."

I nodded.

"Ghosts and psychic entities aren't that far off the spectrum from each other," he said. He reached into the bowl and smeared some ash on Abi's forehead. "And luckily for us in this case, the human body reacts to possession much in the same way, no matter the source. Abi's aura has been wrecked. If we have any chance of removing the parasite, she needs to be strong enough to survive the procedure."

"You're going to remove the parasite?" I asked, careful to not allow relief flood my voice just yet.

"No."

Good thing I held back, huh?

"That's not my area," Luke said, fussing over Abi. Then, satisfied, he stood up. "But there is a Grigori who can take care of it. Evans, the Golem Maker." He nodded at Gil, who tilted her head slightly.

Luke retreated back into the kitchen and I heard the sound of dish-ware clinking.

"Can Evans really do it?" I asked Gil.

She nodded. "He's made golems with organic flesh before. He thinks he can transfer the parasite into a different host."

"Then let's go."

"Sit down." Luke had returned and was setting up the table with knives and forks. "The cleansing I just did needs at least an hour to work to stabilize her. Move her now and you'd do her more harm than good. For now all you can do is wait."

I glowered at him. "Wait? Easy for you to say. She's *dying*."

Luke looked like he wanted to retaliate with something sharp. Instead he said, "I know. But you still need to wait. If you move her, she won't survive Evans' procedure."

Jack came in with a massive pot of curry and the scent wafted through my nostrils.

"You need to eat something," he said. "Erik, I know it's hard, I know you want to spring into action. But you're battered, you look like shit, and you're tired. Abi needs her rest too." He offered me a kind smile. "Take a shower. Eat something. Recover your strength. You can only help others if you are strong enough to do so."

That was something I had told him, a lifetime ago when we had met. Jack had been little more than a hired thug with no training and more issues than you could fit in a book. Unlike Abi, he had never been wizard material. His powers were set and all he needed was a stable life—something I could never provide for him. He was now a blacksmith, and he was happy. Sure, I could pick on his choice of life partners— I mean, *Luke* for God's sake?—but hell, they made each other smile, and wasn't that the whole point?

And he was right.

I stood up and headed for the bathroom, nodding at Jack along the way.

I'll say this about Luke: the guy makes a damn good curry.

After my shower and a change of clothes that was a little too big for me—Jack had *really* bulked out—I sat down with my sister and her boyfriend, my demonic familiar, my former apprentice, and my former enemy.

Yeah. My life made sense.

I ate like I was getting paid to do it. Jack had been right. I hadn't had a moment's rest since I had left Sun Tzu's place, and when I questioned after it, my sister brought me up to speed.

"Sun Tzu retreated soon after, along with Rashid," she said. "Once Ishtar was gone, they had no reason to be there. Sun Tzu has officially withdrawn any help until this matter is brought to a conclusion."

I was glad for that. Having godly beings around this chaos was akin to throwing a grenade in a blender. It might not blow up now, but you know it *will* blow up eventually.

"Meanwhile, your big werewolf friend showed up again," she went on. "Several Vol outposts have been hit, along with cells of Rashid's army. He's not distinguishing between them. Not that there is any distinction after the evidence you found."

I nodded and accented that nod by shoving a spoonful of rice in my mouth.

At least I remembered to chew and swallow before I spoke.

"So now we have a plan," I told her. "We get Abi to Evans, then we find Rashid and kill him."

"I like this plan," Greg said. "Although it is a vague plan."

"More of an outline really," Amaymon interjected.

"A mission statement at best," Jack commented.

I rolled my eyes at all of them.

"We can't kill Rashid," Luke said.

"Correct," added my sister. "He's a stabilizing force. Kill him and you risk another entity replacing him. One without the restraint Rashid has shown." She sighed and set her spoon down. "I know you think otherwise, but we need Rashid to stay in power. He was right about the Grigori not having the manpower to control the vampires. And more importantly, he's the devil we know. Which means he's the devil we can deal with."

Suddenly I lost my appetite.

Quiet settled down around the dinner table. "Doesn't matter what we do."

It was Amaymon that had broken the silence. His voice was calm and smooth, leaving behind most of the usual bravado.

"It doesn't matter what we do," he repeated. "We have something he wants, something that is now inside Abi. He's gonna keep coming after her until he gets it."

"That's not gonna happen," I said.

He nodded, yellow feline eyes hard and terrifying. "No, it won't. Because we will destroy every last one of them who steps on our doorstep. It is what we do. And it is why we were brought into this, Erik." A grin. "Ain't that right, Gil?"

Her lips bore the faintest trace of a smile.

"I know how my brother thinks," he went on. "The Grigori are tied up. So they bring in a third party. Nothing unusual about that. Then one of the enemy gets sworn in, and the bad guys start trying to use the law to their benefit. But see, they're in a hurry. Now, out in the wild, when things get in a hurry it means their advantage is running low. They want to end the fight before the enemy wizens up. Which is why it was the princess and not anyone else that was selected. The one party determined to turn on the bad guys."

It clicked.

"You're waiting until Rashid feels safe," I told Gil. "Until he and I start duking it out. Then Carmilla swoops in and you have every reason to bully your way into their territory. You want her in power."

"No." Gil took a sip of water. "We want Rashid in power. We just want him neutered. Carmilla is a driving force for him. Pushing him to grow stronger. His adversity with her is why he rallied his forces. Then Greede set in motion the events that led up to now and their quarrel was put at bay. But make no mistake, brother, they are quarreling and they love it. They drive each other to reach for greater heights, until one day they will be so strong we will not be able to contain them."

"And out of the two, Rashid is the nuke," I concluded. "So you want him right where he is, minus the god-like power."

"Precisely," she said.

"That's a lot of moving parts," I told her. "And with that many *what-if*s something's bound to go wrong."

She smiled and stood up. I watched her go towards a supply closet and open it. Inside I saw Greg's spear and her wand, along with Abi's Sun Wukong staff. She returned with something wrapped in a blanket. I moved my plate and unwrapped my sword, Djinn.

Feeling its magical hum was like coming back home after a long journey.

"That's precisely why I hired you, brother," she said, with a grin that rivaled Amaymon's. "For when things go wrong."

30

We drove way the Hell outside of town until we reached an abandoned steel mill that was now being used to produce clay. This didn't really surprise me, since Golems were made out of clay and the guy we had come to visit relied on them for pretty much everything. As we walked in, I saw several workers huddled around a giant kiln, while others shaped the clay into a variety of pots, cups, and myriad other utensils.

What I was looking at were the workers. They were all identical—buff humanoids with no hair or facial expression.

Nothing.

Smooth skin with no holes, ridges, or a single hair.

The golems looked at us as we entered, a weird group consisting of myself, Gil, Greg, Amaymon, Luke, and an unconscious Abi. The golems opened the gates for us to allow Luke's SUV inside, and Evans himself emerged.

"Welcome," he said.

Evans calmly opened the door to the SUV and with a

delicateness that did not befit his stature, slowly lifted Abi into a bridal carry and walked off.

"Follow me," he said, leading us through the workshop.

The heat was unbearable as we passed by the forge. Sweat ran down me, soaking my clothes, and I was thinking of taking off my coat, when I reconsidered. This was my backup coat, the first one now in tatters in what was left of Rashid's palace. It did not have the same protective enchantments as the other, but it had some, and some was better than none.

Mercifully, Evans led us away from the kiln and towards a set of stairs. Down and down we went until we reached a place that was literally buzzing with magic. It was another workshop, this one with massive mills that constantly churned clay and other pastes that looked eerily like congealed blood.

I had always been interested in how golems were made. Now I was less interested.

Evans placed Abi on a cot and two other golems, identical to the worker golems outside, proceeded to strip her. We all turned around out of respect.

"She will need to be covered with a paste first," Evans explained to us. "Then we shall mold a golem for the parasite to occupy. This process is long. You may wait outside."

"I'd rather wait here," I told him.

Evans cocked his head. "This is my workshop, Erik. I never allow visitors inside. You must respect that."

"Erik," Gil said. "He's already done enough."

Greg caught my eyes and nodded. They all trusted Evans. Hell, I did too. But I had learnt the hard way when I was a ghost (long story) not to trust the Grigori too much. Sure, things were different now that my sister was running the show, but some lessons you never forgot.

I guess though, I also did not want to admit the real issue here. I was helpless to help Abi in any way. Evans could. I wanted to be her hero. It also didn't help that whenever I wasn't dealing with necrophages, or rabid vampires, or rescuing succubii, I couldn't stop playing our kiss over and over in my brain.

Out of this entire ordeal, it was that one small act that had shattered my reality. That kiss made me question everything, it made me mull over everything Abi and I had ever shared. I had always been attracted to her—she's literally half-sex demon—and she had done what very few people had:

She had earned my respect, I saw her as an equal, and that fundamentally changed the playing field.

Before I could make up my mind, Evans was in my field of vision.

"I would like to speak with you personally," he told me. Then to the others, "There is a kitchen just to the left. An aide will guide you."

Sure enough, a faceless golem was waiting to escort them out, while Evans' massive hand clamped gently on my shoulder. Amaymon looked at me quizzically.

I tilted my head, and said, "Sure thing, Evans. Let's talk."

We waited until the others had left the room. The door clicked behind them.

Then something hissed from the back of the workshop. I turned and watched as a sliding door that had not been there before parted, and a man came in.

He was sitting down on a chair of some kind, a big heavy-duty metallic contraption that encased the lower half of his body. The chair's legs were thick spidery legs, and made a soft clicking sound whenever the chair scuttled about.

The man himself was stick-thin, with a thick frizzled mop of hair and a balding spot at the very back. His stubble was starting to grow into a patchy beard that had shades of salt and pepper. Mid-twenties, maybe early thirties if I had to guess though his disheveled appearance certainly aged him. His eyes were dark brown, the color of the clay he loved so much, and his arms were covered in symmetrical cuts and burns: the telltale signs of an artist who worked past the pain in order to relieve himself of the agony his mind brought along.

The chair scuttled towards me. Evans looked at me through copper-rimmed spectacles. His teeth were yellowed and he didn't exactly smell daisy fresh. The combination of sweat, body odor, and clay was not a popular fragrance.

"So you're the one," he said. I remembered his voice, surprisingly young like a teenager on the verge of puberty, from when I had taken over his golem, back when I had been a ghost. "You're the one who hijacked my battle golem."

He chuckled. "I thought you'd be taller."

I glanced from the massive golem I knew as Evans, down to the real Evans, its creator. The man behind the magic, puppeteer behind the puppet.

"Big guy you built there. Compensating, are we?" I shot back.

Evans glared at me for a second. Then he threw his head back and barked a laugh.

"I never allow people in my den, you know," he said, scuttling over towards a shelf. I heard the clinking of glasses. "But you... Oh boy, did I want to meet you. You always bring in the strange."

He offered me a shot glass with something that was clear

but smelled like motor oil. He saluted with a second glass and downed the shot.

I mirrored him and felt my soul on fire. My hacking amused him.

"The strange?" I echoed.

"The strange, that's what I call it," he said. "People like you are rare, even for our world. Many can do magic. It's not that impressive. But those who bring in the strange are different. They don't need magic because they have that something special churning inside of them."

I had no clue what he was talking about. The only thing churning inside me was whatever the hell was in that shot glass.

"Did Akasha ever mention me?" he asked. I saw his hands shake when he poured another round. His eyes were focused on the liquid. "I knew the two of you were close."

"You could say that."

Normally I wouldn't talk about her with strangers but he —or rather, the big golem now standing idle a few feet away —had been something of an aide to her. I think, seeing him now, that maybe she was also a mother figure to him.

Evans passed me a drink. "She saved me, you know. Saved me from myself." His hands were still shaking but they steadied just enough for him to down the shot. I did the same. This time the liquid didn't hurt as much.

"You're sick," I said, figuring it out.

Evans nodded. "Brain tumor. Inoperable. Got it right around my sixth birthday, just in time for me to start seeing things. You know how it is with magic. It grows on you." He chuckled at his own pun.

Most people get their powers just before puberty. I was eleven when I started exhibiting mine. By that time you literally grow into it. You see things others can't, you do things others can only dream of, but you're old enough to have already grasped some form of reality.

Doing all that at the age of six... The tumor in his head must have accelerated his development. But magic also has a price. That development must have cost him.

I glanced at his legs, then at his face which was looking at me expectantly. It cost him himself, taking from him the only thing he had to give.

"Why golems?" I asked.

"Wanted imaginary friends," he replied. "Then I realized making things is fun so, you know, two birds and all that. I like understanding things, Erik. First I understood magic, then I tried to fix myself, only I couldn't, so then I started building things. Better things."

"You tried to build yourself a new body," I said.

He nodded. "Not yet. But one day. One day I'll be able to figure out how consciousness works." He grinned. "I'm close, mind you. Close enough to understand the thing inside your friend over there."

Our attention turned to Abi, whose whole body was now caked in mud except for her face, which was only smeared with clay in something that resembled runes.

Sigils, I reminded myself. That's what golems used.

"Can you remove it?" I asked. "Or transfer it?"

"It's linked to you and her," he said.

"Me? How?"

Evans shrugged. "Beats me. When was the last time you two linked your powers?" His eyebrows raised. "Unless you decided to have a threesome with a psychic entity or something."

"We did not."

"Good. They can be fickle." He chuckled. "So, then? When did you link powers?"

I cast my memory back. I remembered, but only because we had brought up Akasha. It was the same day as the battle. The same day she died. The same day *I* died.

Abi and her mom had faced off with, ironically enough, a golem. One created out of indestructible bones, the heart of an angel, and as we had discovered now, an Astral Shard.

And I had lent Abi my powers because the golem was a vessel for a powerful psychic entity that Greede had under his control. I remembered the cry of that thing when Abi killed it. I remembered the backlash.

And I remembered how Ishtar jumped in front of her daughter, shielding her.

The parasite was a shard of that psychic entity, something born out of the fragments.

"Shit," I said.

I told Evans the story.

"Shit," he replied. "Then I got some good news and bad news for you. But I want you to understand something first: I'm a genius. I am possibly one of the smartest people on this planet and I don't say that lightly. I don't brag. It's just a fact."

I was about to point out that saying he's a genius and that's a fact *did* technically constitute as bragging but Evans was on a roll.

"So when I tell you I cannot build a body for this thing, I want you to believe me."

"Shit," I said. "Please tell me that's the bad news."

"It depends," he said. "I know someone who *can* build a body. Someone who is, technically, a demon."

"I can handle demons," I told him. "How will you convince him to work with us?"

Evans grinned. "I won't. You will."

I cocked my head. "Who's the demon?"

"Your familiar's brother."

Then it clicked.

Astaroth, Amaymon's more fiery brother, was pretty much like Evans but with fire foxes (totally a thing), a literal castle full of inventions, and, stay with me, a matching pair of talking sock puppets.

"Astaroth won't leave his lair," I told him.

"All the materials we need are here," Evans said.

"Then you gotta bribe him with something," I said. "He's just like you. What would convince *you* to leave this place?"

Evans scowled, then chuckled, then fell in thought. "I got just the thing."

He whistled and one of the faceless golems brought over a hammer. A small silver hammer that looked dainty enough to be one of those hammers they use for jewelry.

"This is made out of orichalcum," he said. "It's an item that can forge things that are both of this world and not." He offered me the hammer. "Tell him I have a whole toolset like this. It's his if he works with me on this project."

I rolled the hammer in my hand and pocketed it.

"Now that we know what the thing is," Evans continued, "I can start working on the preparations. You!"

The massive battle golem walked over to us.

"Tell the fire guy to help steam up the kiln," human Evans said. Golem Evans nodded. "The demon will be going to Hell so make sure the portal is open."

Golem Evans nodded again.

Human Evans had a massive grin on his face. He slapped his chair enthusiastically.

"All right, people. Let's get cracking!"

. . .

FIVE MINUTES later I was watching Luke use the brunt of his pyromancy to make the kiln go from "unbearably hot" to "heart of a volcano".

Amaymon had already left with the hammer after making an inappropriate comment, and promising to be back with his more reclusive brother.

Greg and Gil were at the back, with Gil casually observing. I knew that look. She was studying Evans' methods and filing information away.

I was outside, pacing.

And that's when the ground started shaking. Marching echoed in the distance and came ever closer.

A flapping screeching sound filled up the sky. I squinted and found a massive black cloud of flapping bats contrasting the twilight of the setting sun.

Rashid had found us.

31

It was like the scene in *The Two Towers* when the orcs attack Rohan, that few seconds when both armies are staring each other down before the swords and arrows come into play.

Only in this version, only the bad guys had the massive army. My side had four people: myself, Greg, my sister, and Luke. Plus a whole load of faceless golems that might or might not be battle-effective.

Preceding his army was Rashid. The king had materialized out of the flock of bats (still so *awesome*), longsword in hand, cloak fluttering in a breeze that had not been there a moment ago, and eyeing me with the same gaze that most crocodiles reserved for antelopes.

"Erik Ashendale," he said, aiming the sword at me.

Not one to be out-machoed I pointed my sword at him. *And* my gun. "Count."

"Excuse me?"

"Count. As in Count Dracula." I cocked my head. "Seriously? *That's* the one I have to explain? To *you*?"

Thus far Rashid had been calm and collected,

attempting to outwit before outmuscling his problems. He was cold and granite.

But apparently, he was real sensitive about shitty vampire jokes because he snarled, and suddenly I was bracing myself as our swords met. He swept in with enough force to send me backwards. Bats fluttered over my face, the longsword bizarrely held along by a trio of the flapping critters, and would have impaled my face were it not for Greg parrying the stroke with his spear. The two lifelong enemies began an exchange of blows.

I noticed Gil falling back, casting as she stepped. Luke the Pyromancer was still occupied with the giant kiln, which in battle meant he was literally with his back exposed. She started shielding them both, sigils slipping out of her fingers with an intricacy that I could never manage.

Basically that left me to deal with a *whole freakin' army*.

Thankfully, Evans—the massive golem—showed up next to me. His hands were up. I knew what to expect but it was still an impressive bit of magic. Sigils glowed around his arms, so hot they burned away the sleeves of his dress shirt and jacket, and twin purple streams of pure arcane energy jettisoned into the front ranks of Rashid's army.

The vampires paused.

I turned my grinning face over to the golem. "You are Iron Man."

"Men," he said.

"What?"

In response I saw the most beautiful thing I had ever seen. A dozen Evanses—Evanii?—materialized out of localized teleportation spells that opened up exactly two meters on each side from Evans. Battle golems stood next to each other in perfect formation and watching them work was a thing of beauty.

Only to be cockblocked by General Karim, who like a roach or a case of sexually transmitted infections, refused to just, fucking, die!

He showed up out of nowhere and swung a claymore sword at me, yelling and screaming like a madman. His armor was gold and purple, dented from where Jack had torn through it and also from when Amaymon had brought down a pyramid on top of him.

I blocked his swing and came face to face with him. His fangs had not healed, his mouth was one giant bruise and more hilarious the knife hole in his head had only partially closed.

"Where is your friend?" he snarled. "The one who gave me these wounds? I would like to tear him apart."

I heaved back. "Which one? We all took turns hitting you 'cause you're such an ass. Here, lemme show you!" I struck my forehead into his already mangled nose. A head-butt is a powerful strike but judging from the way Karim leapt back, you would have thought I poured molten lava on his face.

I shot him. The armor did not hold. Karim blocked the second strike with his sword. I swept it aside and thrust Djinn into his stomach. He bit me on pure reflex but with no fangs it was just a disgusting sensation.

Fire exploded from my sword, engulfing the general and finally putting all of us out of our misery from having to breathe the same air as that asshole.

Not that vampires breathed air. Just a metaphor.

My victory was short-lived when someone threw a spear right into my back. I spun and rolled on the ground, painfully wrenching the weapon out, then watched as a few more soldiers leveled crossbows at me.

Greg was sent flying as Rashid hit him with a particularly powerful kick.

The Evans squad had now been reduced to half its force, the fallen golems turning into shattered mounds of clay, surrounded by the ash of the vampires they slew.

It wasn't enough. This was Rashid's full force, and we were simply not enough. This is the sad truth about warfare. You can be the toughest guy on the planet, but if six people surround you, you *are* going to get hit. That's just a fact. A prehistoric fact, in fact. Mammoths were bigger than humans, yet *we* ate *them.* That right there should tell you all you need to know about teamwork and the importance of having numbers on your side.

Someone sliced at my hamstring. I shot them back, missed their head and caught them on the shoulder.

Times like these you'd be grateful for when God—any god—or the fates, or destiny, or whatever cosmic entity you subscribe to—intervenes.

An Act of God, they call it.

Except in our case, salvation was big, hairy, angry, and took the shape of a giant werewolf.

32

The wolf's battlecry shattered the war. The mighty beast stood on two legs with the vampires cowering as it towered over them. Howls emerged from around us. There had to be at least a dozen other werewolves, these ones regular-sized—though admittedly even a regular-sized werewolf is nothing to scoff at.

Only two of the pack were not wearing their furs. A pale woman, reed-thin, was holding back a girl that was just tall enough to reach her mother's hips. Her eyes were jet-black orbs, her skin the color of ink.

Rashid looked at the kid, eyes wider than when he had first seen the alpha wolf.

"The abomination."

I saw the resemblance then. The child possessed both traits of a werewolf—claws, slightly top-heavy as her shoulders and chest bulked out—and a vampire—fangs, flattened face, and elongated, slender limbs.

A Vaewolf. A hybrid.

Someone from the opposing army had the bright idea to

reach out towards the child. The mother was on all fours before I could blink, snarling at him before ripping his throat out as she protected her child in a more bestial form.

The battle resumed.

I watched as the alpha leapt onto Rashid and did the one thing none of us had been able to thus far:

He hit him. Hard.

Long, deep, claw marks furrowed Rashid's face. The werewolf continued to maul him, while a dozen soldiers rushed the wolf. I threw myself in the fray, sword blazing (the gun had flown out of my hands the last time I got hit), and was joined by Greg.

Gil emerged from the workshop, radiant and glowing. Her aura had turned into a series of globes behind her, and from each she shot a bolt of searing white light. The rain of light machine-gunned into the enemy.

Next to her, the burning man carpeted everything in front of him in fire.

"Kiln's done," Luke announced over the roar of his fires. Behind him, even the worker golems were grabbing anything that could be remotely called a bludgeoning weapon and going to town on any vampire that slipped past Gil's and Luke's defenses.

Rashid flocked then reformed around the alpha werewolf and managed to land a strike with his longsword. The alpha's roar punched me in the gut but I still took a step forward to aid the beast. I figured it was better to have the furry Hulk as our ally—enemy of my enemy and all that.

I tried to walk but my healing was having a tough time keeping up with all the injuries. Greg leapt over by the werewolf and they double-teamed Rashid. Again, they struck him, this time Greg landing a searing slice with his spear over to Rashid's sword arm while the werewolf snapped up the limb and sword all in one bite and crunched down. Rashid screamed something foreign and leapt back. His form ebbed into mist just in time to avoid a swipe from the alpha werewolf.

But Greg was a different story.

His war cry was deafened by the sound of booming thunder. I had never seen Greg do his Kresnik thing. His eyes turned into white fiery globes, his hair crackled with static, and rainbow light trailed his spear's every movement. When he struck the mist, the light spread out.

Rashid's cry was agonizing.

He reformed behind a line of his troops, face bloodied and scarred, his right arm missing, and now his armor torn off and his torso burnt and bubbling as if acid had been injected beneath his skin. Whatever he said must have been something along the lines of "retreat" because the vampires fell back.

We let them go. We didn't have the numbers or the power to give chase, and it was getting even darker.

Now we turned our attention to the werewolves. One by one, naked humans replaced the snarling wolves, while the massive alpha sank down, unbothered by the fact that Greg was eyeballing him.

I joined him and we watched as the big wolf shrunk down to a young man a foot shorter than me. His shoulders were massive, his chest a barrel, and frankly, he looked like he could benchpress a freight train. His skin was darker than mine which made me think he must have been of different ethnicity.

But it was his face that bothered me the most. I knew those eyes. Two years ago I had fought a man with those same eyes, the same man that had once served my father and then served Greede until his dying breath.

The werewolf man took a few steps towards me.

"My name is Caleb," he said, "and you killed my grandfather."

33

Okay. So.

There are moments in my life where I feel I need to recap, because everything tends to get bizarre.

But even by *my* standards, low as they might be, this was out there.

Golem factory saved, check.

Big vampire army repelled, check.

Giant werewolves, with pack, plus one child-sized Vaewolf, coming to the rescue, check.

Inigo Montoya quote confirming what I had suspected for a while, check.

Chance of getting mauled by said giant werewolf, check.

We sat around a table at the back of the workshop. Caleb the alpha wolf basically strode in like he owned the damn place and no golem made an effort to stop him. Instead he found a table wide enough to accommodate most of us, sat down, and said,

"We need to talk."

Evans had even provided us with cold beer.

"You're Ubatu's grandson," I said.

Caleb nodded. "My mother was just a child when my grandfather started his contract with Greede. He transferred his pack's leadership to her while he upheld his duties. I grew up in the castle town with her pack."

I grimaced. The bottle was tightly gripped in my left hand. My right tightened around the gun I had re-holstered on my thigh but did not draw.

"I saw what you did there," Caleb went on. "It was... Thorough."

I had been a rampaging black knight with four of Hell's worst at my side, guns blazing through a castle town that had served as Greede's stronghold.

Yes, *thorough* was one way of describing it.

Murderous might be another.

Still, I said nothing.

Caleb gave me a slight nod. "I never liked Greede. I was glad to be free from his obligation."

"What about your family?" I asked him.

"They made their choice," was all he said. Caleb took a swig from the bottle. He didn't look old enough to drink, but I guess you don't argue with the hulking monster who had just saved your life. "Just like I made mine."

His eyes slipped over his crew. His pack. They were all in various states of undress, and all nursing wounds.

"Why did you help?" I asked. "Not that I'm not glad for it, but I have to ask. I'm the one who put Ubatu down after all. Why help me?"

"I'm not," he said. "I'm helping me."

"The Vaewolf," Gil said. "She's part of your pack. You want her safe."

Caleb nodded. "My cousin. On my father's side," he said with a smile. "Rashid wants her." He reached in his pocket.

Greg's hand flew to his spear but made no move to lower it. Caleb glowered at him.

The scar he exhibited in wolf form translated into a long silvery line down the side of Caleb's face, running between his nose and eye, bifurcating most of his handsome face.

Caleb lowered a small jewelry sack on the table. Gil reached out and opened it. She gasped and slowly upturned it.

Bits of black rock tumbled out.

"Astral Shards," I said.

"Got them off some of the Vol Bloodletters that I encountered," Caleb explained. "They guarded them with their lives. Figured they were important. To them, and to you."

Gil picked one of them up. "More will come. Especially now that Rashid knows you have the Vaewolf."

I found myself glancing back. The hybrid child looked no different than any other regular kid, except perhaps for something predatory in her eyes. It was unsettling, seeing something that dark on such a cute face.

"Lily," Caleb said. "Her name is Lily. And she is more than just a hybrid, Miss Ashendale. She is family."

I found myself liking Caleb more and more. The guy was probably too young to be leading a pack despite his strength, but he had stepped up to the plate and he was compromising even now and dealing with outsiders for the safety of his family.

"You want to keep her safe," I said. He nodded. "We will do that."

"No, you won't," he replied. "I will. I'll take my pack and hide somewhere no one will find us."

"Rashid will," Greg muttered.

"Let him come," Caleb snarled.

Yep. The kid was just like I was, all bristle and fire. He probably hadn't been in a fight he'd lost and I didn't want his first time to be when his family needed him most.

"I got you covered," Amaymon drawled from next to me.

The demon had come back from Hell just as the battle ended. He popped out of the portal inside Evans' lab, presumably depositing his brother there and left them to their own devices.

Now, he propped his feet up on the table, rattling the bottles that sat there. "I can make any patch of land you're on warded long enough for these chuckleheads and myself to take care of His Royal Batface."

I knocked his feet off. "You can do that?"

Amaymon shook his head disapprovingly, as if questioning why, after all these years of working together, I still doubted his great prowess, and then looked at the alpha.

"Only if the big guy over there wants me to."

Caleb leaned forward slightly. His eyes locked onto Amaymon's. I'd never seen anyone hold the demon's gaze for so long.

"You are a demon," he said. "But not just any demon. You are the Earth Beneath. You are the Land That Provides, the Mountains That Shelter, the Rocks That Bind." He nodded. "We will trust you, King of Earth, for we are subjects to you."

Amaymon shot me a shark-toothed grin. "See? Wolfy knows who he's dealing with. Respect! King of Earth needs respect, boy!"

"He doesn't have to clean your litter," I responded.

He waved me off. "Silence, peasant, or I'll get my new werewolf pack to piss on your bed."

Caleb exhaled and stood up. "Time to go."

He exited. The rest of the pack followed soon after. Lily

gave me a smile. She had a missing front tooth. It was adorable.

Amaymon yawned and stretched very cat-like, which I found ironic. "Kid needs to relax. Maybe get laid."

He chuckled, before doubling over in giggles.

I rolled my eyes.

"What?" my sister asked.

"He's thinking of a doggystyle joke."

Amaymon sighed. "You people are not my audience." And with that the King of Earth disappeared in a hole.

34

About three seconds after they left, Evans the golem came to find me. I was needed in the basement. Taking the bag of shards with me, because I thought they would be safer that way, I followed the giant mud monster in a suit.

I opened the workshop door and found utter chaos.

The first thing that hit me was a massive blast of heat, like opening the doors to a sauna. I closed my eyes and when I reopened them I was sweating. The second thing was the sound. Never mind the noise of the machine—pop music blared from a stereo somewhere, and there was a demon dancing to it.

Astaroth, fire Elemental demon, one of the most powerful beings in the known universe, was shaking his very skinny rear, making the hasn't-been-white-in-a-while lab coat flare up dramatically behind him. Once again, I was forced to question the events that had led up to me watching a teal-colored, lizard-skinned demon with tiny horns, a grey-white ponytail, a stained lab coat, open-toed shoes, faded jeans three sizes too big, and a shirt saying *I don't give a fox* dance to Taylor Swift.

Bizarrely enough, Evans—the human version—was cheering him on.

Even more bizarre was the fact that they were carrying on a conversation. I stood there at the door for about five minutes, observing the chaos, and I couldn't tell you what they were talking about. Even if the room was dead-quiet—an impossibility with Astaroth—their conversation was not meant for ignoramuses like myself. There is only so much quantum theory I could take. Multiply that by magical meta-physics (meta-magical theory it's called, and it can go fuck itself. It was by far my worst subject when I was still being tutored) and you get one very confused wizard.

And they weren't just working on Abi, who was now decidedly more naked, having had most of the mud and clay wiped off her, and was instead adorned with sigils that Astaroth fussed over with a Magic Marker.

The demon had along with him a whole litter of his favorite familiars: fire foxes. Little cute vulpine creatures made entirely out of fire. And two of them carried sock puppets.

Orange chattered animatedly with one other worker golem, guiding him as he drew sigils on a map. I knew enough to recognize them as artifice. Unless they were planning to build the psychic entity a cyborg body, they were working on a totally different project.

The same went with Black, who in between belting out Britney Spears tunes (don't ask. Please, dear God, don't ask) was yelling out instructions on meta-math (a particularly horrid branch of theory) to an attentive duo of golems.

They all carried different conversations, each at various degrees of volume ("You drive me craaazzyyy... What did I just say? The derivate is on the lower quarter. That's it. Now add the constant. Congratulations, genius..... Craazzzyy!")

Finally I made my way towards the main duo, interrupting a conversation that included time travel and wormhole magic, chilling me to the core. There are some things one does not mess with.

On the other hand, I had never seen Astaroth this happy. The guy was a demonic nerd. Not many of them around.

And Evans... The bottle was long forgotten, and he couldn't stop smiling.

It was a match made in heaven.

Hell.

Whatever.

"Sorry to interrupt the fun," I told them.

Astaroth bounded towards me, giving me a hug. The demon was not a hugger, though he was veritably insane, and you can't exactly count on stability of personality with those people.

"Erik! So good to see you." He pointed at Evans. "I have a new friend."

"So I can see," I said, turning to Evans. "You guys seem busy."

"Yeah," he said. "How's things upstairs? The damn alarm won't stop buzzing."

"Taken care of," I said. "All quiet."

"Aw," Astaroth said. I never thought a lizard could look crestfallen but he managed. "Too bad. I like the music. I should take more of it to my castle."

"I'll hook you up with Spotify," Evans said.

"Is that a potion?"

"Only for the soul, man."

I rolled my eyes. "Abi," I said. "The woman currently in critical condition on the table. What about her?"

Evans waved his hand. Suddenly the noise died down. All other conversations came to a halt. Astaroth stood up abruptly and looked around, spooked.

"Oh," he said after a while. "We're being serious." His eyes, yellow and feline, identical to Amaymon's, burst with azure flames.

"Whoa there, buddy," I said. I had seen Astaroth throw down. He was potentially more dangerous than Amaymon. My familiar was bound to a contract that severely limited his power on this plane. Astaroth was not.

Heck, even in Hell he had to be confined to his own pocket dimension, he was so volatile.

And something told me Evans kept a couple illegal bomb-type-things tucked away here somewhere.

He didn't look too perturbed. "We can continue our talk later," he reassured Astaroth. He leaned forward on his spidery wheelchair. "In fact, I wanna see *your* workshop. Never been to Hell before."

"It's warm," I told him. "At least his part is."

"Good. I like the heat. Can you make a beach?"

The demon's eyes returned to normal and he grinned. "I can now."

That chilled me.

You see, demons like Astaroth and Amaymon were only capable of embodying one element. Yet, I'd seen Astaroth throw both fire and water. The water brother, Baal, was a carcass somewhere in Astaroth's lab.

They weren't supposed to kill each other. The four elements were a balance. Sure, Amaymon and Mephisto were always at each other's throats but it was akin to play-fighting. Trust me, I'd seen Amaymon duke it out for real.

Astaroth had, in a rare fit of lucidity, explained that he had had to break the balance. He never mentioned why.

Guess that was for me to find out. Some other day.

"Okay, back to this," Evans said, taking a swig from the bottle. "Vessel-wise we got a few choices, and we'll need to run a few more tests but it seems to me we're hours away from creating something sustainable for the little critter."

Hours. I wondered if she had that long to live.

"Yes," Astaroth said, after I voiced my concern. "Her life force is tied to that kitsune."

Sure enough, snoring lightly next to Abi's head was a magenta-flamed kitsune. Its flames were dulling but pulsed bright enough in the center. She was stable.

For now.

"You drew out her life force?" I asked the demon.

"Mirrored ethereal morphology."

"Huh?"

"Her life force is mirrored in the fox," Evans explained. "Think Beauty and the Beast. Beast got himself a rose, we got your girlfriend a fox. Or vixen. Guess it's the lady one."

"She's not my girlfriend," I replied automatically. Which in turn brought back *that* particular basket of clusterfuck.

"Vixen," Astaroth replied, completely ignoring me. "I call her Rosy."

"Rhymes with crazyyyyyyy." Three guesses who said that.

The fire foxes carrying the socks bounded off after a withering look from Astaroth.

"You're seriously not sleeping with her?" Evans asked. "Dude, I can't move from the waist down and even I feel empowered enough to walk over to her." He chuckled. "Now I know why your sister calls you thick."

"Can we please," I snarled through clenched teeth and rosy-colored cheeks, "get back to the topic at hand?"

Astaroth leaned in closer to Evans. "This one is called embarrassment, I think. More tests are needed though."

Evans nodded.

"Erik. Do you wish to further discuss your situation? Do you not wish to mate with your companion?" Astaroth asked. "Or is it perhaps an issue of biology? Because I have a solution-"

"There is no issue, thank you very much. And we are *not* having this conversation," I snapped.

Evans winked at his new demonic best friend. "Told you. Insult a man's cock and he tells you all you need to know." He chuckled and took another swig. "Okay, back to business."

I growled my approval.

"Since this is a spiritual entity," Evans said, "we need a particular ingredient. The same thing those Vol bastards are hunting down. That black rock thing Rashid had in his scepter."

I cocked my head. Then I plopped the bag of Astral Shards on the workbench.

"You mean that?"

Evans examined the bag, while Astaroth proceeded to lick each piece. Then he hurriedly went over to the kiln and threw a couple of them in.

"Yes!"

He then proceeded to place them in a cluster around Abi's head.

"We need more," Evans told me. "Where did you get these?"

I glanced back at golem Evans. The big guy had fallen silent into a corner. "He was there."

"I was distracted," he said, gesturing around him. "I have far more interesting things to do than eavesdrop on people."

"A werewolf gave them to me," I said.

"Ah."

I waited for more. He fell silent.

"Erik?"

"Yes?"

"Get out of here and go get more Shards," he said.

Oh. Right.

I cocked my head at him. "How many?"

Evans shrugged. "You got an earth demon, right? So, pretty much all you can carry. And hurry." He glanced over to where Astaroth was fussing with the tiny shards. "That thing inside her... It's struggling to get out now. These shards will buy us some time but the clock's ticking."

I nodded and walked out.

This was familiar territory. This was *my* territory. Racing against time, someone's life on the line, deadly enemies to hunt down—this was what I did.

But it was never Abi. It was never like this.

Shut up, voice of reason. Get the angry guy back.

I found the rest of the team where I had left them. I told them what I needed. Greg immediately sprang into action, saying he would help out by taking one of the other locations. I agreed and silently thanked the universe he wasn't going to be there when I found the Vol. When I found them there was a high chance of me doing some things to them he would find unappealing. Greg was all about justice. I just wanted to rip something apart.

Cooling myself, I told Gil what to look out for, then sent Luke back to his boyfriend. He had done enough for now.

Amaymon, having already taken care of the wolf pack (enchanting land was apparently as easy to him as snapping his fingers) and returned hungry for some battle, sidled next to me as we climbed into one of the spare cars Evans kept around.

"He gave us exactly what we needed," he commented. The demon was currently in cat form and curled on the passenger seat.

I nodded. My hands tightened around the steering wheel without turning on the ignition.

"He's playing his own game," the cat pressed.

"I know," I said.

"Why?"

I looked at him and found his intense cat eyes on me. "I don't know. Maybe he just can't trust us. Or maybe he's got a vested interest in-"

You know those moments when your brain just suddenly clicks?

Maybe it was getting severely confused by the two geniuses below, or maybe I had my noggin clocked during the fight, but suddenly I started forming a theory and the more I mulled it over, the more sense it made.

"What?" asked the cat.

I told him.

He cocked his tiny feline head. "Huh. Well, that would make sense. You gonna tell your sister?"

I shook my head. "Not yet. I need her to focus on getting me the Vol's locations. If I sprung this one on her it would distract her. It's political. That's her wheelhouse so she'll tackle it before anything else."

Amaymon chuckled and nodded.

"So what now, Boss?"

I turned on the ignition and put the car in gear. "Now we do what *we* do best: hunt down those sons of bitches."

35

The hideout we found was just like the rest. Rituals spray-painted on the walls, chanting vampires with tattoos, and a few fledgling Daywalkers.

I coughed up ash and blinked it out of my eyes. Another vampire kicked me in the sternum and we had one flying Erik. As I lay on the gravel I saw Amaymon lazily rip the head off one of the Daywalkers.

You know, the same Daywalkers that threw me in the air. He winked and yawned theatrically. Asshole.

"Behind you," he drawled.

I heard the crunch of boots as soon as he stopped talking. My gun poked out from beneath my coat and I blasted the Daywalker's leg off from the knee down. As he fell I rolled over him and stabbed Djinn all the way down, cracking the concrete below.

Another regular vampire sunk his fangs in my shoulder, ripping flesh and cartilage. My scream echoed and I turned it into a spell, one aimed at the other vampire coming directly at me. The sonic blast was not the sort of refined, controlled magic that aerokinesis required, but you know, vampire on my back.

The pain and blood loss kicked in my survival instincts. A single shadowy arm erupted from my shoulder, manifesting as a clawed hand around the vampire's face before squeezing. I won't bother you with the gory details. Suffice it to say that, it wasn't just ash that hit my mouth.

The arm withered away as soon at the job was done. Which was strange in and of itself. Just a year ago, I would struggle to keep my shadowy curse powers held at bay. There hadn't been enough willpower in the world to stop them from consuming me, shrouding me in power.

Now it was just the minimum effort and back they went.

Was my curse jealous that I had reacquired the full range of my magic? I chuckled internally.

Then again, maybe I was onto something.

My thoughts were quickly interrupted by a jagged spear of granite that Amaymon had thrown at an oncoming Daywalker. It skewered the creature onto a wall where I quickly decapitated it.

Amaymon grabbed the last two vampires and flicked his wrists, snapping both necks at the same time.

"So," he said casually kicking up the ash that fell on the ground beside him. "No Shards."

He was right. The tunnel system had taken us an hour to find, and yet we were still no closer to helping Abi than we had been when we first left Evans' workshop.

Only Abi was now an hour closer to dying.

"There has to be something," I said, knowing I was in denial but refusing to admit defeat. "There has to." I looked up. "Maybe we can go to the crypt again. There was this black crystal. That could be it." I sighed. "Although if I were

Rashid I would have either moved it or locked down the crypt itself."

Amaymon started saying something. A second later he was a blur.

I barely had time to draw my sword again when I saw him wrestle a female vampire to the ground. He ignored the slashes of her curved daggers and the spear jab of her companion, though he did notice when a third one yanked him off by wrapping a whip around his neck. He pulled her and punched so hard his fist tore through her stomach.

Amaymon hates collars.

I sensed someone coming up behind me, the shadows rippling to life, and struck. My blade was parried by a slender rapier point which stopped just short of impaling my throat. I followed the blade to its owner.

Carmilla held her weapon at half-thrust, which meant that Djinn stopped just short of her neck.

Many people think the rapier is the flimsy weak piece of metal they see in Olympic fencing competitions. But real rapiers like the one Carmilla wielded had the exact weight and structure of a longsword. They were just shaped longer and thinner, with all the weight in the handle, making them that much faster.

"Stop!" she barked.

Amaymon tossed the half-dead vampire retainer on the ground and turned onto the other two.

"I said stop," Carmilla said, pressing the tip of her blade into my throat.

Which was good. I would die, but I had a healing factor and the few inches closer would bring her closer to my sword... And no vampire walks away from decapitation.

"I don't take orders from you, babe," Amaymon said. "And I find myself in a killing mood. Erik?"

I glared at the princess.

"I'm not your enemy," she said before I had a chance to speak. The urgency in her voice was the only thing that gave me pause. "I was not with my father when he attacked you, either time, nor was I supporting him. My retainers and I were hiding. He took my army too."

I remained silent, focusing only on holding Djinn straight, waiting for the opportunity.

"I can kill you," she hissed. "I can consume your life-force even while your legendary healing powers kick in."

Her eyes glowed.

"You're an Ergophage," I said, careful not to make too much movement around my neck.

Carmilla nodded.

She was a mutant too then. Vampires usually consumed blood, everyone knew that. But there was a rare sub-species that was often demonized in their culture. Ergophages consumed energy more than they did blood, which also meant they got more 'nutrition' per pint of blood than other vamps did. More than that, they hunted emotions. They preyed long-term on their victims, having no use for them dead. Which made them less bloodthirsty, and therefore less predatory than other vampires.

Now it all made sense. Rashid's disdain of her, why she lived in a different nation altogether, her mindset which, by vampire standards, was almost human.

I lowered my sword. Amaymon made a groaning noise in protest but he stood down as well.

Carmilla stepped back, well out of Djinn's reach, and lowered her weapon.

"I should have opened with that, I suppose," she said, smiling humorlessly.

"You're still not in the clear," I said. "And even with your abilities, very few can handle my magic."

She nodded. "I can sense your... Peculiarity. But rest assured, I have no interest in harming you. Nor stopping you for that matter." She sheathed her rapier and made a show of displaying her empty hands, palms up.

"I want to help."

"How can I trust you?" I asked. "You practically told me you're a backstabber."

"Because you have no other choice," she said. "I overheard your conversation. You need Astral Shards. Astral *Stones* preferably if you are dealing with a psychic entity."

"And lemme guess," I added, "you can provide them for me."

Carmilla smiled fully this time and cocked her head. "Oh no, my dear Erik. I cannot give you anything. I can only guide you. You see, the Brotherhood of the Vol are far more evolved than my father believes. He thinks of them as thugs and fanatics, but I know they are far more dangerous. Which is why they only keep around twenty percent of their forces here, on Earth."

It would explain the lack of Astral Shards or Stones.

Wait, did she say Earth?

Carmilla made a low sensual sound at my confusion. Hell, I didn't know if she was hungry or horny at my confusion—probably both.

"Where are they?" I asked. "Where can I find them?

"The one place someone like my father will never look," she replied. "They are in the Shadows, in what we call the Underworld. Home realm of the Vol entity itself."

36

For the third time since this whole debacle had started, I found myself back in Egypt. Only this time, instead of Rashid's royal palace, we were faced with rubble.

Well, some rubble.

Most of it was a giant sinkhole.

Amaymon grinned at us—myself, Greg (who had joined us right before we departed), Carmilla and her retinue—obviously satisfied with his previous work. Move over Da Vinci, we got a real artist over here.

Carmilla looked at what was once her former home and sighed.

"You don't do anything in half-measures, do you?" I saw a hint of a smile on her perfect lips.

Perfect lips hiding deadly fangs, I reminded myself.

I shrugged. "What can I say, I'm thorough." I glanced at Amaymon and nodded.

The demon stepped forward and raised his arms. Sand swirled around the sinkhole. The entire desert shuddered beneath our feet. Even the vampires, with their unnatural grace, struggled to remain upright. Greg dug the butt of his spear into the ground for purchase. Amaymon chuckled at our discomfort.

The desert spat out the remnants of the palace, littering the surrounding area with mortar, stone, and bits of metal that had once been part of the palace's structure. Carmilla was right—Amaymon had been thorough.

Finally, he stepped back and I peered down into a deep dark hole. The demon grinned.

Then he pushed me in.

Typical.

THE CRYPT WAS JUST like we had left it, minus the crippling magic negation. Incidentally, it was soon tested when I landed badly—then again there isn't really a better way to land when your demonic familiar throws you down a pit.

The others landed beside me while various bits of my legs were being mended and inserted back into where they belonged. Greg thudded heavily, his eyes glowing silver and white. The vampires landed in soft thuds, directly opposite the Kresnik, clearly wary of him. Amaymon did a little skip-dance along the crypt.

"Cute," he said, taking in a deep breath. "Ah, I love the smell of necrophage shit."

I groaned and stood up on shaky legs.

Carmilla nodded at her aides. Two of them drew their weapons and strode forward. Another aide hovered by Carmilla, ready to leap at her retinue's defense. Greg released a low rumble from his throat and closed his eyes. I saw him tightly grip his spear but when he reopened his eyes, his eyes were back to normal—with just a little silver of eyeshine, like you might see on some felines.

Speaking of, Amaymon's yellow eyes glowed in the dark and I heard him stride forward. He tugged me along with him. He might be an asshole but he knew that in this context it was the wizard that was the squishiest. If the demon brought up the rear, few things were bound to sneak up on us.

We walked for a few minutes in complete and utter silence, only the shuffle of our clothes and the clink of our weapons audible. Even so, everything echoed eerily. Carmilla's aides at least had the decency to light some torches along our path, though most did not work. But hey, when in a dark creepy crypt, some light is better than none.

"I met your brother down here," I told her.

If Carmilla was surprised she didn't show it. Instead she hummed in assent.

"I had heard that my father threw him down here," she said. "I think we can both agree it was high time that vermin was removed."

It's nice to hear that sort of compassion from family.

"Why did Rashid chuck him here?" I pressed. "I mean, not that he didn't deserve it, but your father didn't seem perturbed with his son's actions last I checked."

The vampire princess cocked her head, flicking a rogue strand of hair from her face.

"He crossed a line. That is all I can say."

"Valen crossed a line your father thought was too much?" I asked. "Damn, what did he do? Piss in the castle's entire supply of blood?"

Her snicker echoed around us, morphing into something sinister.

"Vampires like my father are fickle, Erik," she said. "One moment they are pleased with their power, another they throw it all away in search for more. Valen was always spoiled, and he grew up knowing there would not be any consequences to his actions. He pushed the envelope. I cannot say more."

"Sworn to secrecy, are you?"

"No," she replied. "It is simply a matter of familial obligation." She stopped to look me in the eye. "I love my father, just as I love my brother. Yes, I wish to dethrone one, and I do not weep for the death of the other—but that does not make them any less family. Valen did something that besmirched our name, an act that went against everything my father was or wanted. Thus, he was punished, and rightly so."

And she kept on walking.

"I think you ruined your shot, boss," Amaymon commented undertone.

I rolled my eyes at him. "What's with this place? And what's the Underworld, exactly? I know there's a hundred versions of it out there but where does it sit, cosmically speaking? A pocket dimension?"

The demon shrugged. "Sure, you could say that. As far as I know, it's one of the doorways to Hell, a vast system of tunnels and caves that can lead to a few different places. All of them different flavours of underworlds or hells from your mythology."

"So what's so special about this one? Other than one creepy go-between."

"This one was once a place of worship, when it was on the surface," Greg interjected. "The civilization that would eventually become the Egyptian Kingdom revered the Underworld as a direct path to the afterlife. Later on, their gods claimed their own afterlife, which became the abode of Osiris. By that time, this place was lost to the surface as it was repurposed into something other than what it once was."

"Which is?" I pressed.

The Kresnik gave me a hard look, looking extra menacing thanks to his eyes. "A prison, one meant to house a being of extraordinary potent."

"Vol."

Instantly, both vampires and Kresnik hissed at me.

"We do *not* mention his name," snarled Carmilla's bodyguard.

"The last thing we need is to give away the element of surprise," Carmilla added.

Greg exhaled softly. "Nor do we wish to open ourselves to its fear. For what we are facing is not a mere monster, Erik. Our enemy is no mere deity. It is the unknown itself. The Underworld exists in Chaos space and only one creature may call it home."

We kept on walking. I tried not to shiver.

I had been lost in Chaos once, for a total of three seconds. That experience broke me but not instantly. No, it just left me mentally vulnerable to Envy's Island, where I then broke down. That chain of events led me to depression, PTSD, and eventually being so broken I was ripe for being possessed by one of the Seven Deadly Sins.

And in those three seconds, I learnt of the only type of creature that could live in Chaos.

Greg was right. Vol wasn't just a deity.

It was an Outsider.

37

When a place is called the Underworld, you're bound to come across some nasty surprises.

For example, it was mostly dark with the only light source coming from crystal mounds growing at intervals.

Oh, and insects.

The Underworld was insect-central if the several I inhaled were anything to go by.

Second surprise: no potable water. Every pool we came across was rancid and only used as a feeding source for thick pus-filled mushrooms. Luckily, Carmilla had thought ahead. Her pals carried along a travel rucksack filled with blood bags and water bottles—the latter I was assured were for me.

And for Greg, who at first refused just on general principle (Heaven forbid a Kresnik accept a drink from their sworn enemy) before relenting to basic human necessity.

Meanwhile Amaymon splashed happily in the bog water.

Because... Amaymon.

We settled down for a little while.

"We're lost, aren't we?" I kept my voice low, so that only Greg was hearing me, but this was the Underworld and secrets carried far and wide here.

The Kresnik barely had time to shrug before a flustered Carmilla replied with,

"We are *not* lost."

I glanced at her. "Keep your panties on, princess," I said. "I was merely expressing my frustration at the fact that we've been in this place for hours and still haven't found squat. Oh, and in case you didn't know before, I'm on a bit of a time crunch here."

She glared at me. "I do know, Erik. And rest assured, time flows differently here. One hour in the Underworld is less than a minute above it," she replied. "This is a place designed to age you, frustrate you, and turn you insane." She narrowed her eyes. "And I do believe it is working."

I patted my face. "Are you saying I've aged?"

Despite herself, she chuckled. "We are all on edge," she said. "This is what this place does." Her eyes shifted to the side and louder she said, "And it does not ease our anxiety knowing we are being followed. Show yourself."

Nothing happened but now that she mentioned it, there was a certain void in that area. Usually things had a way of flowing: in a forest you looked for signs of silence and stillness. That was usually where the big hungry predator was hiding. No bird wants to chirp around a ravenous tiger.

"Amaymon," I said.

Before the last syllable had exited my mouth, the demon was leaping from the water. I heard a high-pitched squeak which reminded me of a plastic toy and then Amaymon threw something before us.

It was a mushroom.

Well, it was a human mushroom. A mushroom-man.

It scrambled up on two comically short legs, with two hands that could not reach one another across its round mushroom stalk body. Just beneath the mushroom cap, which was too big for its head, were two slanted eyes the color of moss. Its mouth was a slit from which it wheezed thin whistling breaths.

"A myconoid," Carmilla said.

"A mushroom man?" I asked. No one seemed perturbed by the walking squeaking mushroom. This was my reality now.

I suppose they had worse in Woodstock.

Carmilla kicked the myconoid, toppling it over with ease, and set her foot on its head.

"Why are you following us?"

In between shrieks that sounded like a kazoo fucking a whistle, the myconoid managed to say,

"Sorry. Curious. Sorry."

So, not the type to speak in full sentences. Of course, Erik, it's a talking-fucking-*mushroom*.

By now we were all surrounding the poor guy, who was flailing his tiny limbs in a way that reminded me of an upturned beetle. Carmilla's foot was still on the rim of his head and she rotated him before kicking him away. The force made him tumble and finally the myconoid was upright, only for Amaymon to seize him and raise him aloft.

"Shall we eat him?" he asked.

In between the myconoid's screams, I managed to say,

"Wait. Can he guide us?"

That made everyone, including the mushroom man, stop.

"We need a guide," I said. "If the Underworld is an endless series of tunnels and caverns, and God knows what else, then we need someone who knows a shortcut. And I don't know about you guys, but I don't wanna spend the next twenty years looking for bad guys while they tickle some Lovecraftian god's tentacle."

Carmilla looked from me to the myconoid. "Fine." She unsheathed her rapier and pressed the tip into the underside of the creature's head.

"If you betray us, I will fillet you and eat bits of your body while the rest watches."

It didn't say anything but whistled a lot. At Carmilla's prompt—another kick—the mushroom man took the lead.

Amaymon fell next to me. "Tickle the tentacle?" he quoted.

I shrugged. "I have the heart of a poet."

He chuckled. "So what are the chances of that little shit actually leading us the right way?"

"I reckon he'll lead us," I said. "My issue is through what."

He grinned. "Figured it out too, huh?"

I nodded.

The cave we walked into was dead-silent.

38

Our first clue should have been the skittering. But then again, if the Underworld had a soundtrack, it would have been a symphony of skittering and clicking mandibles, eerie silence, hissing, rough breaths of creatures watching you while they hid in shadows that seemed a little too solid to be the real thing, and basically anything that could be classified under "horror".

The myconoid just kept walking, unaffected by the gloom, the smells, the sounds, and remained pretty much oblivious to our surroundings. Which pretty much confirmed my fears: the mushroom man was leading us towards the Vol, all right, but he was doing it in the most straightforward way.

As in, through a massive enclave filled with cobwebs.

Amaymon stopped in his tracks, which instantly made me hug a wall. Greg raised his spear.

The myconoid kept on walking.

Something reached down from the ceiling and scooped up the mushroom man.

Ever chopped a fresh plump mushroom? You know that

squeaky noise it makes? That was pretty much what our guide sounded like when the creature that snagged it tore it into several chunks.

The worst part was that the chunks of the myconoid that fell out were still mobile and trying to scramble away.

Two creatures leapt onto the bits.

When they rounded on us, I could make out their shape. Or shapes.

Think of a centaur. Now replace the horse bit with a giant spider's thorax and eight spindly legs. Bits of gelatinous webbing trailed from their... Buttholes, I suppose. Or web holes.

What am I, an arachnologist?

The top half was humanoid, with bluish skin and long gangly limbs waving spears and swords. The faces were perfectly human—except for the multitude of eyes that blinked at random, covering their entire foreheads.

I knew these ones: Arachno-fiends, scions of the original Arachne, the Greek goddess of weaving and, you guessed it, spiders. They came in two versions, Weavers and Stingers, one for spiders and the other for scorpions.

The first was a lot friendlier than the second.

The skittering tripled and now everything around us was *moving*. I didn't think. My gun was out and I started blasting.

My reasoning was simple: fire. Loud and bright, taking advantage of their low-visibility environment. Creatures who lived here had to be light-sensitive and judging from the way they screamed and skittered, I was right.

I channeled fire magic through the gun and every bullet transmuted into a bolt of angry red light that seared a baseball-sized hole through the nearest Weaver.

One of Carmilla's handmaidens pulled out a pair of

sickles from across her back and threw herself violently towards a Weaver that took half a step towards the princess. The vampire leapt onto the creature's back and dug her blades into the small of its back where the human torso ended and the spider parts began. The Weaver reared up and shrieked.

A second Weaver leapt onto his back, trying to dislodge the vampire aide. She deftly leapt away and watched as the pair of monsters now snapped at one another.

Two more scuttled towards the two sources of light in the cavern: myself and Greg. The Kresnik swung his spear, deflecting a sword coming down on him, and retaliated by chucking a glass ball at the monster. It shattered against its head, and something like chaff exploded from the potion ball, covering the Weaver in phosphorescent dust that made him glow against the gloom.

Following his tactic, I fired at an oncoming enemy, aiming for its eyes, but instead caught it on the shoulder. Still, there was enough force in the blast to send it toppling sideways. The two Weavers collided and mine started tearing into the one covered in whatever Greg had doused it in.

From the side, another Weaver flew. I mean one moment, it was attached to the wall, scuttling towards Carmilla—the next, Carmilla flinched and her rapier was out, and the spider creature was filleted and tossed aside. I saw her turn and lock eyes on the one who had snatched our myconoid guide. In the wild, it was the leader who ate first. Sure enough, this one was wearing a crown—a twisted, dull metallic, half-formed circlet that stopped just short of its forehead (and the extra eyes).

Carmilla strode calmly towards her target, while her aides made short work of a trident-wielding Weaver that guarded the king. I spotted a third Weaver on the ceiling. He hissed and let go.

A jet of white flame exploded into the Weaver, shooting out from my gun and straight towards the free-falling monster. My spell turned it into a crisp. Dust showered the princess and her handmaidens. She turned to look at me. I half-expected a glower ("How dare you, lowly peasant, ruin my outfit!") but instead was met with a nod of gratitude.

The Weaver leader turned around and scuttled away, and came face to face with Amaymon who was casually leaning against the entrance of the cave.

"Boo!"

You would have thought from the leader's reaction that Amaymon had ripped all eight of his legs off one by one. He screamed and ran back at double speed and then Carmilla actually did cut off two of his legs.

He crashed down and two things happened.

First, Carmilla grabbed his head and held the razor-sharp edge of her rapier against his throat.

Second, about a bazillion Weavers scuttled out of their various hidden holes. If we were in trouble before, we were in a quagmire of shit now.

Carmilla took stock of our situation and pressed the blade even further.

The Weaver was almost in tears now. "Cease," he said. Have you ever heard someone speak while they had a fork in their mouth? That was precisely what he sounded like.

His kin kept on coming.

"Cease!" snapped Carmilla.

At her command the Weavers stopped. They watched her. She turned her attention back to the leader.

"Our fight is not with you," she said. Her voice had enough ice in it to freeze a bonfire. "We only seek passage to our true enemies." She leaned closer. I can't imagine the creature having anything but bad breath, but even with her enhanced senses, Carmilla didn't flinch.

"You know of whom I speak," she said. Much to my surprise, she actually released her prisoner. "We only seek them, not you."

The leader rose and reclaimed his crown. Now that he wasn't running and hiding, I could actually see how tall he was. At least twice the size of the others, reaching almost ten feet. His body was narrow and slender, all the more perfect to slither in and out of the caves, and when he moved I noticed the thick barded stinger at the end of his... Web hole.

"Yes," he said, his weird voice echoing throughout the cavern. "Your darkling kin. We have seen them. We have eaten them."

At the last statement the other Weavers started shifting excitedly.

"But they are foul and deadly," the leader went on. "They are most foul. Their master turned them vile, so now their meat is vile. And we are now most hungry."

Now I could practically hear them salivating. I pressed back and bumped into Greg, who was grabbing his spear as if he was preparing to die with it in his hands.

"You seek passage, vampire," the leader said. "The way is ahead. But we require payment."

Carmilla sighed. "Of course you do," she said, somehow managing to sound bored. "And let me guess, you are hungry."

"So very hungry."

"How does forty humans sound?"

You know when someone says something, and your brain doesn't quite catch up, and then it does, and you just stare at them? I did that with Carmilla casually offering forty innocent people to these monsters.

Amaymon gave me a look that made me stay put. Not that I was about to object. I could smell Carmilla's bullshit a mile away. She was lying.

The question was, how much?

"Four hundred," the Weaver bargained. "We are many. I have many sons and daughters to feed."

"Forty," Carmilla insisted. "Every fortnight."

My jaw dropped. I really, really hoped she was bullshitting him.

The Weaver struggled with the multiplication but maybe he was just that hungry, because he practically yelled, "Deal!"

The rest of the nest scuttled and clicked in their approval.

Five minutes later we were ushered on our way out of the nest with two Weaver escorts.

"You weren't serious," I whispered to Carmilla. I had practically pulled her to the back of the group.

She shrugged.

"Carmilla," I began. "You know I can't let you sacrifice eighty people a month."

She looked at me deadpan. "Why not?"

Holy crap, she was serious.

"Because it's wrong," I said, firmly kicking myself for forgetting even for a second that she was a *vampire.*

Not human. No matter how lovely she was when she batted her eyes at me.

She was a deadly, manipulative creature and every word out of her mouth was poison.

"Wrong?" Then she smiled. "Oh, you are under the assumption that I was going to capture people off the street, weren't you?"

"Um..."

"Silly hero," she said. "I'll have you know that my castle has a dungeon that can feed this nest five times over. And before you get judgmental, please understand that these are not your typical humans. They are magic-users, and they have abused their powers. I have serial killers, rapists, thieves, terrorists—at least two of them captured within this decade were found guilty of mass murder in order to enact their necromantic rites. The abominations we had to face consisted of entire families sewn together into Fleshlings. One of them had an army of no less than seventy. And then there are the vampires, the were-changers, the shamans—do you know that some of them can induce demonic possession? We had a rampage not twenty days ago in the city. Twelve dead, all females under twelve. The demon proclaimed to find their blood most decadent."

She glared at me.

"So tell me, what am I to do with them? They deserve their death many times over. But I pride myself on not being a wanton, *wasteful* killer like my father and my dear departed brother. Death—even that of the vile creatures I imprison—should have a purpose. And if it helps me make allies, then so be it."

I was lost for words.

See, this is why I fucking *hate* politicians.

On the surface, she was right. Hell, I have killed many more for less worse things. Carmilla had lived for centuries, so her list had to run miles longer than mine. I found myself in conflict between the justification of playing god, and the necessity to take final action against things that had no such qualms about who lived or died.

And I hated her for it. I hated that she could put me in such a place where I would have to *agree* with the sacrificial murder of thousands.

Fortunately, I didn't have time to raise my objections. We all sensed the foul magic, confirmed by the fact that the Weavers scurried back from where we had come from.

We had reached the Vol.

39

It was a sea of vampires. A *sea*.

Of vampires.

There were so many of them that I could hardly distinguish between one vampire and the other. They were clustered together around a ziggurat of sorts, raised several feet above them, and wide enough to fit six Vol priests. All six were bald, their fangs so over-grown that they jutted out towards their chins like saber teeth. Their bodies were emaciated and somehow still strong. They reminded me of twisted steel, narrow but almost indestructible.

Tattoos snaked down their skin, pulsating faintly with a color that hit my eyes like ultraviolet.

"What are they doing?" I asked.

No one answered me. Honestly, I was hoping for someone to know. Hell, I didn't need much, just some damn pointers.

Instead all I got was dark energy.

I don't mean dark, as in bad. I mean *Dark*, as in, capital D. The primordial Dark. The end-all-life Dark.

Incompatible-with-being-alive, Dark.

And these bastards were shaping it right on top of that altar.

After that I got my answer.

Reality in the Underworld, already a tricky concept, ripped open. The six priests no longer existed as separate individuals. I closed my eyes. I had enough nightmare fuel, and what I was about to witness was not meant for human consumption.

I had learnt that lesson the hard way. I may be a wizard but I am first and foremost a human being. My body could heal but not my mind. Not the thing that made me, me.

The Vol aberration, a tiny portion of the Outsider itself, slopped on top of the altar. A mass of flesh that constantly shifted—a leg here, tentacle appendage there, several eyeballs, mouths that were wide and grinning, or tubular and expounding noxious gasses.

For a brief moment I was reminded of Lilith, the Sin of Lust. The first creature I had ever fought. I realized later just how lucky I had been. Lilith was also a primordial, maybe closer to the Outsider than I was comfortable thinking about. It took the might of my unrestricted curse powers, along with an archangel's grace to put her down.

I later found out that she had acted prematurely. Her original form had not yet assimilated the full powers of the Sin mantle, which in turn had severely weakened her. It made her weakness very obvious—Lilith needed fresh bodies to refuel her biomorphic changes.

But the Vol... This guy had no such weaknesses. This thing was an Outsider, effectively a god. There was no way I could unplug this guy.

At least not without crossing over to his dimension, and even with all my powers I would never be able to survive there.

And yet you keep missing the obvious.
"Wha-"

"-t?"

The landscape was familiar, like a recurring dream that you've had since childhood.

The sky was red, the landscape was red and sandy, and before me, spanning from root to stem, was a massive obsidian tree, wider than any tree I had ever seen, with roots thick as telephone poles that dug into the earth beneath. They looked like mangrove branches, with some gaps big enough to be mistaken for cavern mouths.

Standing before the tree were two figures.

The first was a child covered from head to toe in a robe that flapped in a wind that was not there.

The second was my alter ego.

My dead alter ego.

Well, maybe not so much.

Dark Erik, a being of living fire and obsidian, of light and shadow, stepped forward. He looked less solid than any of the times I had met him previously.

"I thought I assimilated you," I said.

"No," he replied. "And yes."

Dark Erik tends to be cryptic. He waited. So did I.

"Time is running out," he finally said.

"Isn't it always?" I replied. Then I sighed. "What are you, exactly? You keep saying you're my inner potential or whatever. When I assimilated you into me, brought you to the forefront, you ceased to exist. You and I became one."

The avatar nodded.

"So why are you here?" I asked.

"I am your potential."

"Which I made real," I said. "By the aforementioned assimilation."

"No, Erik," he said. "You did not. You took your potential and aimed it at a singular being. You died as a result, and your power—our power—became corrupted."

At that he stepped aside.

Behind him, sitting inside one of the hollow mangroves, was a knight. Not just any knight.

I recognized it, from the protrusions on the pauldrons, to the angular curvature of helmet, right down to the oversized broadsword that was chipped and rusting, resting against the vambraces.

The Knightmare.

The Sin of Wrath.

"No, it is not," Dark Erik said. "This is no longer Wrath. This is now an empty shell."

"Then what's it doing there?" I asked. "Last I checked that thing was corruption. You said so yourself."

Dark Erik shook his head. "*That* is your power. It took that form because the Cacodaemon reshaped it. Your magic returned, unbound from the confines of your fear. Now it is time to retake your *true* powers back."

As he spoke, I realized what had been missing. It was like a little dark corner in my peripheral vision, unknown until someone points it out, and then it is the only thing you can think of.

Ever since I had got my magic back, I had relied less and less on my shadowy-curse powers. Sure they sporadically came out, but I saw them less frequently and less potently. Which I had assumed was just a natural thing since I had been told that the shadows came from my magic, which until then had been trapped in my body.

But I knew fundamentally that was wrong. It had been

convenient, a nice way to put my problems aside and just fix myself after several years of taking beatings and being put through the wringer.

I didn't tackle my problems head on like I usually did.

This time I dodged them.

I was scared of them.

Dark Erik, who was me, which meant he was along for the ride on this particular train of thought, nodded.

And then I looked at Dark Erik.

"You're not my alter ego anymore, are you?"

The fire inside him changed color, going from yellow and orange to a kaleidoscope of colors, many of which we did not yet have a name for. The granite and obsidian, crusted like lava, molted and became wind and water, earth and fire, and then something else.

"I am," the creature said. "But also not. I am something else. In time the answers will be revealed to you, Firstborn, but not today. Not until all the pieces are gathered."

And it was gone.

I glanced back at the armor. It just sat there, a dead hunk of metal and infinite power, the magic of Life and Death, the primordial magic somehow bestowed upon me—and I had left it there.

And now I knew who the kid beneath the robe was.

"How long have you been here?"

A thought formed in my head. It wasn't English, just a set of sensations. I knew instinctively that the kid had been here since its inception. That my powers and my inner world, Ashura, had provided it with much-needed shelter.

But now it was time for it to leave. It just needed... Something.

"A way out," I said. "Without hurting... Abi..." I looked up. "Your mom."

The words felt weird and out of context, but they made sense in that moment.

This psychic entity was my child. I had made it—my powers, my magic, *me*—had made it, in combination with Abi.

And it was begging me to fight. It was begging me for a way out without hurting anyone.

Psychic entities were not bothered by things like space and time. The kid I was seeing here was the same one currently tearing Abi apart from the inside. It was being nourished from both ends, and only once they met could it be birthed properly.

It just needed one very crucial thing.

"A name," I said. "Every child needs a name."

Happiness ensued forth.

I had thought of one, a name that fit, and the child was happy. I didn't say it yet. Words have power, especially in this context.

Thoughts are just ethereal until we make them real with words. Ideas are nonexistent until we speak them. Until we give them form.

Until we birth them into our reality.

The kid nodded and stepped aside.

Up until this point I had never really considered the idea of fatherhood. I mean, anyone who knew me pretty much consigned me to the "should never breed" department. The last thing the world needed was another maniac with magic.

But hadn't I changed?

"Not about me," I said.

That was my problem. Even now I was talking only about me, me, me. How selfish was that?

Here was my kid begging for my help, and I was worried about being a father.

I sighed.

No. I am not that selfish, I decided. I am not a piece of shit like my own father.

And now I have a reason to fight—for something far greater than me.

I reached out and touched the armor. It sprang to life.

"Erik. Whoa."

Amaymon backed away. His eyes were wide. I saw his nose twitching. He was smelling my magic, acclimatizing to the new scent.

Everyone was looking at me.

The Knightmare's armor was on me, covering me in living black shadow. Metal that was both solid and not gleamed off the torches from the altar beneath.

Djinn was already in my right hand. Magic enveloped it, growing the weapon into a longsword. Blue and black intermingled.

"Erik?" I heard Carmilla ask.

I turned to face her. It made me chuckle when she recoiled.

"Relax, princess," I said. My voice remained the same—just more solid. "Just gearing up for the fight. Listen."

I turned my attention to the Vol. It looked at me. I looked at it. There was no point in hiding anymore.

I called up my magic into my left arm, forming a shield, and held my sword before it.

Magic flared.

Not a sound.

At least not until I roared,

"With me!"

40

We charged the Vol vampires.

I led the team in a V-formation, shield first, sword pointed out beyond it. Shadows flared on both sides, sparking light and power in their wake.

We crashed into the first ranks of the Vol. There was no time to think of formations. No strategy. Instead I kept pushing forward, a (mostly) human arrow against a sea of monsters, shooting directly towards the ziggurat.

Through my shadows lapping onto my teammates, I received enough sensory information to know what each was doing.

Amaymon had morphed into his wildest shape yet: a giant cat with skin like granite and crystals growing on his back along the spine. Claws the size of fully-grown humans raked at the vampires, while the earth around us shook. Rock piled onto his sides, forming two hands with hammers for fists, and he began swinging, sweeping a dozen Vol vamps aside with each attack.

Light seared around Greg, white and glowing like the sunlight reflecting on ice. His eyes, beard, hair, and spear were all the same white color, and when he swung he barely had to touch the enemy with his weapon. It was *swing!*, dust, *swing!*, dust.

Carmilla and her aides were the slowest of the team, which speaks volumes to the power-ups Amaymon, Greg, and I had unleashed. One of the handmaidens was overwhelmed, torn to shreds. The other two fought back to back with their liege, who thrust her rapier in a fast series of jabs, each jab dusting another Vol vampire.

Through my shadows I sensed a power in Carmilla. The princess was leagues more powerful than she let on, as witnessed by the fact that nothing could hit her. Her aides were getting cuts and jabs, and hits and bruises, while she just... avoided them.

But that was a problem for another time.

I pressed my shield forward, piling on more vampires before it. A mass of twenty were holding me back at least, and no matter how powerful I was, there was no way to out-muscle twenty Vol-enhanced vampires.

So I changed tactics.

The energy of the shield, for it was just a shadow construct after all, morphed into a horizontal blade of energy that sliced through the vampires. The resulting squelches were very satisfying.

I roared and grabbed my longsword with both hands. Djinn's blade was now a blaze of azure fire. I knew vampires were slashing and clawing at me, some even trying to bite through the armor, but each attempt only left them in dust.

Slicing and cutting and thrusting, I finally took one step onto the ziggurat. The Vol aberration glared down at me (as much as a mass of eyes, teeth and limbs can actually glare) and the psychic assault was like a weighted net on me. It actually stopped me and I stood there, swinging my sword at vampires while stuck in place.

No. I had to push through.

I had to.

For my family. For my child.

Strength returned to me. Shadow tendrils flared out, each containing fire and ice and lightning. My magic. My spells. My powers.

I pushed even further. More steps crossed. I turned and released a massive crescent wave of power at the vampires climbing after me. The blast cut a furrow miles long, dividing the ranks. Amaymon and Greg picked up the slack from either side, giving me a moment of reprieve where I could race up.

And up.

Until I was at the altar, facing the aberration.

I grinned, before remembering I was wearing a helmet. Ah, well, I guess it's the thought that counts.

"It's just you and me now, Ugly," I said. It roared and screeched at my taunt. I lowered my sword until the tip was aimed right at its center. "Come on!"

You cannot fight a god.

Luckily, I didn't have to.

Vol was an Outsider, a being of Chaos and anti-life. So how do you force it down? You don't. You just create enough of a chain reaction, like when fire and ice meet. It wasn't the boom I was after—it was the scalding steam.

My shadows were Life magic, and I threw everything I had at that aberration. Had it been the real Outsider, I would have been out-classed. After all, I was a molecule compared to this thing.

But the aberration was a *physical* manifestation. It was on Earth (or as close to Earth as the Underworld got) which meant it had to play by our rules of physics.

And inside Earth's playing field, I was a heavy-hitter.

Shadows enveloped my sword and as I thrust, the power pierced into the aberration. Something clicked. Power surged.

And then we were sucked into Ashura.

I felt red sand crunching beneath my feet. The aberration sat unnaturally on the sand like a blob of roiling fat. I could feel it reaching out with its magic, trying to make sense of where it was. Worse, it was trying to reach out to its magic source.

"Ain't gonna happen, Ugly," I said.

The tip of my sword trailed lines in the sand as I strode languidly towards it.

"You're cut off," I went on. "This is my power base now, and I have no need for you and your shit."

Ugly started writhing. It found the black tree and made a reach for me. A shadow shot from my body, and severed the tendril before landing with a thunk on the tree trunk and I recognized the shape of a bat projectile.

Sweet. I had batarangs now.

The aberration screeched and a mass of tentacles, each tipped with a scythe-like nail, whipped towards me.

I didn't even flinch.

From my back, a veil of shadows encased me, deflecting the nails. A second later the veil sprouted a mass of blades that severed the tentacles. The aberration slumped even further. From its shoulder I saw a face emerge. I recognized the head of one of the six priests that the Vol had assimilated.

Realization dawned on me. This thing should have been

conserving its energy. It should have struck only when it saw its way out.

But that was assuming it was an intelligent being. All the aberration encompassed was the rage and hatred that the priests had. The instinct to kill and destroy.

Which meant the aberration would just keep coming at me, keep spending what little precious energy it had, until there was none left.

Fine by me.

I swung Djinn. A beam of energy sliced across the priest's bald head. Blood, black and goopy, sluiced down. The aberration shrunk even further.

I kept hitting it, claiming a second priest along the way, and then I ran out of time. Power like mine always came at a cost, and worst of all, it came with a limitation.

One moment we were in the red desert, the next, I was slumped down against the altar on top of the ziggurat.

But a few things had changed.

One, Amaymon had *wrecked* the place. There were places where the floor and ceiling were just one. Entire walls of stone had been erected, then broken through.

Two, I was not alone.

Carmilla offered me a hand up. As I reached, I noticed I was no longer covered in shadows or armor. I was back to my familiar, *vulnerable* self. If Carmilla thought along those lines, she didn't show it.

Greg was right next to her and the Christmas ornament power was still active in him.

Amaymon was closest to the aberration.

And he was winning.

With impunity he ripped two entire chunks of flesh from the aberration. It was connected to the real Vol once again but no matter the power surge, it still needed time to recuperate.

Amaymon cocked his huge feline head towards us.

"Heads up!"

Greg and Carmilla lunged forward just as the aberration flew towards me. Their weapons pierced the remaining priests and now the aberration was just a flopping pile of goop.

Which landed past me. It splashed on top of the altar. The Astral Stone on top of it, the one originally used to summon the power of the Vol, pulsated with power.

The sludge swelled up in size.

I raised my sword. "Oh no, you don't."

And with all of my remaining strength, I stabbed Djinn down. The blue blade sank through the sludge and into the Stone itself. There was a primordial shriek followed by a backlash of energy.

I was thrown off the ziggurat and landed in a pile of ash. No vampire remained alive. No Outsider came through.

Huge chunks of Astral Stone—Shards now, technically—rained all over the place.

I stood up shakily and found Amaymon, back in his human form, grinning at me. He palmed a Shard.

"Well, I guess that solves the transportation issue," he said, tossing the Shard at me. Greg and Carmilla, along with her two aides, strode down the ziggurat.

"I ain't cleaning this up," Amaymon said. He plucked the Shard back and sniffed it. Then he held it up over his open mouth and swallowed the whole thing.

And to this day, I never told anyone how we got those Shards out of the Underworld and onto Evans' table.

41

"They're slimy," Evans commented. He frowned from one of the larger Shards and back to me. "Why are they slimy?"

I shrugged and tried not to think about it too much.

"We, um," I began. "We had some transportation issues. Can you use them or not?"

"Hmm." Evans frowned some more before a big smile crept over his face. "Sure we can. After a wipe down."

Astaroth fussed over Abi, whose entire body was now covered in sigils. He laid the Astral Stone over what I first thought was a body in the slab next to her. It was a golem, an exact replica of Abi. Astaroth placed the Astral Stone in the golem's chest. One of the fire foxes he commanded leapt over the golem and its clay skin started cracking. The Stone began to melt as if it were nothing more than an ice cube, the black ethereal substance slowly absorbed into the body.

The demon looked up.

"It is time," he said.

He stood up and backed over to where Evans was. The two of them observed me.

"What do I do?" I asked.

They exchanged a look and shrugged. "I guess," Evans supplied, "you be yourself."

Helpful, as always.

I sat down next to the slab Abi lay on and took her hand. "I don't know if you can hear me," I told her. "But I want you to know you're gonna be okay. We're getting this thing out of you, Abi, and you're gonna be okay."

Of course.

The words echoed in my mind and I was no longer sitting inside Evans' workshop, deep underground.

I was in a world of clouds and multicolored strings and endless fragments of thoughts that once were part of a greater cohesive tapestry that had long since been dissolved.

Before me on the ground lay Abi, naked as the day she was born. She would have been a very pleasant distraction were it not for the fact that I too was in a similar state of undress... And also blue.

No, not in the metaphorical sense.

My skin was a translucent sapphire and purple, as if I had ultraviolet light coursing beneath my skin. On the surface I was my regular self, but beneath I was this weird thought-form. I realized what this was. This wasn't my first time literally living as two states of matter: one physical, the other, thought.

Abi was likewise admiring her new state of being, and I must admit I too was admiring her. So sue me.

Welcome, Father. Mother.

There was no warning, or puff of smoke. The psychic entity just appeared, blue and purple and indigo all crumpled together into something that resembled a human child. The outline was perfect but the features were blank. I felt it reach out to us, lightning branches of blue and purple playfully zapping around me and Abi.

The entity's face became more solid. Its features were elven and sharp, lips that resembled Abi's, full and slightly thin, with a perpetual bend that made her look like she was smiling. I realized that was one of my favorite features about her—and the entity emulated that.

It had my eyes, green and intense. Abi had commented about them before. I guess the entity had heard that too.

Its hair was long, growing until it cascaded down to its ankles. The child wore something of a tattered robe. The ends flapped in a way similar to my coat. I half-expected to see Djinn's handle poking from its right side, the way mine did sometimes, but the child was weaponless.

Yes. I am unarmed. Defenseless.

Defenseless in this realm—as soon as it said that, I knew just how much danger it was in.

The realm of thought, the psychic plane, was not a place of predators and prey. Rather it was a place where one became lost. It was where all fleeting thoughts originated from and where all thoughts ended.

Our psychic child was holding itself together, struggling against its home plane, which wanted nothing more than to spread it thin and recycle it, turning it into nothing more than a fleeting thought.

Truly lost forever.

Abi stepped towards the child. She reached out with her hand and the child emulated her movements. A bright, warm spark of purple erupted from where they made contact. Abi smiled as she held the child's hand.

"How?" she began.

I reached out too. My heart was in my throat. I touched

the child's—*my* child's—hand. It was warm and loving, and *forgiving.*

The psychic entity, born of me and Abi, had forgiven me.

You knew not, it said. *You knew not what would happen. You know not about me. Now you do. Now you took action. It is all that matters, Father.*

The last thing I expected to do was break down in front of the kid but there I was bawling my eyes out. I was on my knees and pressing the kid's hand to my lips, and crying.

Do you know what really got me? The tone of voice. This kid had my tone of voice when I was telling someone to stop blaming themselves, to stop being stupid. I said it to others plenty of times, but I rarely heard it myself.

I guess we all need to be told to breathe once in a while.

"It was when we fought Greede's psychic entity," I told Abi, once I regained enough control to speak. "You remember that?"

She nodded.

"I had just witnessed everyone die in front of me," I said. "I made a deal with Dark Erik. I gave into the powers. I transformed." More nodding. "We faced the thing Greede created. The reason he killed all of those poor creatures and harvested their bones. The reason he pulled out the angel's heart from his chest. The reason he messed with your mom."

Now she started trembling.

"I gave you my power," I kept going. "And you used your psychic powers to fight the entity, since the body was indestructible. You almost had it. Your mom helped you."

"I remember," she whispered.

"When thoughts die, they leave echoes," I said. I reached out and plucked one of the strings. It resonated and fizzled out. "Literal afterthoughts. That entity was so large, its afterthoughts had enough power to reach out. And one of those fragments found our power — mine and yours. It merged with them, taking our psychic DNA for nourishment. It grew into a living being of pure thought."

I looked at the child.

"It grew into you."

The child smiled, green eyes all too familiar sparkling. *Indeed, Father. I am your child. And you, Mother, I am yours too.*

It released my hand and hugged Abi tightly.

I am so sorry for hurting you.

"What needs to happen now?" I asked. "What will happen to Abi if you aren't born?"

The child threw its head back and laughed. *But I am born already, Father. I am complete. Well, perhaps not so much. I still require one last thing.*

"A name," I said.

Yes. The one you gave me in the Dark Place. The one you fought so hard for. Give me a name so that I may be... It grinned at me. *"Real."*

The last word echoed so loudly in the psychic plane that thought fragments glowed purple and scattered, leaving us in darkness. Only our bodies were the source of light.

I glanced at Abi. "Boy or girl?"

She shook her head. "I can't tell." She turned to the child. "What are you?"

The child cocked its head, *exactly* the same as its mother does when she was annoyed. *"Psychic entities have no gender. We are one and both. We are what we are."*

"A unisex name then," she said.

"Father knows," the child said.

Abi turned to me.

"I wasn't sure," I said, "but when I spoke with you in the Underworld, I thought it was only fitting for you to have a name that meant something. Names have power, they carry history, and most importantly they help give us an identity. And I don't ever want you to be lost, Zeke."

42

The stark contrast of suddenly appearing back in Evans' workshop was jarring to the senses. Everything was so solid, so rigid and defined. My mind liked the comfort of physicality but somewhere deep down I missed what could have been infinite potential.

Turns out we didn't actually teleport anywhere. The conversation with Zeke happened inside our minds after all.

Then I heard Evans mutter something in Yiddish and realized that Zeke had materialized before us. In the physical world.

Astaroth cocked his head, lizard nostrils flaring. "Most curious."

Zeke, still purple and blue and ethereal, offered him a smile. That seemed to quell any further questions from the demon.

"I cannot remain here for long," said Zeke. "My form is at an interstice between two worlds. But rest assured, Father, Mother, I will not be lost now that I know who I am."

I glanced at Abi. She was crying. I guess I was too.

"What happens now?" I asked. "You leave? Will we ever see you again?"

The child laughed, a beautiful sound that resounded joyfully around the dull, grey room, filling it with light.

"Of course. I may be different. We psychic entities tend to age sporadically." Zeke looked at themselves self-consciously. "What age do I appear to humans?"

"About eight," I suggested.

"I was going to say you looked just like I did when I was eight or nine," Abi said. "Or same as Erik, I guess."

Now that she mentioned it, it was kind of like looking through a looking glass and seeing your younger self. With bits of Abi thrown in.

Man, this psychic stuff was starting to give me a headache.

Zeke nodded. "I suppose that is fair. I shall likely be older when we next meet." They smiled. "Think of me for I shall be thinking of you. And sorry for the discomfort I have caused you. I understand you have a bit of a vampire problem."

Abi and I chuckled. Yeah, our kid all right.

Our kid.

Holy psychic kittens.

Zeke tilted their head towards the two of us. "She calls for help, you know?" they said. "The one like me."

"Huh?" I asked.

"The one born of two worlds, yet is of neither," Zeke went on. They seemed like they had entered a trance. "Why do all bad things happen to her? Why was she the one chosen? Why did her father have to be so cruel? Punished, yes, but no retribution was given to the victims. No, they are nothing but whelps to hunt for sport."

"Zeke," Abi said. "You're starting to scare me."

"Yeah, ditto, kid," I said. "What are you talking about?"

Zeke turned to look behind them. The door swung open, snapping the heavy bolt that held it shut, and Amaymon strode in.

"Ah, come on, more people in this fucking lab?" Evans snapped. He grabbed a piece of sheet metal to cover his face.

Zeke and Astaroth both reacted in the exact same way: they leapt towards Amaymon with an anime-esque joy, yelling,

"Uncle Amaymon!"

"Brother!"

Amaymon threw his hands up, swatting away his brother, and grabbing Zeke by the collar with the other, holding the child aloft.

"And who in the mind-fucking fuck are you-" He stopped. Glared at us. Looked back at the child. Glared at us some more. Huge grin. "Well, fucking finally. It was about time you dumb-asses got laid." He shook the child a little, eliciting childlike glee from Zeke. "Why'd ya call me uncle?"

"Oh," Zeke said. Their feet were dangling. Amaymon was still holding them high by the collar in the air. Zeke didn't mind. "Has it not happened yet? Sorry, I am having a tough time acclimatizing to physical thought."

The demon set my child down and sighed. "You and me both, lil' kitten," he said. "But stick around. Life ain't that boring around here. Plus, Uncle Amaymon's got a lot to teach you about mortal life. Burgers are awesome. Alcohol makes people fun to be around. And *boobs*. Boobs are amazing."

"Oh, come on!" I snapped. "The kid's just been born. Let them have a second before introducing junk food, alcoholism, and porn in their life, will you?"

Zeke laughed again and I swear I saw them exchange a conspiratorial wink.

Oh, awesome.

Amaymon turned his attention to Astaroth who was all but crying. "Get up, you overgrown lizard," he said, pulling his brother up and hugging him. "There, stop your trembling."

"Thank you, brother," Astaroth said, joy returning to his reptilian features.

"Yeah, yeah," Amaymon said. "And you, Rabbi." Evans peered from behind the sheet metal. "Yeah, you. Put that shit down, we got actual work to do. Plus, I scouted you out months ago. I know what you look like. How old are you anyway? You look anywhere between eighteen and thirty?"

My jaw must have hit the ground. Amaymon is not what you might call subtle but he was being impatient even by his usual standards.

"I have a condition," Evans supplied with a small voice.

"Is it that you can't make golems worth shit?" Amaymon retorted. "I can fart better clay in my sleep." To prove his point, he spat in his hand and tossed a lump of wet clay toward the Golem Evans who thus far had been silent as a post. "There. Improve your constructs please, since we're about to head into some real shit."

"What happened?" I asked.

"Rashid just stormed Caleb and his pack," Amaymon said. "We need to move. Your sister is already on her way, and she'll shut us down. I heard her say something about Rashid being exempt from us pulling his head apart from his neck."

I swore and grumbled something about political bullshit.

"Okay, crunch time," I said. This part was easy for me.

This part I can do. "Astaroth, thank you for your help, but I need you to go home. The last thing I need is a planar shift because an elemental demon is unbound on ours."

Judging by the way he looked at me you would have thought I had taken away his ice cream and slapped him, but I didn't have time to be nice. The fact of the matter was, the demon was dangerous.

"Ah, don't worry about it," Evans said. "I'll call you anyway. We got that orbital cannon to finish."

Astaroth grinned. "Oh, yes we do."

"Orbital what?" I asked.

Evans waved me off. "Don't worry about it. We'll point it at the Russians."

I decided I'd rather not argue.

Speaking of which:

"Abi, stay here."

Wouldn't you know, she argued.

"What? You can't do that!"

I sighed heavily. "Yes, I can," I said. "You're grounded on account that you just birthed a psychic entity, and have been nourishing it for the past forty-odd hours."

"Thirty-six by my estimation," Evans supplied.

"More like thirty-four hours and nineteen minutes," Astaroth whispered loudly.

"However many hours," I said. "Abi, please. You're tired. You need to recover. Didn't a wise woman once tell me that you can't help others if you don't help yourself first?"

She scowled at me.

"Who was that woman, Abi?" I pressed.

"Me." She growled. It was cute. "Fine. But only because I made that argument, and I'm always right."

"There's logic in there, and I'm not prepared to argue with it," I said. "Zeke."

I looked at where the child was last. Now there was only empty space. I looked around.

"Where's Zeke?" I asked. Everyone shrugged. "Anyone see Zeke leave?"

I am still here, Father. But I am going now. You should be going too. We both have journeys to take if we are to meet again.

Judging by the way Abi started crying, I was guessing they also left her a farewell message.

My throat seized. It wasn't the words so much as the emotions that Zeke sent over. Psychic entities communicated in feelings. I *felt* Zeke's goodbye and the way my heart tightened was more real than any words they could have imparted.

I knew I would see my child again.

But for now, I had bigger, furrier things to occupy myself with. I turned to Amaymon.

"Let's go."

43

The landscape was a bloodbath. Everywhere I looked was covered in red, viscous liquid, bits of fur, and viscera.

I am used to death and dismemberment. I am used to horror. Hell, I *know* better than anyone what it's like to give into your primal instincts, to rip, kill, and hunt.

But there was something evil about this. I could tell from the wounds, from the werewolves still left alive, from the way they were scattered and strewn about—whoever had done this had not done it out of need, or rage, or a hunter's instinct.

They had done it out of spite.

Pure, unfiltered malice.

Evil for the sake of evil.

"Erik." Amaymon was just standing there. I realized I hadn't moved.

"Tend to the wounded," I told him. "Where's Caleb?"

Amaymon sniffed the air. "There's a cave down there," he said, pointing to the east. "And he's not alone."

I nodded and followed the path, drawing my sword as I

did. My mind raced with possibilities, until I finally settled on one: the vampires must have brought some true sickos along for the ride. There are things that could outclass a werewolf, especially given what I knew now about the Underworld. Likely some horror had taken the alpha down to the cave to torment him.

I found the cavern mouth. It was silent. I cast a spell to make the blade glow and in the sudden illumination I found Caleb in his bestial form, half-dead on the ground.

Behind him were a dozen children, some human, some not.

"Holy shit," I said, lowering the weapon. Caleb snarled at me. "Easy, easy."

He was twice my size but laying half-sprawled on the ground, there was nothing he could do from stopping me approaching him. Still, I sheathed my sword. No need to incite violence with a wounded beast.

I carefully examined the wounds. There was a cut so deep in his stomach it would have ruptured if I dared move him. The ground was soaked with his blood. One of his eyes had burst. They were all injuries that would heal if he reverted back, but you needed energy for that, and the kid had none. Plus, there was a chance his intestines would spill out from the sudden size change, before his body had had a chance to close.

"Okay, okay."

I turned to look at the kids. Two of them in wolf form, little cubs barely larger than a Labrador, snarled at me.

"I'm here to help," I told them. That didn't placate them, which was understandable. I was an intruder, the same kind that had just massacred their families no more than a few meters away from here.

Caleb released a low whine.

"Don't," I told him. "I can give you some healing energy but you can't change. Not yet."

Amaymon appeared in the cave mouth. The snarls doubled, followed by whimpers of fear.

He ignored them. "We've got company."

"Gil?"

He nodded.

I gritted my teeth. My sister will tell me to curb my rage and *not* attack Rashid just yet. She'd also provide shelter for the cubs and had a lot more to offer Caleb in terms of saving his life.

The kid needed urgent help. Sometimes it's not about you.

Amaymon was also gearing up for the fight.

"Get them in here," I told him. "They can help these people better than I can."

He cocked his head quizzically at me.

"Trust me," I told him.

Amaymon held my stare for a while. Then he nodded and melted into the ground beneath him. A few seconds later several of Gil's soldiers made it to the cave. They surrounded Caleb and a team of medical people started tending to him.

All the while I petted his snout and told him it was going to be okay. The big wolf went unconscious straight away. I would like to think he heard me.

Then the soldiers rounded up the kids. Amaymon stepped in between them.

"What are you going to do with them?" I demanded.

Gil stood outside the cave mouth. "Find them shelter, of course," she said. "We have a mansion, don't we?"

"A mansion formerly used to lock up monsters for experimentation," I pointed out.

My sister glared at me testily. "I have all the werewolves I might need, brother. But yes, by all means, let us leave them here, open to the elements and the viscera of their parents just meters away. By all means, let us do that."

I let out a long exhale. My sister and sarcasm are a deadly combination. "Fine. Amaymon, can you help them?"

"Can do." He turned to the cubs. They were scared of him until he started making wolf noises. I didn't know he could speak their language—guess you learn something new every day.

I turned to my sister.

"No," she began, clearly reading my intent.

"He's going to die for this," I said.

"He's the king."

"Fuck the king," I said. "And the army he rode in with."

"I agree with you," she said. "Rashid will pay for this. But if you attack him, he will actually have a reason to invade Eureka."

"Dammit Gil!" Everyone stopped to look at the crazy shouting man. I didn't care. "Look at what he did. Right under your nose! You keep playing politics with him—a vicious fucking predator! Creatures like him understand force, and nothing but. So I say we go in, stake the asshole and dust his entire species like the fucking rats they are!"

I was breathing heavily by now.

"You think I don't know that?" Her voice was low, a hiss of rage. "You think I don't see what he is?" When she looked at me her eyes were filled with wrath. "You think I will let him do this without some form of retribution?"

"The fact he did it at all means you don't have him under control," I told her. "It means you *can't stop him*. Plain and simple. You are not in control here. He is. And he's killing people."

She could have slapped me. She could have hit me—Hell, I wanted her to. I wanted her to show me she had some kind of fire in her.

But Gil was not like that. Gil remained calm. Gil, the Ice Queen.

"He is," she said, her voice emotionless. "I have a solution. Come to the mansion if you want to be a part of it."

She spun on her heels and left.

44

Amaymon and I could have entered the house via the front door, but I was angry at my sister and Amaymon never needs justification for wanton destruction.

So we burst through a wall.

Every person there turned to look at us, eyebrows raised.

"Told you," said Greg. "Pay up."

Luke, Jack, Abi, Gil, Evans (the golem, of course), and Emrys chuckled. They all reached for their wallets.

My sister sighed heavily.

"What?" I asked. Clearly, this had not gone as intended.

"I bet them all twenty American dollars that you would burst through wall," Greg said.

"I had ceiling," Luke interjected.

"Fireball," Jack said.

I sagged my shoulders. "Am I that predictable?"

"Yes," Greg said, greedily pocketing the money I had just made him. "You are like child. You get angry, you smash things. Is temper tantrum. Is funny."

Gil shot him a withering look.

"What? It is."

My sister closed her eyes, and I heard her grumble something about children, and then she sighed dejectedly at me. "Please, brother, won't you join us? We were just discussing the intel Caleb gave us as soon as he woke up."

"How is he?" I asked, sitting down on an armchair. Amaymon turned into a cat and hopped on Abi's lap. She started stroking him lovingly.

"Alive," Gil replied. "Remarkably well-healed for someone in his condition. He will not be joining us in the fight."

"Fight?"

Gil pursed her lips. "You are right, brother. The time for politics is over."

I blinked at her. "I'm sorry, I must be having a stroke. I am pretty sure I heard you say I was right."

My sister was not amused.

"Abi," I went on, "was there a news report of a snowstorm in Hell? Or pigs flying?"

She chuckled.

"Gil, did you find yourself on a spaceship and agree to some alien foreign-exchange program?" I asked. "Are you even my sister?"

Her eyebrow soared. "If you're quite done..."

"No, wait, I have another." I paused. "Dammit, I lost it."

"Thank Heavens for that," my sister said.

"Something about water and people in Hell," I said.

"Plenty of water in Hell," Amaymon said. "You just gotta talk to the right people. Also, I think your sister's vein is about to pop."

Now everyone was forcing down giggles. Gil chose to ignore us and sigh some more.

"If we're all quite done," she said, shooting me a threatening look, "we have some news. This time Rashid killed only twenty werewolves, but abducted two. Caleb says that he was forced back by his compatriots, but he clearly saw the vampires take two of his pack: the Vaewolf cub and her mother."

Shit.

Apparently I wasn't the only one thinking that because both Greg and Emrys said the same thing.

"This makes him an enemy then," Luke said. "And Carmilla along with him. Her seat is renounced."

Gil cocked her head. "Perhaps. Our intel about Rashid is almost null. But if someone were to know for sure, it would be her." She sighed. "There are hostages now. We need to tread carefully."

"He won't kill them," Emrys said. "Not if he needs them for the ritual."

"Just the kid," Luke said. "Not the mother. She's likely there as a scare tactic. Greede used them all the time. Kidnap a package, main target plus the family. Threaten the family to put pressure on the target. It's very effective."

I felt my hand shaking. God only knows what that kid was going through right now.

"We need some way to convince Carmilla to part with that knowledge," Gil was saying.

"She can be bribed," Greg said. "She is very power-hungry. We can figure out way to give her some leverage against her father."

"Which would only replace one despot with another," Abi interjected.

"Better the devil you know," Evans said, speaking for the first time. "Carmilla is not as crazy as her father. She is willing to negotiate."

I stood up, and took out my phone. My fingers were

dialing without any direction.

"Hello?" said a person with a hint of an Eastern European accent.

"It's me," I said. The entire room was watching. "Put her on."

I waited less than a breath before Carmilla's sultry voice came on. "I was wondering when you'd call me."

"It's about your father."

The sultriness dropped. "How gauche. What about him?"

"I'm putting you on speaker," I told her. "It's Carmilla," I informed the rest of the room, setting the phone on the coffee table. "You're on."

"Lovely," her voice filled the room. "I assume this is about my father's latest attempt at forcing you into open war."

"He took a kid, Carmilla," I said. "A Vaewolf child. And her mom."

She hummed in assent.

"He's not going to get away with harming them," I told her.

"No," she said. "I suppose he won't. Which is why you are calling me, likely the only person with the means to locate him."

"Yes."

"Make me an offer."

The room stilled again.

"No." My voice was calm and quiet.

"No?" she echoed.

"My offer is this," I said, ignoring the looks of horror from those around me and staring at the phone with nothing short of hate. "You get to live in peace, far the fuck away from me. You get to settle your colony."

"Doesn't sound like much of an offer," she said coolly.

"Then how about a counter-offer?" I said. "I dust you first. If your father harms a single hair on the child, knowing you could have helped us prevent it and you didn't, I go rogue. I won't find him, but I will find *you*. And I dust you first, then your colony, then I find your father and end your entire race."

This time I snatched my phone from the table and held it to my mouth.

"You know I can do it," I said. "You saw me cut loose. And I promise you, Carmilla, if I decide to enforce my threats, I will make my actions in the Underworld look like a goddamn party trick." I paused. "If you think you can survive that, end this call. If not, help us."

I set the phone back down and walked away.

Laughter cackled from the device.

"Ah, finally," Carmilla said. "Finally, a man with balls. Such a rare find these days. Do not assume your threats have any sway on me, Erik, but unlike my father, I am willing to consider my subjects. I will not stand for you to harm them." She snickered. "And truth be told I was just about to launch a strike attack against him anyway. Can't have my rival become a demigod, now can I? This way, you attack, and I shall sit back and reap the rewards after."

A low throaty noise echoed loudly. I don't know if it was predatory or sensual—likely both.

"Gil, dear, check your inbox," Carmilla said. "Oh, and do make sure to finish it this time, Erik darling. Now, I am ending this phone call. Please do not kill any of my kin now that I've helped you." Her sarcasm made me want to punch her. She knew that, so she laughed again. "See you at the endgame, Handsome."

The line went dead.

45

What I really wanted was a drink but we were getting ready for battle and I needed my wits about me.

Coffee it was.

The kettle was just about done brewing when Abi entered the previously-vacant kitchen.

"Hey," she said.

I nodded. "Hey."

Wordlessly, she picked up a mug and dropped a tea bag in it. Something fruity and sweet-smelling. I poured my coffee and offered her the kettle.

"Thanks," she said.

We drank and stared at one another.

"So," she said. "That was one interesting phone call. Quite the power move you pulled on Carmilla." She sipped. "She seems to like you."

I snorted in my coffee.

"Is this a will-they, won't-they scenario?" she pressed.

"It's a won't-they," I said. "Carmilla is a predator, a monster. I can't trust her, but I can tell you she's manipulative, she's deadly, and she'll stop at nothing to fulfill her goals."

"Sounds like quite the catch," Abi said, with a grin that never touched her eyes.

"Yeah, if you're into getting killed," I said. "She's not my type, Abi. Like I said, I'm not into monsters."

She lowered the cup.

"What about me?" she asked in a small voice.

My heart did some gymnastics. "What about you?"

"You know what I mean."

"Are we finally going to talk about that whole situation?" I asked. "I was instructed not to overthink it in the crypt, remember?"

She smiled. "We were also being chased by a crazed vampire if I remember correctly. Not exactly the right time and place for a heart-to-heart."

"Right."

More silence.

"Man, we suck at this," she muttered.

"Yeah, we do," I said.

"Why is this so hard?" she said. "We have a kid together." She set the tea down. "Erik, we have a kid. A child. That we made."

"With our minds," I added.

We both burst out laughing.

"Fuck, our lives are weird," she said. "I would have never thought in a million years that this is what I was signing up for all those years ago."

"Oh, yeah. The college party."

"Lilith."

"Seems like a lifetime away," I said. "Literally, in my case."

"It wasn't only you," she said. "Death rarely affects the

dead. It's the ones left behind who really suffer."

She looked at me. Her eyes were big and brown and utterly beautiful.

"I missed you. There were a thousand things I wanted to tell you, and there was never a right time after."

She flicked a strand of red hair away.

"There was always something stopping me," she said. "First, it was the island, and then you met Akasha and you were happy, so I didn't say anything. I mean, you were *happy* — I didn't want to mess with that. And then, she died and then *you* died. You *died,* Erik. You went away and you were never supposed to come back. But you did. And when you came back you brought back with you so much darkness. And now..."

She stopped and looked at me.

"I love you, Erik."

Four words.

Funny how the universe works.

Words have power, don't let anyone tell you any different. But it's power we assign to them. Anyone can sing your praises but when it comes from your parents or your loved ones—the ones who really matter—then it counts for real.

I had never heard those four words being uttered to me by anyone. Akasha and I had skirted around them for a while, but it had never been real between us. We had liked each other but this was a whole new level.

Four words, and Abi was the only one I ever wanted to say them to.

The world stopped spinning. The coffee cup met the floor. The sound rang, the clock ticked slow, her tea billowed smoke, and none of it mattered.

I kissed her.

My hand found her face, pressing her onto me. She

squealed a little when she bumped into the kitchen counter. I was just about to pull back and apologize, when I felt her hands all over me. There was hunger there, primordial and needy. I distinctly remembered Amaymon saying something about her not feeding her succubus side recently.

She had been starving herself. Because of me. Because she only wanted me and was willing to weaken herself for that. She was willing to *die* for that fact.

I kissed her and did not mind when she fed on my energy. I had plenty to spare. I had magic galore and it felt right.

This wasn't something sexual either (though there was plenty of that desire). This was history, a seemingly random series of events, all leading up to this one climactic moment.

We pulled apart an eternity later. Her lips and cheeks were flushed, her eyes wide with passion, and I wanted her. She wanted me.

But the world hadn't stopped for us.

Amaymon made his presence known by whistling.

"Day-yum," he commented.

Now me and Abi separated like high-schoolers caught in the act. He clapped slowly.

"About damn time," he said. "Now holster it for a second while we kill us some vamps."

He turned and left, and when we emerged, the rest of the group was looking at us smugly. Most were grinning.

Heat flushed my cheeks once more.

Greg even gave me a thumbs-up. I sighed.

"Not, one, word," I growled at them.

Needless to say, they all ignored me and more chuckling ensued.

46

You had to hand it to King Rashid: the prick knew how to pick a stronghold.

I had no idea how he had managed to get an army barracks in the middle of the damn forest but there we were, hidden among the trees and scouting out the area. Our plan of attack had already been formed:

Emrys, Greg, and Evans were at the rear of the barracks, ready to enter when I gave them the signal.

Abi went off. Her job was to get the Vaewolf and her mom, camouflage them under an illusion spell and get the hell out of dodge. Just to be safe, Luke and Jack were situated just adjacent to her where they would make enough noise for her to slip past.

Me—I was the bait. I was the big chaotic distraction, entering through the front door guns blazing, along with Amaymon. I sent the demon ahead to scout the area. If the king had managed to transport a stronghold all the way here, then I had no doubt he had some powerful magic-users in his fold.

I never heard them. The crossbow bolts punched

through my coat and into my body, one at the shoulder, the other just above my kidney. My lungs tightened and then, *whack*, I was on the ground, with a duo of vampire soldiers looping lengths of chain around my arms. When the world stopped spinning, I saw a vampire with a crossbow placing a foot on my chest.

"Make sure he cannot get to his weapons," he told the ones holding my arms spread-eagled through the chains. Then he grinned at me, fangs bared. "The wizard who cannot use magic. So powerless. And yet you dare attempt to infiltrate our stronghold."

Well.

Shit.

They say no plan ever survives first contact. Now I just needed to know how much shit I was really in.

"Careful," I told the leader. "I might have a few tricks up my sleeve. We humans are tricky like that."

He pressed harder on my chest. I made a sound that was somewhere between an exhale and a moan.

"You are powerless," he said, icily. "And you are alone."

Bingo. The others were safe.

"Yes, I am," I said. "What now? Kill me and get a promotion? Maybe upgrade you to a weapon that has seen use in the last, say, two decades?"

The vampire snarled. He reached in, found my gun holster and unsheathed the weapon, setting his crossbow aside.

"I shall take this," he said, operating the slide. "So unwieldy, yet so powerful. I can see why you like it. It shall be mine. And behold." He pressed the weapon against my leg.

Calmly he pulled the trigger.

My gun uses a big caliber. You need to when dealing

with things that have natural armor up the wazoo. Jack had built that weapon for me, and he had made sure to front-load the bullets with as much gunpowder as he could fit.

The bullet hurt.

A lot.

I opened my mouth to scream but thanks to the bolts in my back and the vampire's foot on my chest no sound came out.

He set the gun on my other leg.

"Who uses 'behold' any more?" I said through gritted teeth.

The vampire's response was shooting my other leg. I nearly passed out. The vampire noticed my first leg and saw the healing magic take effect.

"Ah, yes," he mused. "So annoying." The gun barrel rested on my forehead. "I wonder, how far can we play with you? If I were to shoot you in the head, wizard, and then bring you before the king, will you be a blabbering mess?"

His eyes were lustful.

"Shall we find out?"

I saw his finger tighten around the trigger in slow motion. I could practically hear the mechanism inside working.

And I could feel the magic inside me leaping into action.

A pool of shadow manifested between the gun and my forehead, absorbing the impact of the shot. A tendril of shadow, so thin it was barely larger than a single strand of hair, carried the kinetic energy from the point of impact and onto the gun, and the wrist holding it.

My gun is a beast. It had taken me hours to learn how to work with the recoil. Now add the punch from a bullet to that force, and no wrist—not even a vampire's—can handle it. Hands are fragile things.

The vampire's hand was now a mangled mess. The gun fell on my chest where a shadowy hand grew and took control of the weapon. At the same time, that single thread of shadow turned into a garrote that beheaded the vampire leader.

I turned to look to the chain-holder on my right. The shadow hand turned the gun in the same direction.

Blam!

Look left, zero in on the other one.

Blam!

Look forward, see a vampire raising his crossbow.

Blam! Blam!

I sat up, gritting my teeth against the pain, and whipped both chains forward. They took to the air, two lengths of untethered metal links that rattled as they looped around a vampire each.

I snarled something that resembled a spell. The chains coiled tighter and tighter. They began heating up, and soon they were searing into the vampires' flesh.

Screams filled the air for a split second.

I stood up, my head spinning from the expended energy.

I heard a crossbow locking behind me and spun. The vampire soldier was there one second, dust the next.

Amaymon stood behind him, claws extended and curled around where the vampire's head had been.

He cocked his head at me.

"What did I miss?"

47

There are times for intrigue and politics, where words are daggers, and looks convey more than any dictionary could describe.

These are not my sort of times.

But this... I lived for moments like this, moments where I could be truly myself, and walk towards the vampire stronghold and yell,

"HEY RASHID, YOU COCKLESS SACK OF SHIT!"

Not my best work but I was working under a time crunch. Besides Astaroth had been right: the way to a man's ego is his dick.

And they say people are complicated.

The sound of a bolt slamming echoed loudly, and the doors to the barracks opened. A pair of vampires walked out. Their skin was the color of a deep bruise, with snow-white hair and eyes of pure-red hatred.

"Who dares call out our king?" said the male. His—and I was making an educated guess here—twin sister, because they looked identical, stopped exactly beside him, her arms to her side. I did not miss the tattoos on her arms. Vol magic then. These two clowns must be on Rashid's magic-user payroll.

After all, who better to take out a wizard than a pair of wizard vampires? Clearly the regular foot soldiers weren't cutting it.

"My brother asked you a question, meat," the sister asked.

"Meat?" I echoed. "That's new. Degrading, but new. Okay then, Ash, I'm Erik Ashendale. You've heard of me. And my business is with the king, not his whelps."

"It dares speak to us so horridly, brother," the sister said.

"Indeed," said the brother. "Perhaps it does not know who we are. It knows not we are blood-brood to Prince Valen himself."

"That psycho?" I said. "And blood-brood... You mean his *kids*?"

I shouldn't have been surprised, give the prince's behavior around anything wearing a skirt.

"Not merely his offspring," hissed the sister. "We are his favored, his strongest, his-"

"Yeah, yeah, I get it," I interrupted. "Daddy issues. We all have them. Now step aside so I can talk to... Your grandfather, I guess."

"The king is far too important for a lowly worm like yourself," the brother said. "What can you do alone?"

The sister snickered.

I cocked my head. "Okay, I gotta ask: why do you think I'm alone?"

The vampire twins stared at my blankly. "We have studied you," the sister said.

"You are always alone," the brother said. "We know you, wizard. We studied you like an eagle studies a rat. We know how you operate."

I sighed. "Why do people always assume I'm alone? Am I that much of a loner? Do you think I should see someone for that?"

The vampires became even more confused.

"I mean I guess it's good that it worked out for me this time," I said. "But you know, long-term I'd like to maybe not have that assumption hanging around me."

"Enough of this." The brother raised his arm. Magic flared. I recognized the necromancy spell, a bolt of death energy. Mid-level spell but that's the trick with those: you can scale them up by pumping as much power as you want to them.

"Gotcha," I said, turning my head behind me. "Here, kitty, kitty."

And…

Nothing happened.

I tapped the ground beneath me. "Um, did I say it wrong? Amaymon?"

"That is not the code we agreed on," came the familiar's voice from beneath the ground itself.

The vampire brother lowered his hand and blasted the ground beneath my feet. A corona of decay marred the edges of the hole.

Whoa. All kidding aside, these two were top-class magic-users, to say the least.

Amaymon climbed out from the hole, completely unaffected by the spell, and raised his eyebrows expectantly at me.

"I am not saying it," I said.

"But it's the code phrase," he insisted. "You gotta commit to the code phrase."

"I am not saying 'Daddy's home', Amaymon."

"Why not?"

"Because if you have to ask, then clearly you should not be in a situation where that phrase ever needs be uttered for real," I snapped.

"Funny you should-"

A second necrotic bolt slammed into Amaymon, shearing a good chunk off his shoulder. The sister lowered her arm, a smug smile on her face.

Rightly so. I can count on one hand all the creatures that can manage to land a hit on the demon. I needed to start taking these vampires seriously.

Amaymon had other plans. He glanced down at his shoulder, shrugged and turned.

"Bitch, I'm talking here. Wait your turn. Also, you dropped this."

He scooped up bits of his own flesh, which had solidified into something resembling granite, and threw them with inhuman speed at the sister. I never saw the projectile, but I heard the sonic boom as it broke the sound barrier.

The sister's head exploded.

"NO!" wailed the brother. Her body fell onto him and he cradled her all the way down.

"SISTER!"

Power welled from the brother. His tattoos became fiery, while somehow getting darker. Death and decay spread from around him. My ears popped as more magic coalesced into and around him.

"Amaymon," I began.

"Say it."

"Goddammit, man. Daddy's home. There."

Amaymon sighed. "You didn't say it right. Here, lemme show you."

A dust cloud kicked up as he bolted towards the brother just as the latter was reaching his critical point. Amaymon slammed into him, then into the doors, the walls and the front entrance of the barracks.

Purple and black energy rose into the sky, churning clouds and causing yellow lightning to burst forth. Down on the ground half the barracks was in ruins, with Amaymon spreading his arms theatrically as debris and corpses fell around him.

He craned his neck and shot me a grin that turned my insides cold.

"Daddy's home," he said.

48

I would have stayed staring at my familiar's wanton destruction for longer, were it not for the crackle of the radio in my pocket.

"We got your signal," came Emrys's voice. "Going in now."

"Wait, what signal?" I said.

"The big purple explosion thingie just a few seconds ago."

"That wasn't me."

"Oh." More static. "We just figured, you know, big explosion, clearly it has to be Erik. So, is that the signal or not?"

I sighed. "Yes, it's the signal. You guys suck. Over and go fuck yourselves."

Just before I clicked the radio off, I heard the three of them chuckling.

So now we had Emrys, Greg and Evans storming the building from the side. Awesome. Luke, Jack and Abi were just going to watch for a few minutes until we created enough damage.

I walked past Amaymon, calling up my shadow magic as

I did. Sword in one hand, gun in the other, my familiar and I strode towards the enemy fortification and proceeded to, in all senses of the phrase, bring the house down.

Amaymon has no concept of doors and walls. To him they are just additions to be used and discarded. That was why instead of blasting through the wall, he simply made a section of it leap forward, crushing a small battalion of vampire soldiers in the process.

I swept in, magic and weaponry slicing and slashing and shooting and blasting. We had the advantage of surprise. Clearly, they never thought we'd make it past the creepy magician twins, or the first rank of fortifications.

Carmilla's information had also been eerily accurate. I recognized the landmarks as Amaymon and I pressed on, rushing to reach the central plaza.

This was also where we became surrounded.

"Ah fuck, where are the others?" I snarled as vampire soldiers leapt at me from all angles.

The Grigori love an entrance. I think they were waiting just so they could come to my rescue.

Luke fell like a comet from the skies, all raging fires and carpet bombs. Jack hugged a wall and did his Colossus impression, with one very cool exception. Spikes shot from his legs and into the ground, bracing him tight. His right arm morphed into a giant bazooka, and with his left he fed the weapon a whole bunch of weapons and armor from the fallen vampires. The metal Elemental had clearly improved his skill set because in a matter of seconds he was deconstructing the arms and armor, turning them into giant missiles and firing them at the enemy ranks.

Suddenly, everyone stopped and listened. The wall to

the right creaked and groaned. A vine the size of a telephone pole poked out like a worm emerging from shelter, wriggling for purchase. More vines came out, ever expanding, until a literal tree grew from the wall and blasted it as the vines and roots pushed the mortar apart.

Racing up the tree was Greg, screaming a Slavic war cry as he dove off the vines and into the vampire soldiers.

Evans was right behind him, the golem's arms glowing with green and purple sigils.

And then a bear showed up.

A big shaggy, honest-to-god bear that mauled a vampire and tossed the carcass away before it exploded into ash.

The bear leapt away and a second later Emrys took its place.

Ah. So *that's* what a Druid does.

Asked and answered.

He caught my eye and winked.

"Nice costume," I said. "Green and brown leathers. What, no Robin Hood hat?"

He raised an eyebrow. "Yeah, like you're any better. You look like the Lone Gunman picked up his coat and then just settled for sweatpants."

I grinned at him, then looked over to Luke and Jack.

"Yo, B-Team, time to split off," I yelled.

Luke shot me a dirty look, while Jack abandoned the bazooka for a machine-gun (yes, the guy had machine-guns for arms!) and raced off. They were Abi's exit point.

"Erik," cried Greg. "Go find the king. We have it covered here."

"Are you sure?"

To prove his point, Greg turned on his holy Christmas light show on and pulverized ten vampires with one swing.

"Touché," I said.

"Lemme get the door for you," Emrys offered. He tossed what looked like a handful of acorns at the doorway. Vampires stormed over them. The Druid snapped his fingers.

The acorns took to the air and exploded, shooting out multiple thorn-like spikes. The corridor was now filled with dust.

Landmine acorns. I filed a mental note not to get on Emrys's bad side. Mother Nature had some nasty tricks up her sleeve.

As I raced up the stairs, I was left unmolested by vampire enemies. Then again, I did notice Amaymon rushing ahead of me. Well, not so much notice, as feel the walls roil with his presence and a demonic energy form preempt my path. We dashed all the way to a throne room.

I felt something punch me in the gut. Magic, pure condensed raw magic, just hit me like a truck.

I looked up.

Rashid had his sword drawn, and was raking it down. Amaymon leapt up. The vampire king struck, just as Amaymon dodged and countered. The king disappeared, a thick fog in his place, and then the sword was slicing along Amaymon's chest.

The demon did something I had never heard him do before: he screamed in agony, and fell away like a rag doll.

King Rashid stood up, reformed, and raised his sword at me.

"You have interfered with my plans for the last time, Erik Ashendale. Time for you to die."

He charged.

49

I blocked. Barely.

My feet found air. I slammed into the wall. Colors were too bright.

Another sword-strike. This one nicked my flesh, only for the shadows around me to absorb the burn of the impact. Bones cracked. Lungs emptied.

I rolled, wildly shooting at him. I bumped something. A vampire. It pushed me.

"No!" snarled the king. He stopped attacking, giving me a moment of reprieve.

The throne room was a vast hall. Vampires stood hidden among the shadows. I could only see their eyes glowing red, save for two pairs. Both of these were yellow and they were almost on the ground.

The werewolf mother and the Vaewolf child. They had to be on their knees.

Rashid's cloak flapped as he unclasped it and tossed it aside. He swung his longsword about him.

"The wizard is mine," he declared. "No one is to interfere. I shall be the one to slay him." He spread his fangs at me. "And drink his blood."

I stood up. Somehow during the exchange my gun had flown out of my hand, leaving me with only my sword. I glanced to the side. Amaymon had swayed up, earth caking his wound. Rashid had hurt him badly. Which meant the rumors were true to some extent. I remembered what Turtle had told us, that Rashid considered himself equal to the Avatars. I wasn't exactly sure what that meant on the power scale but I could safely place Rashid in the demigod section.

I was just a guy. A guy with a load of magic, sure, but nowhere near a demigod.

Right?

But wait...

What if I was more than just a guy? Didn't they all keep saying that I was something *more*?

Amaymon, Mephisto, Sun Tzu, Turtle, Dark Erik, even my own child, Zeke—they all kept pushing me to be more. I thought that meant fight harder because that had been the default setting all my life.

That was what I did.

I fought.

But what if I could do more?

I stood up and faced an enemy I had no hope of defeating. But I stood up anyway and did something I had not done since I was eleven years old. Something that had cost me my magic, and that had required an archangel to heal, some two decades later. Something I had started with Anael's help, but never quite committed myself to.

I opened myself up to magic.

It was like turning on an old faucet. Things started out rusty, glugs of water spurting out, and then, if everything held, water rushed forth.

The power welled up inside me. From the center of my chest red and yellow vines snaked out. Shadows solidified over my body into an armor that was less bulky than that of the Knightmare. That had been armor meant to intimidate and protect. It had been the armor of something weak and scared. It had been a shell.

This was my second skin, as my body transformed into a living manifestation of my own magic.

Djinn blazed high, elongating into a longsword.

I didn't feel powerful. I didn't feel like a berserker. I felt the one thing I rarely ever was in my life:

I was in control.

"So this is what your resolve has turned to?" King Rashid paced ahead of me, sword held lightly by his side. "Where is the fearsome warrior, Erik Ashendale? Where is the being that broke Alan Greede?"

I looked up. "I'm right here, Rashid. Come face me, if you dare."

The king grinned. "With pleasure, wizard."

Our swords clashed. His strength overwhelmed me. I spun and slid along the block, extending my left hand. Shadows draped over his head, forming a visor which instantly turned into stone.

Blinded, the king swung wildly and a flock of bats replaced him. A single bat smashed on the ground, shattered, and the king reformed with one eye blinded and hollow.

He roared and swung at me again. I dodged the first, countered the second and extended my left hand again. This time he swung his sword to sever my arm—only I saw it coming.

I back-pedalled, held Djinn out in front of me, and let loose. Blue fire and energy intermingled into a massive cone in front of me. In the midst of the roar of energy, I heard Rashid scream.

Cold swept over the throne room.

Rashid held his arms in front of him, and I felt Vol magic take effect. He was 'killing' the heat, turning the fire into ice, and a massive steam bomb went off. Water splashed all around us.

I spread my shadows over it and raised it, encasing Rashid. He struggled and began pushing his way out with just brute force.

Which meant he was too distracted when I threw lightning at him. The water in the spell conducted the electricity like a charm. Rashid screamed, and then *poof*, cloud of smoke.

What?

His fist nearly tore my head off. He reformed nearly intact. I noticed his sword speared into the ground. The bastard must have used it as a lightning rod.

He grabbed my sword arm, and his head shifted into that of a large wolf. Rashid bit down, crushing bones and sinew into pulp. Djinn went flying. I screamed. My free fist punched at his good eye. He caught it and held my arm high. His jaws snapped open and he bit down on my collarbone.

My pain and agony turned into rage, which empowered my magic. As Rashid went forward, I snapped both hands—and realized that my healing was also supercharged. My right arm hurt something bad and it was all I could to hold his jaws just far enough from tightening around my throat.

A battle which I was losing, fast.

I extended both index fingers, tips touching. A blast of power shot from both, creating an opposite force. Rashid's wolf jaw snapped open violently. I reeled back, both my hands broken.

My healing took effect, creating more agony as bones were snapped in place and tendons tightened.

Rashid fell to the ground. His head was back to normal. His lower jaw was bloodied and half his teeth were missing, but he managed to stand back up.

Vol magic charged around his arms. I never gave him a chance. Shadows roped around my arms, ending in a blade on each, and I went in swinging. The shadow blades only lasted one hit each, but I managed to dispel his Vol magic, tearing new gashes in his arms along the way.

I uppercutted his face. Rashid swung his fist at me. It connected. It hurt. I made my cross-punch hurt more. His head reeled back. He leapt up and threw his fist down. I charged in, shooting from beneath his guard.

We grappled. I fired elbows at him. He punched me in the gut so hard I felt my stomach rupture. As I doubled over, I threw my body weight into a heavy stomp kick. He avoided that and shifted into bats again, flocking behind me.

I tapped my foot, releasing a little magic. The floor behind me cracked and broke, creating a little hole, just the size of a shoe, and when Rashid reformed, his foot got caught in the hole.

He toppled forward. I swung my elbow back into his throat.

The king fell back. I stumbled forward.

The doors burst open and a voice charged full of power and authority cried,

"Enough!"

I turned and saw Abi. I saw the long dagger held against her throat.

And I also saw Carmilla's triumphant face behind her.

50

Carmilla pushed Abi forward.

"Enough of this farce," she said.

"Carmilla," Rashid snarled. "What is the meaning of this?"

I chuckled.

"Something funny, wizard?" he snapped.

"Yeah," I said. "Your daughter is a piece of work." I stood up and reclaimed the fallen Djinn. All the while I kept looking at Carmilla.

"Hello, princess. Your blade seems to be at my friend's throat."

Carmilla purred. "It does, doesn't it?"

"So you really are committed to going along this route?" I asked.

"Carmilla," Rashid snapped. "Cease this at once and help me."

"Be quiet, father," she hissed. The venom in her words made the vampire king recoil. "I shall deal with you shortly. And as for you, Erik, it seems we are in need of a *renegotiation*."

"The bitch is screwing you over," Amaymon said. He was healed by now, and he stretched his arms high over his head.

I grinned. "Oh, I know."

"You do?" Carmilla asked.

"Of course, princess," I said. "I got your number the moment you walked into my office with your damsel face on." I sighed. "And the fact of the matter is, as much as I underestimated you, you also underestimated me."

"I did not," she said. "I calculated every possibility, including the militia you assembled downstairs."

"But did you account for me having lived with my sister and actually learning something?"

She looked behind her.

Gil, along with the rest of the team I had brought along, was right behind her. She flicked the black, meter-long wand.

A sigil glowed beneath Abi's feet and white energy consumed her. A spatial displacement spell, one of Gil's specialties. It used to take her a while to get those going. Now it was barely an afterthought. I felt my shadows stir as my sister used her magic. White smoke clung to her like a shroud, the same curse endowing her with powers much like it did mine, albeit better-tailored to her needs.

Abi vanished from Carmilla's grasp and reappeared next to Gil. Carmilla snarled and took half a step forward.

Mephisto bitch-slapped her into a wall so hard she left a crater. The demon glanced at me and Amaymon, gave us a little nod, and sauntered casually over to his master.

I chuckled as Carmilla picked herself up.

"We knew you were watching us," I said. "Do you know why? Because you and my sister have the same thought process. You value intelligence over everything else. So I thought, what would a morally-corrupt evil version of my sister do?"

"We found your listening devices in my mansion and Erik's office weeks ago," Gil said. "As well as the eavesdropping spells around the forest and the territories where we secured the werewolf tribes. We know it was you who fed your father information about the location of Caleb's tribe and the Vaewolf child."

Rashid looked at his daughter.

"Did you know she also set Valen up?" I told him. "It took me a while to figure it out, but that was the reason he got sent to the crypt, wasn't it? Because you didn't care who he got his jollies with so long as it wasn't a werewolf. Except you don't know addicts. They will always push their limits, always try to get a bigger high."

I looked at where I had last seen the werewolf mother and the Vaewolf child.

"I bet you were a servant here once, I'm guessing about nine years ago," I said. "I noticed a few werewolf fledglings in your palace when I came to visit. They were the day guard, correct? A Vaewolf means one of the parents has to be a vamp." I turned to Rashid. "And I bet you had no idea until a few days ago. Until your daughter brought evidence against her own brother."

"Right after you left my palace," Rashid murmured.

"Exactly," I said. "Princess Psycho saw her opportunity. I bet she was the one whispering all about power too. If it were me, I'd set about a few rumors that my power was growing. If I had a rival, say my father, it would be sure to drive him towards more power to stay ahead. Even if it meant open war. And, oh look, a big power vacuum just presented itself. How well the fates align."

Rashid turned to his daughter. "You betrayed me? You set Valen up? Your own brother?"

Carmilla smiled at him. "Of course I did. Did you ever stop to consider who your firstborn was? Did you ever stop to think about *ME*?"

Power blazed from her.

"All my life, I was a side story to you," she said. "I was just the woman, the girl, a tool to be married off, or bargained with, or an option for seduction. My own father never saw in me my true power. I am a queen, you miserable old fool, and I have outwitted you at every step. Observe."

The shadows around the room warbled. I heard the sounds of a dozen crossbows go off. Carmilla's handmaidens walked out, carrying hand-crossbows and knives. Ash lay at their feet.

"I have taken your court from you."

Clicking and clacking rose from behind the throne. A pair of Weavers, the half-spider monstrosities we had met in the Underworld, emerged, their spindly legs arching over the throne.

"Your throne is mine," Carmilla declared. "Just as soon as I kill you, Father. Take up your sword." She drew her rapier, and held her dagger in her left hand. "I challenge you, Father. For a crown that has long been my due."

Rashid retrieved his longsword. He laughed at her as she settled into a rapier fencing pose.

"You foul, foul child," he said. "I am your father, I am your *king*. You seem to have forgotten that. Allow me to rectify your mistake."

51

"Don't interfere," Amaymon told me. "This is some of that destiny shit. This goes beyond all of us."

I stiffened. I hadn't realized I was ready to leap to action. Instead, I sheathed Djinn and went over to where Abi was. She nodded at me.

"Who are we rooting for?" I heard Emrys ask.

"There is a devil we know, who needs to be stopped, and one we do not know," Greg said.

"Frying pan, meet fire," I said.

Amaymon was right. This was some destiny shit. All we could do was sit back and enjoy the show.

Rashid was fast. Lightning fast, literally. But Carmilla kept up with him, blow for blow. She hadn't fought like that in the Underworld. She had held back. She had always been holding back.

And still I felt she was holding back.

Rashid was not. He was injured and tired, and he needed to end this duel quickly.

His daughter also knew that. She danced around his

sweeping strokes, not so much parrying with her daggers as redirecting the energy. Her rapier snaked in a couple of times, thrusting deep into her father, but so far neither had scored a killing blow.

And then they went ballistic. Their movements were a blur. By the time I heard their swords clash they were already four moves ahead.

Blade, blade, blade, *CLANG*.

These two were fighting at speeds faster than the eye could see. Blood splattered all around them, flying towards us. Gil cast a spell undertone and cleaned us up.

The fighting slowed down a beat. Both were tired. Rashid charged in. Carmilla had her sword down, her dagger up. The swing disarmed her. She flicked the dagger up with the tip of her rapier and caught it-

Just as her father turned into a flock of bats and rushed her. She stuck her dagger back, stabbing behind her. Her father reformed and grabbed her hand just before the tip reached his eye. He kneed her in the back. We heard her spine crack. Then he raised her arm up and spun her around, tip of the longsword pressed into her sternum.

"It is over, daughter."

He thrust forward.

And found a flock of bats.

Carmilla reformed behind him and thrust both rapier and dagger into his back. The tips of the weapons emerged from her father's chest.

"Indeed it is, father," she said, withdrawing her weapons.

Rashid sagged to his knees, sword clattering on the ground.

"How?"

Carmilla paced around and stopped in front of him. "I told you, father, all those centuries ago when I left your palace, to never underestimate me. I have grown far stronger than you could ever imagine. Strong enough to rival and beat you, the King of Vampires."

Rashid spat blood as he laughed. He looked up at his daughter.

"Ah, yes, I see now," he said. "I see the error of my ways, daughter mine. I have been so blind. Hurry, daughter. Hurry and drink my blood before my body regenerates. Hurry and claim your prize."

Carmilla cocked her head. "No," she said flatly.

When her father looked up, she said, "I will not take your power, father. I never needed it." She smiled maliciously at him, eyes full of hatred and bloodlust.

"I grew strong by my own means, unlike you and your predecessors who took power from those you felled and added it to your own. I relied solely on myself, and I have surpassed you and all who came before you. So no, father, I will not take your blood. I shall not taint myself with you or your foul legacy. Your line ends now."

She thrust the rapier deep into her father's collarbone, pressing down until she reached the heart. Rashid gasped. With one final exhale, he turned to dust and ash.

And thus ended the reign of King Rashid.

Carmilla sheathed her dagger and walked over to the throne. She took no note of the Weavers or vampires on either side. She ignored the werewolf and her hybrid daughter. She ignored us.

She just sat on the throne, rapier across her legs, and settled back with a jovial smile, eyes closed.

Then she opened her eyes and looked to the side. Her vampire handmaidens were all on their knees.

"All hail Her Vampiric Majesty, Queen Carmilla," said the nearest one.

"All hail," chanted the others.

They kept repeating it over and over again, hailing the dawn of Carmilla's reign.

She was staring straight at me and that's when I knew I had lost the game. She had been playing us from the start, that much we knew, but we didn't know just how good she was at the game.

She had wiped the court clean, manipulated us to weaken her father, downplayed her own powers, and then swooped in to finish us all off.

Being crowned meant the Grigori could not touch her now. Not without inciting the very war they had been trying to prevent.

And the Weavers. I knew she had bargained with them, but I figured it would take her a while to see their advantage and leverage them against us.

Nope. She had assimilated them into her plan seamlessly. Hell, she didn't even need Earth anymore. She could just take her army and start dominating the Underworld one piece at a time. I shuddered, thinking of all the monsters and allies she could potentially have.

And just in case she had lost the duel with her dad, there was no way he would have survived the Weavers attacking him, along with all the handmaidens, and our interference when he tried to kill the Vaewolf for his ritual.

All the moves led to her win.

She conveyed all of that with her sinister smile and triumphant pose, sitting on the throne after millennia of skullduggery. She had played the game and won.

The devil we don't know.

All hail the queen.

52

Lily held my hand. The Vaewolf kid was strong, stronger than her mother. Abi was next to her, whispering calming words to counter the poor mother's hysteria.

The kid had this smile on her face, like she was calm. Something caught my eye on her other side. Zeke walked beside her, and the two kids giggled at some inside joke. I felt something catch in my throat. It felt strange, being proud of my kid.

Hell, it just felt strange having a kid at all.

The helicopter Gil had prepared for us took us to the mansion. No one wanted to go through a portal again, and I doubted we had the juice for it. Defeating demigod vampire monarchs is hard work.

As soon as we landed, Caleb came out the gate. Lily ran up to him, shouting "Uncle Caleb", and rushed him into a hug that knocked the air out of the alpha. The tearful reunion lasted for a while, and Caleb joined us in Gil's study afterwards, while the rest of us gathered around some tea and refreshments.

"Carmilla has made good on her promise," she was saying. "She pulled out her troops from Eureka, and even took a large number of vagrant nests with her to Prague. My sources tell me that she's doing exactly what she said she would: rebuilding the vampire kingdom in Eastern Europe."

"So does that mean we can't tease them with an accent anymore?" I joked.

I heard some snickering going around, while Gil rolled her eyes at me.

Only one person did not laugh.

"I will kill her," Caleb said. His tone was soft and low but we all heard the resolution there. The werewolf had steel in his words. "For what she has done to my pack, I will kill her."

"We all want to kill her," Gil said flatly. "But as part of our peace treaty, Queen Carmilla remains a member of the Grigori."

"She still has the tenth seat?" I asked.

As I said that, I glanced at the other members of the Grigori. Evans stared blankly at the tray of food before him, while Emrys and Greg were competing for World's Grimmest Expression. Luke drummed his fingers impatiently on the crook of his arm.

Not a popular opinion then.

"She does," Gil said. "Her Majesty intends to honor any and all terms of our peace treaty." She sighed and joined the Grim Parade. "Until it suits her."

"Which is good news for you, wolfie," Amaymon interjected. "When the queen fucks up, you get the first crack at her."

I expected my sister to comment but she stayed silent. Which meant Amaymon had hit the nail on the head. They were all waiting for their new ally to turn on them and get the drop on her before she invaded the planet or something.

"What about Lily and her mother?" Abi asked.

"They are safe," Caleb answered. "The Vol are no more."

"Indeed," Gil said. "Carmilla has been thorough. But threats for a hybrid are always real. Which is why I have set up new identities for them, as well as housing, education, and a protection detail."

Caleb cocked his head.

"What's the catch?"

Smart kid. Gil never gives out free lunches.

My sister pursed her lips and turned to me. "Brother, have you given any thought to the reward I offered you in exchange for helping me?"

"You mean the third seat at your little Camelot reenactment group?" I said. "No thanks. I'd rather bite off my own toes one by one."

"Graphic," Emrys commented.

"I see," Gil said. "Well, that is good news then. I have a seat to give out and technically you were employed by Ishtar. So I don't have to pay you."

Then she grinned at me. "Just kidding. There's a cheque on your way out."

I gave her a thumbs-up. "Gee, thanks."

Gil turned to Caleb. "My condition is that you take the third seat on the Grigori. I could use a man of your power and influence over the packs, and you are young enough to be trained and taught."

She forgot "manipulated".

Then again, my sister wasn't about to get outdone by some vampire princess—sorry, queen. If Carmilla had got some new spidery allies, Gil was about to get control over every wolf pack in North America. Also, with both Caleb and Carmilla on her team—officially—they were duty-bound to avoid tearing each other's throats the next time they saw each other.

And the pieces keep moving.

If I said it once, I said it a million times:

I really fucking hate politics.

Caleb growled, literally growled, before nodding.

"I have not forgotten my vengeance, and mark my words I will have her blood," he said. "But my pack needs aid. Help which you can provide. So yes, I will join you."

Gil beamed at him. "Excellent."

POP!

All seven of us turned, some of us reaching for weapons.

Amaymon and Mephisto stood side by side. The latter held a tray of champagne flutes and wore a tired sigh on his face. Champagne foam covered the front of his butler suit.

Amaymon held the bottle he had just popped, nearly giving us all a heart attack, and shrugged at our collective glare.

"What, we ain't poppin' this sucker?"

It was late by the time we got home. Amaymon had turned feline and disappeared somewhere, leaving me and Abi alone for the first time since our awkward confession in the mansion's kitchen.

"I, uh..." I cleared my throat and found her looking expectantly at me.

Oh, boy. Picked a Hell of a time to freeze.

"I...I..."

When had she gotten closer? Not that I was complaining. Amazing what moonlight could do to a pretty woman.

"Um..." she began. She was starting to turn bright red. "Yeah."

"Yeah."

More silence. I mean, we just stood there like two awkward teenagers. This was ridiculous. We were adults. Adults who had just saved the world from a vampiric invasion.

Adults who had a kid together, for crying out loud.

"So, um, I was thinking..."

Yes, Erik, good. More words. More words is good. Finish the thought.

"Of food, you know."

On second thought, maybe shut up.

Abi cocked her head. Because, that's what every woman wants to hear from a guy she's been pining over: that during this most romantic of moments, he's thinking about food.

"Food, you know, to eat..."

Holy kittens, there was no stopping me.

"For us," I said. "To eat. Together. You know, like... um... Like the thing..."

She gave me a look, which pretty much solidified any voice in my head telling me I was going to die alone.

Then, miraculously, a smile. Oh, she had a beautiful smile. I always loved that smile.

"Yeah, like a date, you mean?"

"*Yes!*"

Abi shrugged. "Sounds like fun."

Now that I was no longer in danger of giving myself a brain aneurism, I opted for brain damage via enthusiastic nodding.

"Uh, huh, a date, yes, exactly that," I said. "So, what d'you think?"

Abi's smile turned into a grin. "You are so bad at this."

"Oh come on!"

"What, you are!"

"Well, you- you're," I stammered. "You're just standing there looking all perfect... How am I supposed to think?"

Her smile got closer and then her lips were on mine.

"That's the idea," she purred. When we parted, her eyes were wide and full of lust. "And not that I don't love your suggestion for a proper date, but I haven't fed in a long while."

It should tell you a lot that it took me a whole of two long, painful seconds to realize she was not talking about food.

"Oh," I said.

"Oh," she echoed, grinning mischievously.

"That."

"That, indeed."

She kissed me again. It lasted longer. The room spun but for a very different reason.

We came up for air. Now I was grinning.

"Yeah," I said. "We can do that."

We kissed again. We went upstairs. We had a good night.

And for the first time in a long while, when I fell asleep with her in my arms that night, there weren't any nightmares.

***

ERIK ASHENDALE RETURNS in **SHATTERED** - *What party isn't complete without a few kidnapping attempts?*

When Erik is hunted down by angels, he knows he's on borrowed time. His sister and her familiar are gone, his list of allies can't be counted on and the only one who can help him is none other than Greede.

There's just one problem: the man is in jail, the Grigori will only release him if Erik and Greede will help them with a super demon that's days away from waking up, and the item they need to to stop it happens to be a super weapon...

Hidden in Heaven...

*TURN the page on for an excerpt **or get the book online!***

∽

SHATTERED - PREVIEW

"Amaymon, no! Put the champagne down! Put it dow- Oh, crap. Everyone, *duck*!"

I watched in horror as the demon slid a claw across the half-opened champagne bottle—'sabering' it in his unique way—and bubbly foam that cost way more than I wanted to think about went sailing across my office. Most of it found the wall, the furniture, my desk and computer, but some of it also splattered our party guests.

Which leads us to today's teachable moment: always keep an eye on your demon, especially during festivities.

Despite Amaymon's havoc, this was turning out to be a fairly good shindig, particularly since the person for whom it was thrown—my former apprentice, and current girlfriend, Abi—had not stopped smiling.

This was a long time coming. It was not every day you got to graduate from magical apprenticeship along with nearly a decade of online college.

So, yeah, I threw her a party.

A woman with whom I had lived for nine years, a woman who had stood by me through thick and thin (and there was a lot of thick—or thin, whichever is the bad one). A woman who had still found time to get a college degree, help me kick monster ass whenever the need arose, and who last year confessed her feelings for me.

We've been dating ever since and I have to say, I've never been happier.

"You're smiling at the sandwiches," Amaymon said. I looked up to see him leaning on the kitchen door frame, broken champagne bottle in one hand. "It's getting creepy. Did you piss in them?"

I frowned at him. "What? No, what's wrong with you. I did not piss in the sandwiches."

"Too bad," he said. "That would have been funny."

I sighed. "I'm just preparing some more snacks. Go clean up that mess before someone slips and breaks their neck or something."

"This crowd? Psh! If someone here gets taken down by some bubbly they'll never hear the end of it."

He took a massive swig from the bottle as his eyes travelled over to where Abi was talking to Jack, another former student of mine who had retired from active duty of almost daily mortal danger to pursue the calm and serene life of a blacksmith.

Both of them were giggling over something, while Jack's boyfriend, Luke, surreptitiously glanced over in my direction.

The rest of the partygoers consisted of the Grigori, a group of wizards and specialists that made up the bulk of the magical policing community.

I had only invited the cool ones.

Or, you know, the ones who did not petition to have me tried and executed.

I'm petty like that.

Emrys, an honest-to-god Druid wearing a not-what-you-pictured-when-I-said-'druid' three-piece suit, was telling a dirty joke and not bothering to keep his voice down. Next to him, Evans, a golem eight feet tall and nearly as wide, nodded while scarfing down three sandwiches from the previous tray.

The other two listening in were not Grigori but that did not make them any less powerful.

Turtle was a giant Chinese man with a rotund belly and an equally round shaved head, permanently etched with a Buddha-like smile. He wore his usual forest-green Chinese suit, and carried an oak staff.

Next to him was an angel.

A literal angel.

Yeah. Let that sink in for a moment.

It helped that Anael looked nothing like her winged, majestic self, instead opting for the guise of Doctor Annalise Tompkins, therapist extraordinaire. A pretty, if somewhat mousy, brunette with killer eyes and a heartbreaker smile. She had once been my therapist, before revealing the fact that she had been sent by a rogue faction of angels to spy on me and my friends, while waging a civil war in Heaven.

She had also helped me get my magic back after my depression.

All in all, not a bad egg.

She and Abi had just begun chatting about therapy (Abi had just majored in Psychology) when Amaymon nudged me.

"Who's the angel chick?"

I glanced from him to her and back to him. "Dude, forget it. You have no chance."

Amaymon shot me a look. "That's the one who gave you your mojo back, right? Angel of love."

"Virtue," I said, sighing in surrender. I knew where this was going. "Virtue of Love."

Amaymon wasn't listening. He was already on his way towards Anael, grinning in the exact same way every self-confident jock did before asking out the head cheerleader. I followed along just for giggles, stopping next to Abi and pecking her lightly on the side of the head. She leaned into my chest and we watched the show.

"Hey," Amaymon drawled. He did that alpha-male thing where he placed one arm on the wall, half-trapping her in. "I'm Amaymon. But you've heard of me already."

Anael, to her credit, kept her expression bored and peered at him through her spectacles.

"Hello, Amaymon. Yes, I have heard of you. However, you are currently interrupting the lovely conversation I was having with Abigale. Unless of course you have something to contribute on the subject of behavioral therapy."

"Only when I spray him with a hose while he's in cat form," I interjected.

The glare he shot me contained little more than the promise of feline retribution.

"I've been meaning to catch you," he went on. "You're the angel of love, right?"

She raised an eyebrow. "Virtue of Love."

"Told you," I added.

"And what does that entail?" he asked. "Do you govern *all* forms of love?"

The angel sighed. "Yes," she replied. "All love. Family, friends, straight, gay, sexual, non-sexual—why, even the bond between wizard and familiar. Any and all forms. And yes, that does include lust, which is why you asked that question."

To his credit, Amaymon remained unfazed.

"That's amazing, you must have quite the repertoire. Maybe share one or two tricks with these two," he said, nodding at me and Abi.

"Hey!" she snapped.

"Yeah, hey!" I added. "We're doing just fine, thank you."

"That's your problem, dude," he said. "*Just fine* ain't gonna cut it. I banged many a succubus, including Abi's mom-"

"Please don't remind me," Abi interjected.

"And *fine* don't do the trick anymore," he went on. "Magic chicks need magic sex. You gotta broaden your horizons. Speaking of which..." He turned to Anael and wiggled his eyebrows. "What say you and I break a few universal laws and teach these kids how it's done? For educational purposes, of course."

Anael closed her eyes, exhaled softly and fully turned to the demon.

"Amaymon." Her dulcet tones only conveyed her ire more. "I have never been more repulsed by a single creature in my entire life. Excuse me."

And without another word she pushed past him and walked away.

We all just stood there, stunned, before I—grinning so much my cheeks hurt—pointed at him and started laughing.

"Denied!"

Everyone else joined me in laughing at the demon.

Amaymon glanced after Anael and shrugged. "That ain't a no," he said.

"No, that was a put-down and a verbal castration rolled in one," Abi told him. "Now I have to go apologize to her and keep the only woman in this party from leaving. Where's your sister anyway?"

I shrugged. "I left her a message but no answer. Maybe she got stuck in traffic or something."

Abi raised her eyebrows. Wizards as powerful as my sister don't get stuck in traffic.

"Okay, maybe she's fooling around with Greg," I said. "Payback for the last time *we* were late for dinner."

Abi chuckled at the memory. To be fair, it was a really good memory. She pecked me on the lips and ran after the angel.

I was about to tell Amaymon off for annoying my party guests when my phone rang. I walked to my desk and picked up.

"Erik!" I recognized Greg's panicked tones.

Greg was a Kresnik, sort of an anti-vampire. He was old, he was powerful, and he was a Grigori. Greg and I had been through multiple missions together and the guy was reliable. And, even if he was dating my sister, he was a good guy and I trusted him.

"Erik, she was taken," he spat in a thick Slavic accent that came out even stronger with emotion. "Gil and Mephisto, both were taken by angels."

"What?"

A cold wave rushed through me.

"No time," he said. From the background I heard the sound of a car honking and tires screeching. "They are coming for you next, Erik! I'm on my way."

"What?" I cried. Now everyone was looking at me. "Greg, what's going-"

I heard a sudden pulse of feedback and the phone died. The lights went out half a second later, plunging the office into darkness.

Light flashed from outside.

"Erik." I saw Anael's worried face from across the room. "Erik, they're here."

I ran to the window and watched as angels rained from the sky.

They were like little meteorites with wings and armor, white flashes that took shape and floated around my office, surrounding the building.

A voice boomed loudly in my head with overbearing, otherworldly power.

"Erik Ashendale. Come out and surrender to Heaven's Army. Your time of judgement is now!"

***

Get Shattered - The Warlock Legacy Book 9 today!

FREE NOVELLA

Get a FREE prequel story
Wolf's Bane - The Warlock Legacy #0
as well as private giveaways, early access to future
books, and MORE!

Click the image or visit http://eepurl.com/bkDPGr

BEFORE YOU GO...

This is the part where I kindly ask you to leave a review for *Blood Rites*. Reviews are hugely important for authors because we depend on word-of-mouth and enthusiasm from readers like you.

So please help spread the word and leave a review!

Thanks! :)

ABOUT THE AUTHOR

Ryan Attard is the author of the Warlock Legacy series and a host of other fantasy works.

Hailing from a faraway island, it was only a matter of time before he began creating imaginary friends and writing down their adventures.

Nowadays you can find him toiling over his next project, rolling dice in D&D campaigns, looking up stuff online that surely garnered the attention of the authorities, and cackling when his fans shake their fists angrily at him for playing with their heart strings.

He also enjoys writing about himself in the third person. Say hi on Facebook, Instagram, or email at ryanattardauthor@gmail.com

THE WARLOCK LEGACY

DO YOU HAVE THE ENTIRE *WARLOCK LEGACY* SERIES?

Firstborn
Birthright
Lost Ones
Judgement
Nemesis
Resurrection
Broken
Blood Rites
Shattered
Fallen

Click HERE to check out the whole series!

Or here to get the BOX SET (at a discount)!!

Printed in Great Britain
by Amazon